the sky is everywhere

Jandy Nelson

WALKER
BOOKS

This is a work of fiction. Names, characters, places and incidents are either the product of the author's imagination or, if real, are used fictitiously. All statements, activities, stunts, descriptions, information and material of any other kind contained herein are included for entertainment purposes only and should not be relied on for accuracy or replicated as they may result in injury.

First published in Great Britain 2010 by Walker Books Ltd
87 Vauxhall Walk, London SE11 5HJ

2 4 6 8 10 9 7 5 3 1

This book has been typeset in Fairfield

Printed and bound in China by XingJiaYi

British Library Cataloguing in Publication Data:
a catalogue record for this book is
available from the British Library

ISBN 978-1-4063-2630-7

www.walker.co.uk

Part 1

1

Gram is worried about me. It's not just because my sister Bailey died four weeks ago, or because my mother hasn't contacted me in sixteen years, or even because suddenly all I think about is sex. She is worried about me because one of her houseplants has spots.

Gram has believed for most of my seventeen years that this particular houseplant, which is of the nondescript variety, reflects my emotional, spiritual and physical wellbeing. I've grown to believe it too.

Across the room from where I sit, Gram – all six feet and floral frock of her, looms over the black-spotted leaves.

"What do you mean it might not get better this time?" She's asking this of Uncle Big: arborist, resident pothead and mad scientist to boot. He knows something about everything, but he knows everything about plants.

To anyone else it might seem strange, even off the wall, that Gram, as she asks this, is staring at me, but it doesn't to Uncle Big, because he's staring at me as well.

"This time it has a very serious condition." Big's voice trumpets as if from stage or pulpit; his words carry weight, even *pass the salt* comes out of his mouth in a thou-shalt-Ten-Commandments kind of way.

Gram raises her hands to her face in distress, and I go back to scribbling a poem in the margin of *Wuthering Heights*. I'm huddled into a corner of the couch. I've no use for talking, would just as soon store paper clips in my mouth.

"But the plant's always recovered before, Big, like when

Lennie broke her arm, for instance."

"That time the leaves had white spots."

"Or just last fall when she auditioned for lead clarinet but had to play second chair again."

"Brown spots."

"Or when—"

"This time it's different."

I glance up. They're still peering at me, a tall duet of sorrow and concern.

Gram is the town of Clover's Garden Guru. She has the most extraordinary flower garden in Northern California. Her roses burst with more color than a year of sunsets, and their fragrance is so intoxicating that town lore claims breathing in their scent can cause you to fall in love on the spot. But despite her nurturing and renowned green thumb, this plant seems to follow the trajectory of my life, independent of her efforts or its own vegetal sensibility.

I put my book and pen down on the table. Gram leans in close to the plant, whispers to it about the importance of *joie de vivre*, then lumbers over to the couch, sitting down next to me.

Then Big joins us, plopping his enormous frame down beside Gram. We three, each with the same unruly hair that sits on our heads like a bustle of shiny black crows, stay like this, staring at nothing, for the rest of the afternoon.

This is us since my sister Bailey collapsed one month ago from a fatal arrhythmia while in rehearsal for a local production of *Romeo & Juliet*. It's as if someone vacuumed up the horizon while we were looking the other way.

2

The morning of the day Bailey died,
she woke me up
by putting her finger in my ear.
I hated when she did this.
She then started trying on shirts, asking me:
Which do you like better, the green or the blue?

The blue.
You didn't even look up, Lennie.
Okay, the green. Really, I don't care what shirt you wear...
Then I rolled over in bed and fell back asleep.

I found out later
she wore the blue
and those were the last words I ever spoke to her.

(Found written on a candy wrapper on the trail to the Rain River)

My first day back to school is just as I expect, the hall does a Red Sea part when I come in, conversations hush, eyes swim with nervous sympathy, and everyone stares as if I'm holding Bailey's dead body in my arms, which I guess I am. Her death is all over me, I can feel it and everyone can see it, plain as a big black coat wrapped around me on a beautiful spring day. But what I don't expect is the unprecedented hubbub over some new boy, Joe Fontaine, who arrived in my month-long absence. Everywhere I go it's the same:

"Have you seen him yet?"

"He looks like a Gypsy."

"Like a rock star."

"A pirate."

"I hear he's in a band called Dive."

"That he's a musical genius."

"Someone told me he used to live in Paris."

"That he played music on the streets."

"Have you seen him yet?"

I have seen him, because when I return to my band seat, the one I've occupied for the last year, he's in it. Even in the stun of grief, my eyes roam from the black boots, up the miles of legs covered in denim, over the endless torso, and finally settle on a face so animated I wonder if I've interrupted a conversation between him and my music stand.

"Hi," he says, and jumps up. He's treetop tall. "You must be Lennon." He points to my name on the chair. "I heard about – I'm sorry." I notice the way he holds his clarinet, not precious with it, tight fist around the neck, like a sword.

"Thank you," I say, and every available inch of his face busts into a smile – whoa. Has he blown into our school on a gust of wind from another world? The guy looks unabashedly jack-o'-lantern happy which couldn't be more foreign to the sullen demeanor most of us strove to perfect. He has scores of messy brown curls that flop every which way, and eyelashes so spider-leg long and thick that when he blinks he looks like he's batting his bright green eyes right at you. His face is more open than an open book, like a wall of graffiti really. I realize I'm writing *wow* on my thigh with my finger, decide I'd better open my mouth and snap us out of this impromptu staring contest.

"Everyone calls me Lennie," I say. Not very original, but better than *guh,* which was the alternative, and it does the trick. He looks down at his feet for a second and I take a breath and regroup for Round Two.

"Been wondering about that actually, Lennon after John?" he asks, again holding my gaze – it's entirely possible I'm going to faint. Or burst into flames.

I nod. "Mom was a hippie." This is *northern* Northern California after all – the final frontier of freakerdom. Just in the eleventh grade we have a girl named Electricity, a guy named Magic Bus, and countless flowers: Tulip, Begonia and Poppy – all parent-given-on-the-birth-certificate names. Tulip is a two-ton truck of a guy who would be the star of our football team if we were the kind of school that had a football team.

We're not. We're the kind of school that has optional morning meditation in the gym.

"Yeah," Joe says. "My mom too, and Dad, as well as aunts, uncles, brothers, cousins … welcome to Commune Fontaine."

I laugh out loud. "Got the picture."

But whoa again – should I be laughing so easily like this? And should it feel this good? Like slipping into cool river water.

I turn around, wondering if anyone is watching us, and see that Sarah has just walked – rather, exploded – into the music room. I've hardly seen her since the funeral, feel a pang of guilt.

"Lennieeeee!" She careens toward us in prime goth-gone-cowgirl form: vintage slinky black dress, shit-kicker cowboy boots, blond hair dyed so black it looks blue, all topped off with a huge Stetson. I note the breakneck pace of her approach, wonder for an instant if she's going to actually jump into my arms right before she tries to, sending us both skidding into Joe, who somehow retains his balance, and ours, so we all don't fly through the window.

This is Sarah, subdued.

"Nice," I whisper in her ear, as she hugs me like a bear even though she's built like a bird. "Way to bowl down the gorgeous new boy." She cracks up, and it feels both amazing and disconcerting to have someone in my arms shaking from laughter rather than heartbreak.

Sarah is the most enthusiastic cynical person on the planet. She'd be the perfect cheerleader if she weren't so disgusted by the notion of school spirit. She's a literature fanatic like me, but reads darker, read Sartre in tenth grade – *Nausea* – which is when she started wearing black (even at the beach), smoking cigarettes (even though she looks like the healthiest girl you've ever seen) and obsessing about her existential crisis (even as she partied to all hours of the night).

"Lennie, welcome back, dear," another voice says. Mr James – also known in my mind as Yoda for both outward appearance and inward musical mojo – has stood up at the piano and is looking over at me with the same expression of bottomless sadness I've gotten so used to seeing from adults. "We're all so very sorry."

"Thank you," I say, for the hundredth time that day. Sarah and Joe are both looking at me too, Sarah with concern and Joe with a grin the size of the continental United States. Does he look at everyone like this, I wonder. Is he a wingnut? Well, whatever he is, or has, it's catching. Before I know it, I've matched his continental USA and raised him Puerto Rico and Hawaii. I must look like The Merry Mourner. Sheesh. And that's not all, because now I'm thinking what it might be like to kiss him, to *really* kiss him – uh-oh. This is a problem, an entirely new un-Lennie-like problem that began (*WTF-edly?!*) at the funeral: I was drowning in darkness and suddenly all these boys in the room were glowing. Guy friends of Bailey's from work or college, most of whom I didn't know, kept coming up to me saying how sorry they were, and I don't know if it's because they thought I looked like Bailey, or because they felt bad for me, but later on, I'd catch some of them staring at me in this charged, urgent way, and I'd find myself staring back at them, like I was someone else, thinking things I hardly ever had before, things I'm mortified to have been thinking in a church, let alone at my sister's funeral.

This boy beaming before me, however, seems to glow in a class all his own. He must be from a very friendly part of the Milky Way, I'm thinking as I try to tone down this nutso smile on my face, but instead almost blurt out to Sarah, "He looks like Heathcliff," because I just realized he does, well, except for the happy smiling part – but then all of a sudden the breath is kicked out of me and I'm shoved onto the cold hard concrete floor that is my life now, because I remember I can't run home after school and tell Bails about a new boy in band.

My sister dies over and over again, all day long.

"Len?" Sarah touches my shoulder. "You okay?"

I nod, willing away the runaway train of grief barreling straight for me.

Someone behind us starts playing "Approaching Shark", aka the *Jaws* theme song. I turn to see Rachel Brazile gliding towards us, hear her mutter, "Very funny," to Luke Jacobus, the saxophonist responsible for the accompaniment. He's just one of many band-kill Rachel's left in her wake, guys duped by the fact that all that haughty horror is stuffed into a spectacular body, and then further deceived by big brown faun eyes and Rapunzel hair. Sarah and I are convinced God was in an ironic mood when he made her.

"See you've met The Maestro," she says to me, casually touching Joe's back as she slips into her chair – first chair clarinet – where I should be sitting.

She opens her case, starts putting together her instrument. "Joe studied at a conservatory in *Fronce*. Did he tell you?" Of course she doesn't say *France* so it rhymes with *dance* like a normal American-speaking human being. I can feel Sarah bristling beside me. She has zero tolerance for Rachel ever since she got first chair over me, but Sarah doesn't know what really happened – no one does.

Rachel's tightening the ligature on her mouthpiece like she's trying to asphyxiate her clarinet. "Joe was a *fabulous* second in your absence," she says, drawing out the word *fabulous* from here to the Eiffel Tower.

I don't fire-breathe at her: "Glad everything worked out for you, Rachel." I don't say a word, just wish I could curl into a ball and roll away. Sarah, on the other hand, looks like she wishes there were a battle-ax handy.

The room has become a clamor of random notes and scales. "Finish up tuning, I want to start at the bell today," Mr James calls from the piano. "And take out your pencils, I've made some changes to the arrangement."

"I'd better go beat on something," Sarah says, throwing Rachel a disgusted look, then huffs off to beat on her timpani.

Rachel shrugs, smiles at Joe – no not smiles: twinkles – oh brother. "Well, it's true," she says to him. "You were – I mean, are – *fabulous*."

"Not so." He bends down to pack up his clarinet. "I was just keeping the seat warm. Now I can go back to where I belong." He points his clarinet at the horn section.

"You're just being modest," Rachel says, tossing fairy-tale locks over the back of her chair. "You have *so* many colors on your tonal palette."

I look at Joe expecting to see some evidence of an inward groan at these imbecilic words, but see evidence of something else instead. He smiles at Rachel on a geographical scale too. I feel my neck go hot.

"You know I'll miss you," she says, pouting.

"We'll meet again," Joe replies, adding an eye-bat to his repertoire. "Like next period, in history."

I've disappeared, which is good really, because suddenly I don't have a clue what to do with my face or body or smashed-up heart. I take my seat, noting that this grinning, eye-batting fool from Fronce looks nothing like Heathcliff. I was mistaken.

I open my clarinet case, put my reed in my mouth to moisten it and instead bite it in two.

At 4.48PM on a friday in April,
My sister was rehearsing the role of Juliet
and less than one minute later
she was dead.
To my astonishment, time didn't stop
with her heart.
People went to school, to work, to restaurants;
they crushed crackers into their clam chowder,
fretted over exams,
sang in their cars with the windows up.
For days and days, the rain beat its fists
on the roof of our house —
evidence of the terrible mistake
God had made.
Each morning, when I woke
I listened for the tireless pounding,
looked at the drear through the window
and was relieved
that at least the sun had the decency
to stay the hell away from us.

(Found on a piece of music paper, spiked on a low branch, Flying Man's Gulch)

3

The rest of the day blurs by and before the final bell, I sneak out and duck into the woods. I don't want to take the roads home, don't want to risk seeing anyone from school, especially Sarah, who informed me that, while I've been in hiding, she's been reading up on loss and according to all the experts, it's time for me to talk about what I'm going through – but she, and the experts, and Gram, for that matter, don't get it. I can't. I'd need a new alphabet, one made of falling, of tectonic plates shifting, of the deep devouring dark.

As I walk through the redwood trees, my sneakers sopping up days of rain, I wonder why bereaved people even bother with mourning clothes when grief itself provides such an unmistakable wardrobe. The only one who didn't seem to spot it on me today – besides Rachel, who doesn't count – was the new boy. He will only ever know this new sisterless me.

I see a scrap of paper on the ground dry enough to write on, so I sit on a rock, take out the pen that I always keep in my back pocket now, and scribble a conversation I remember having with Bailey on it, then fold it up and bury it in the moist earth.

When I break out of the forest onto the road to our house, I'm flooded with relief. I want to be at home, where Bailey is most alive, where I can still see her leaning out the window, her wild black hair blowing around her face as she says, "C'mon, Len, let's get to the river pronto."

"Hey you." Toby's voice startles me. Bailey's boyfriend of two years, he's part cowboy, part skate rat, all love slave to my sister, and totally missing in action lately despite Gram's many invitations. "We really need to reach out to him now," she keeps saying.

He's lying on his back in her garden with the neighbor's two red dogs, Lucy and Ethel, sprawled out asleep beside him. This is a common sight in the springtime. When the angel's trumpets and lilacs bloom, Gram's garden is positively soporific. A few moments among the blossoms and even the most energetic find themselves on their backs counting clouds.

"I was, uh, doing some weeding for Gram," he says, obviously embarrassed about his kick-back position.

"Yeah, it happens to the best of us." With his surfer flop of hair and wide face sun-spattered in freckles, Toby is the closest a human can come to lion without jumping species. When Bailey first saw him, she and I were out road-reading (we all road-read; the few people who live on our street know this about our family and inch their way home in their cars just in case one of us is out strolling and particularly rapt). I was reading *Wuthering Heights*, as usual, and she was reading *Like Water for Chocolate*, her favorite, when a magnificent chestnut brown horse trotted past us on the way to the trailhead. *Nice horse*, I thought, and went back to Cathy and Heathcliff, only looking up a few seconds later when I heard the thump of Bailey's book as it hit the ground.

She was no longer by my side but had stopped a few paces back.

"What's wrong with you?" I asked, taking in my suddenly lobotomized sister.

"Did you see that guy, Len?"

"What guy?"

"God, what's wrong with *you*, that gorgeous guy on that horse, it's like he popped out of my novel or something. I can't believe you didn't see him, Lennie." Her exasperation at my disinterest in boys was as perpetual as my exasperation at her preoccupation with them. "He turned around when he passed us and smiled right at me – he was *so* good-looking … just like the Revolutionary in this book." She reached down to pick it up, brushing the dirt off the cover. "You know, the one who whisks Gertrudis onto his horse and steals her away in a fit of passion— "

"Whatever, Bailey." I turned back around, resumed reading, and made my way to the front porch, where I sank into a chair and promptly got lost in the stampeding passion of the two on the English moors. I liked love safe between the covers of my novel, not in my sister's heart, where it made her ignore me for months on end. Every so often though, I'd look up at her, posing on a rock by the trailhead across the road, so obviously feigning reading her book that I couldn't believe she was an actress. She stayed out there for hours waiting for her Revolutionary to come back, which he finally did, but from the other direction, having traded in his horse somewhere for a skateboard. Turns out he didn't pop out of her novel after all, but out of Clover High like the rest of us, only he hung out with the ranch kids and skaters, and because she was exclusively a drama diva, their paths never crossed until that day. But by that point it didn't matter where he came from or what he rode in on because that image of him galloping by had burned into Bailey's psyche and stolen from her the capacity for rational thought.

I've never really been a member of the Toby Shaw fan club. Neither his cowboy bit nor the fact that he could do a 180 Ollie into a Fakie Feeble Grind on his skateboard made up for the fact that he had turned Bailey into a permanent love zombie.

That, and he's always seemed to find me as noteworthy as a baked potato.

"You okay, Len?" he asks from his prone position, bringing me back to the moment.

For some reason, I tell the truth. I shake my head, back and forth, back and forth, from disbelief to despair, and back again.

He sits up. "I know," he says, and I see in his marooned expression that it's true. I want to thank him for not making me say a word, and getting it all the same, but I just remain silent as the sun pours heat and light, as if from a pitcher, all over our bewildered heads.

He pats the grass with his hand for me to join him. I sort of want to but feel hesitant. We've never really hung out before without Bailey.

I motion toward the house. "I need to go upstairs."

This is true. I want to be back in The Sanctum, full name: The Inner Pumpkin Sanctum, newly christened by me, when

Bailey, a few months ago, persuaded me the walls of our bedroom just had to be orange, a blaringly unapologetic orange that had since made our room sunglasses optional. Before I'd left for school this morning, I'd shut the door, purposefully, wishing I could barricade it from Gram and her cardboard boxes. I want The Sanctum the way it is, which means exactly the way it was. Gram seems to think this means: *I'm out of my tree and running loose through the park*, Gramese for *mental*.

"Sweet pea." She's come out onto the porch in a bright purple frock covered in daisies. In her hand is a paintbrush, the first time I've seen her with one since Bailey died. "How was your first day back?"

I walk over to her, breathe in her familiar scent: patchouli, paint, garden dirt.

"It was fine," I say.

She examines my face closely like she does when she's preparing to sketch it. Silence tick-tocks between us, as it does lately. I can feel her frustration, how she wishes she could shake me like she might a book, hoping all the words will just fall out.

"There's a new boy in honor band," I offer.

"Oh yeah? What's he play?"

"Everything, it seems." Before I escaped into the woods at lunch, I saw him walking across the quad with Rachel, a guitar swinging from his hand.

"Lennie, I've been thinking … it might be good for you now, a real comfort…" Uh-oh. I know where this is going. "I mean, when you were studying with Marguerite, I couldn't rip that instrument out of your hands— "

"Things change," I say, interrupting her. I can't have this conversation. Not again. I try to step around her to go inside. I just want to be in Bailey's closet, pressed into her dresses, into the lingering scents of riverside bonfires, coconut suntan lotion, rose perfume – her.

"Listen," she says quietly, reaching her free hand out to straighten my collar. "I invited Toby for dinner. He's quite out of his tree. Go keep him company, help him weed or something."

It occurs to me she probably said something similar to him about me to get him to finally come over. Ugh.

And then without further ado, she dabs my nose with her paintbrush.

"Gram!" I cry out, but to her back as she heads into the house. I try to wipe off the green with my hand. Bails and I spent much of our lives like this, ambushed by Gram's swashbuckling green-tipped paintbrush. Only green, mind you. Gram's paintings line the walls of the house, floor to ceiling, stack behind couches, chairs, under tables, in closets, and each and every one of them is a testament to her undying devotion to the color green. She has every hue from lime to forest and uses them to paint primarily one thing: willowy women who look half mermaid, half Martian. "They're my ladies," she'd tell Bails and me. "Halfway between here and there."

Per her orders, I drop my clarinet case and bag, then plant

myself in the warm grass beside a supine Toby and the sleeping dogs to help him "weed".

"Tribal marking," I say pointing to my nose.

He nods disinterestedly in his flower coma. I'm a green-nosed baked potato. Great.

I turtle up, tucking my knees to my chest and resting my head in the crevice between them. My eyes move from the wisteria cascading down the trellis to the several parties of daffodils gossiping in the breeze to the indisputable fact that springtime has shoved off its raincoat today and is just prancing around – it makes me queasy, like the world has already forgotten what's happened to us.

"I'm not going to pack up her things in cardboard boxes," I say without thinking. "Ever."

Toby rolls on his side, shields his face with his hand trying to block the sun so he can see me, and to my surprise says, "Of course not."

I nod and he nods back, then I flop down on the grass, cross my arms over my head so he can't see that I'm secretly smiling a little into them.

The next thing I know the sun has moved behind a mountain and that mountain is Uncle Big towering over us. Toby and I must have both crashed out.

"I feel like Glinda the Good Witch," Big says, "looking down on Dorothy, Scarecrow and two Totos in the poppy field outside of Oz." A few narcotic springtime blooms are no match for Big's bugle of a voice. "I guess if you don't wake up, I'm going to have to make it snow on you." I grin groggily up at him with his enormous handlebar mustache poised over his lip like a grand Declaration of Weird. He's carrying a red cool box as if it were a briefcase.

"How's the distribution effort going?" I ask, tapping the cool box with my foot. We are in a ham predicament. After the funeral, there seemed to be a prime directive in Clover that everyone had to stop by our house with a ham. Hams were everywhere; they filled the fridge, the freezer, lined the counters, the stove, sat in the sink, the cold oven. Uncle Big attended to the door as people stopped by to pay their respects. Gram and I could hear his booming voice again and again, "Oh a ham, how thoughtful, thank you, come in." As the days went on Big's reaction to the hams got more dramatic for our benefit. Each time he exclaimed "A ham!" Gram and I found each other's eyes and had to suppress a rush of inappropriate giggles. Now Big is on a mission to make sure everyone in a twenty-mile radius has a ham sandwich a day.

He rests the cool box on the ground and reaches his hand down to help me up. "It's possible we'll be a hamless house in just a few days."

Once I'm standing, Big kisses my head, then reaches down for Toby. When he's on his feet, Big pulls him into his arms, and I watch Toby, who is a big guy himself, disappear in the mountainous embrace. "How you holding up, cowboy?"

"Not too good," he admits.

Big releases him, keeping one hand on his shoulder, and

puts the other one on mine. He looks from Toby to me. "No way out of this but through … for any of us." He says it like Moses, so we both nod as if we've been bestowed with a great wisdom. "And let's get you some turpentine." He winks at me. Big's an ace winker – five marriages to his name to prove it. After his beloved fifth wife left him, Gram insisted he move in with us, saying, "Your poor uncle will starve himself if he stays in this lovelorn condition much longer. A sorrowing heart poisons recipes."

This has proven to be true, but for Gram. Everything she cooks now tastes like ashes.

Toby and I follow Big into the house, where he stops before the painting of his sister, my missing mother: Paige Walker. Before she left sixteen years ago, Gram had been painting a portrait of her, which she never got to finish but put up anyway. It hovers over the mantel in the living room, half a mother, with long green hair pooling like water around an incomplete face.

Gram had always told us that our mother would return. "She'll be back," she'd say like Mom had gone to the store for some eggs, or a swim at the river. Gram said it so often and with such certainty that for a long while, before we learned more, we didn't question it, just spent a whole lot of time waiting for the phone to ring, the doorbell to sound, the mail to arrive.

I tap my hand softly against Big, who's staring up at The Half Mom like he's lost in a silent mournful conversation. He sighs, puts an arm around me and one around Toby, and we all plod into the kitchen like a three-headed, six-legged, ten-ton sack of sad.

Dinner, unsurprisingly, is a ham and ash casserole that we hardly touch.

After, Toby and I camp out on the living room floor, listening to Bailey's music, poring over countless photo albums, basically blowing our hearts to smithereens.

I keep sneaking looks at him from across the room. I can almost see Bails flouncing around him, coming up from behind and dropping her arms around his neck the way she always did. She'd say sickeningly embarrassing things in his ear, and he'd tease her back, both of them acting like I wasn't there.

"I feel Bailey," I say finally, the sense of her overwhelming me. "In this room, with us."

He looks up from the album on his lap, surprised. "Me too. I've been thinking it this whole time."

"It's *so* nice," I say, relief spilling out of me with the words.

He smiles and it makes his eyes squint like the sun is in his face. "It is, Len." I remember Bailey telling me once that Toby doesn't talk all that much to humans but is able to gentle startled horses at the ranch with just a few words. Like St Francis, I'd said to her, and I believe it – the low slow lull of his voice is soothing, like waves lapping the shore at night.

I return to the photos of Bailey as Wendy in the Clover Elementary production of *Peter Pan*. Neither of us mentions it again, but the comfort of feeling Bailey so close stays with me for the rest of the evening.

Later, Toby and I stand by the garden, saying goodbye. The

dizzy, drunk fragrance of the roses engulfs us.

"It was great hanging out with you, Lennie, made me feel better."

"Me too," I say, plucking a lavender petal. "Much better, really." I say this quietly and to the rosebush, not sure I even want him to hear, but when I peek back up at his face, it's kind, his leonine features less lion, more cub.

"Yeah," he says, looking at me, his dark eyes both shiny and sad. He lifts his arm, and for a second I think he's going to touch my face with his hand, but he just runs his fingers through the tumble of sunshine that is his hair.

We walk the few remaining steps to the road in slow motion. Once there, Lucy and Ethel emerge out of nowhere and start climbing all over Toby, who has dropped to his knees to say goodbye to them. He holds his skateboard in one hand, ruffling and petting the dogs with the other as he whispers unintelligible words into their fur.

"You really are St Francis, huh?" I have a thing for the saints – the miracles, not the mortifications.

"It's been said." A soft smile meanders across the broad planes of his face, landing in his eyes. "Mostly by your sister." For a split second, I want to tell him it was me who thought that, not Bailey.

He finishes his farewell, stands back up, then drops his skateboard to the ground, steadying it with his foot. He doesn't get on. A few years pass.

"I should go," he says, not going.

"Yeah," I say. A few more.

Before he finally hops on his board, he hugs me goodbye and we hold on to each other so tightly under the sad, starless sky that for a moment I feel as if our heartbreak were one instead of two.

But then all of a sudden, I feel a hardness against my hip, him, *that*. *Holy freaking shit!* I pull back quickly, say goodbye, and run back into the house.

I don't know if he knows that I felt him.

I don't know anything.

Someone from Bailey's drama class
yelled BRAVO at the end of the service
and everyone jumped to their feet
and started clapping
I remember thinking the roof would blow
from the thunder in our hands
that grief was a room filled
with hungry desperate light
We clapped for nineteen years
of a world with Bailey in it
did not stop clapping
when the sun set, moon rose
when all the people streamed into our house
with food and frantic sorrow
did not stop clapping
until dawn
when we closed the door
on Toby
who had to make his sad way home
I know we must have moved from that spot
must have washed and slept and ate
but in my mind, Gram, Uncle Big and I
stayed like that for weeks
just staring at the closed door
with nothing between our hands
but air

(Found on a piece of notebook paper blowing down Main Street)

4

This is what happens when Joe Fontaine has his debut trumpet solo in band practice: I'm the first to go, swooning into Rachel, who topples into Cassidy Rosenthal, who tumbles onto Zachary Quittner, who collapses onto Sarah, who reels into Luke Jacobus – until every kid in band is on the floor in a bedazzled heap. Then the roof flies off, the walls collapse, and when I look outside I see that the nearby stand of redwood trees has uprooted and is making its way up the quad to our classroom, a gang of giant wooden men clapping their branches together. Lastly, the Rain River overflows its banks and detours left and right until it finds its way to the Clover High music room, where it sweeps us all away – he is *that* good.

When the rest of us lesser musical mortals have recovered enough to finish the piece, we do, but as we put our instruments away at the end of practice, the room is as quiet and still as an empty church.

Finally, Mr James, who's been staring at Joe like he's an ostrich, regains the power of speech and says, "Well, well. As you all say, that sure sucked." Everyone laughs. I turn around to see what Sarah thought. I can just about make out an eye under a giant Rasta hat. She mouths *unfreakingbelievable*. I look over at Joe. He's wiping his trumpet, blushing from the response or flushed from playing, I'm not sure which. He looks up, catches my eye, then raises his eyebrows expectantly at me almost like the storm that has just come out of his horn has been for me. But why would that be? And why is it I keep catching him watching me play? It's not interest, I mean, *that* kind of interest, I can tell. He watches me clinically, intently, the way Marguerite used to during a lesson when she was trying to figure out what in the world I was doing wrong.

"Don't even think about it," Rachel says as I turn back around. "That trumpet player's accounted for. Anyway, he's like so out of your league, Lennie. I mean, when's the last time you had a boyfriend? Oh yeah, never."

I think about lighting her hair on fire.

I think about medieval torture devices: The Rack, in particular.

I think about telling her what really happened at chair auditions last fall.

Instead I ignore her like I have all year, swab my clarinet, and wish I were indeed preoccupied by Joe Fontaine rather than by what happened with Toby – each time I recall the sensation of him pressing into me, shivers race all through my body – definitely not the appropriate reaction to your sister's boyfriend's hard-on! And what's worse is that in the privacy of my mind, I don't pull away like I actually did but stay wrapped in his arms under the still sky, and that makes me flush with shame.

I shut my clarinet case wishing I could do the same on these thoughts of Toby. I scan the room – the other horn players have gathered around Joe, as if the magic were contagious. Not a word between him and me since my first day back. Hardly a word between me and anyone at school really. Even Sarah.

Mr James claps to get the attention of the class. In his excited, crackly voice, he begins talking about summer band practice because school's out in less than a week. "For those who are around, we will be practicing, starting in July. Who shows up will determine what we play. I'm thinking jazz" – he snaps his fingers like a flamenco dancer – "maybe some hot Spanish jazz, but I'm open to suggestions."

He raises his arms like a priest before a congregation. "Find the beat and keep it, my friends." The way he ends every class. But then after a moment he claps again. "Almost forgot, let me see a show of hands of those who plan on auditioning for All-State band next year." Oh no. I drop my pencil and bend over to avoid any possible eye collision with Mr James. When I emerge from my careful inspection of the floor, my phone vibrates in my pocket. I turn to Sarah, whose visible eye is popping out of her head. I sneak out my phone and read her text.

Y didn't u raise ur hand??? Solo made me think of u – that day! Come over 2nite???

I turn around, mouth: *Can't.*

She picks up one of her sticks and dramatically feigns stabbing it into her stomach with both hands. I know behind the hari-kari is a hurt that's growing, but I don't know what to do about it. For the first time in our lives, I'm somewhere she can't find, and I don't have the map to give her that leads to me.

I gather my things quickly to avoid her, which is going to be easy because Luke Jacobus has cornered her, and as I do, the day she mentioned comes racing back. It was the beginning of freshman year and we had both made honor band. Mr James, particularly frustrated with everyone, had jumped on a chair and shouted, "What's wrong with you people? You think you're musicians? You have to stick your asses in the wind!" Then he said, "C'mon, follow me. Those of you who can, bring your instruments."

We filed out of the room, down the path into the forest where the river rushed and roared. We all stood on the banks, while he climbed up onto a rock to address us.

"Now, listen, learn and then play, just *play*. Make *noise*. Make *something*. Make *muuuuuuuuusic*." Then he began conducting the river, the wind, the birds in the trees like a total loon. After we got over our hysterics and piped down, one by one, those of us who had our instruments started to play. Unbelievably, I was one of the first to go, and after a while, the river and wind and birds and clarinets and flutes and oboes mixed all together in a glorious cacophonous mess and Mr James turned his attention from the forest back to us, his body swaying, his arms flailing left and right, saying, "That's it, that's it. *That's it*!"

And it was.

When we got back to the classroom, Mr James came over to me and handed me Marguerite St Denis's card. "Call her," he said. "Right away."

I think about Joe's virtuoso performance today, can feel it in my fingers. I ball them into fists. Whatever it was, whatever that thing is Mr James took us in the woods that day to find, whether it's abandon or passion, whether it's innovation or simply courage, Joe has it.

His ass is in the wind. Mine is in second chair.

5

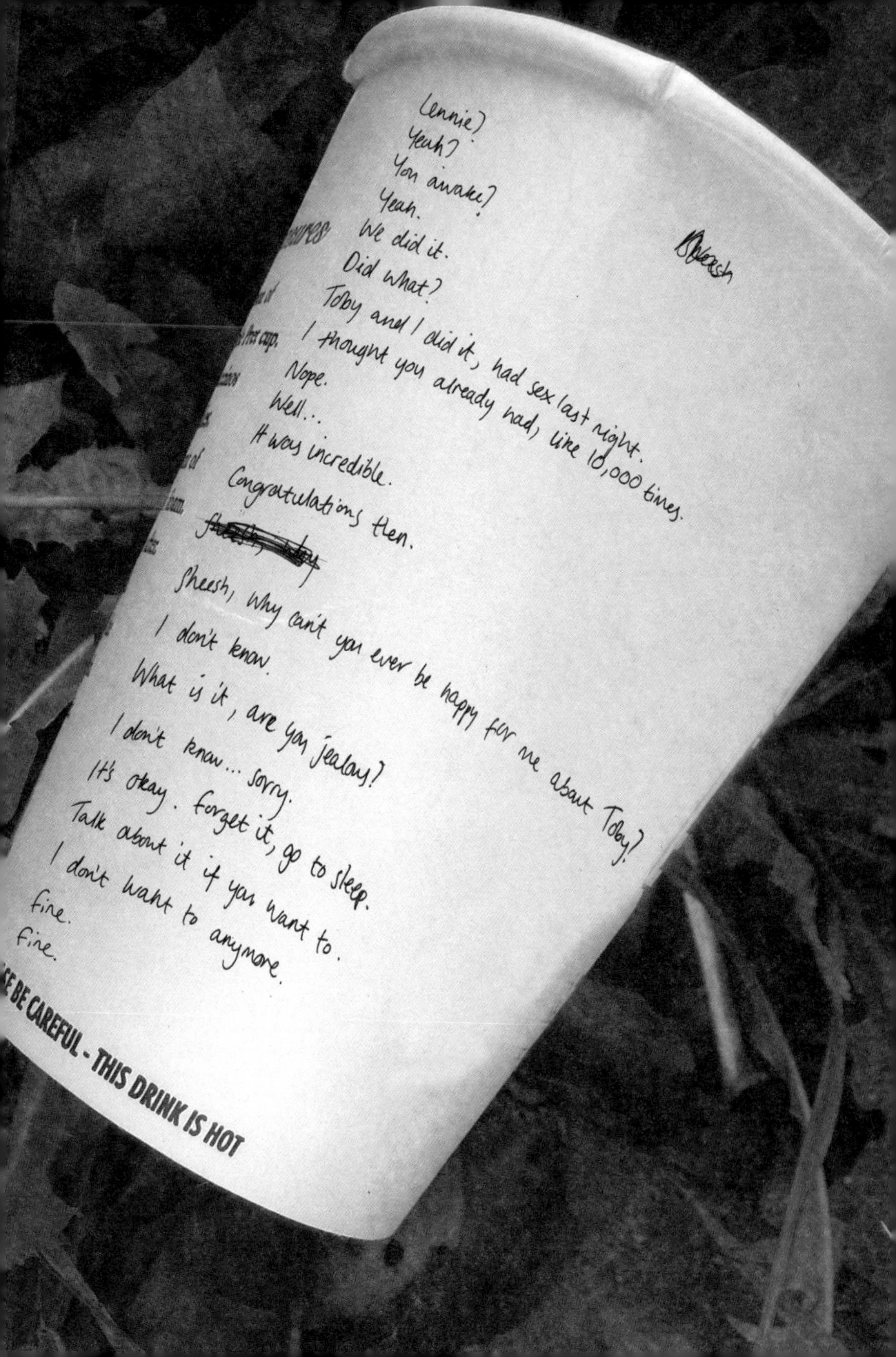
Lennie?
Yeah?
You awake?
Yeah.
We did it.
Did what?
Toby and I did it, had sex last night.
I thought you already had, like 10,000 times.
Nope.
Well...
It was incredible.
Congratulations then.
~~Sheesh, why~~
Sheesh, why can't you ever be happy for me about Toby?
I don't know.
What is it, are you jealous?
I don't know... sorry.
It's okay. Forget it, go to sleep.
Talk about it if you want to.
I don't want to anymore.
Fine.
Fine.
Sheesh
E BE CAREFUL - THIS DRINK IS HOT

(Found on a takeaway cup along the banks of the Rain River)

I know it's him, and wish I didn't. I wish my first thought was of anyone in the world but Toby when I hear the ping of a pebble on the window. I'm sitting in Bailey's closet, writing a poem on the wall, trying to curb the panic that hurls around inside my body like a trapped comet.

I take off the shirt of Bailey's I'd put on over mine, grab the doorknob, and hoist myself back into The Sanctum. Crossing to the window, my bare feet press into the three flattened blue rugs that scatter the room, pieces of bright sky that Bailey and I pounded down with years of cut-throat dance competitions to out-goofball the other without cracking up. I always lost because Bailey had in her arsenal The Ferret Face, which when combined with her masterful Monkey Moves, was certifiably deadly; if she pulled the combo (which took more unself-consciousness than I could ever muster), I was a goner, reduced to a helpless heap of hysterics, every time.

I lean over the sill, see Toby, as I knew I would, under a near full moon. I've had no luck squelching the mutiny inside me. I take a deep breath, then go downstairs and open the door.

"Hey, what's up?" I say. "Everyone's sleeping." My voice sounds creaky, unused, like bats might fly out of my mouth. I take a good look at him under the porch light. His face is wild with sorrow. It's like looking in a mirror.

"I thought maybe we could hang out," he says. This is what I hear in my mind: *boner, boner, erection, hard-on, woody, boner, boner, boner* – "I have something to tell you, Len, don't know who else to tell." The need in his voice sends a shudder right through me. Over his head, the red warning light could not be flashing brighter, but still I can't seem to say no, don't want to. "C'mon in, sir."

He touches my arm in a friendly, brotherly way as he passes, which sets me at ease, maybe guys get hard-ons all the time, for no reason – I have zero knowledge of boner basics. I've only ever kissed three guys, so I'm totally inexperienced with real-life boys, though quite an expert at the kind in books, especially Heathcliff, who doesn't get erections – wait, now that I'm thinking about it, he must get them *all the time* with Cathy on the moors. Heathcliff must be a total freaking boner boy.

I close the door behind him and motion for him to be quiet as he follows me up the steps to The Sanctum, which is soundproofed so as to protect the rest of the house against years of barky bleating clarinet notes. Gram would have a coronary that he's here visiting me at almost 2 a.m. on a school night. *On any night, Lennie*. This is most definitely not what she had in mind by reaching out to him.

Once the door of The Sanctum is closed, I put on some of the indie-kill-yourself music I've been listening to lately, and sit down next to Toby on the floor, our backs to the wall, legs outstretched. We sit in silence like two stone slabs. Several centuries pass.

When I can't handle it anymore, I joke, "It's possible you've taken this whole strong silent type thing to an extreme."

"Oh, sorry." He shakes his head, embarrassed. "Don't even

realize I'm doing it."

"Doing it?"

"Not talking… "

"Really? What is it you think you're doing?"

He tilts his head, smiling squintily, adorably. "I was going for the oak tree in the yard."

I laugh. "Very good then, you do a perfect oak impersonation."

"Thank you … think it drove Bails mad, my silent streak."

"Nah, she liked it, she told me, less chance of disagreements … plus more stage time for her."

"True." He's quiet for a minute, then in a voice ragged with emotion, says, "We were so different."

"Yeah," I say softly. Quintessential opposites, Toby always serene and still (when not on horse or board) while Bailey did everything: walk, talk, think, laugh, party, at the speed of light, and with its gleam.

"*You* remind me of her…" he says.

I want to blurt out: *What!? You've always acted like I was a baked potato!* but instead I say, "No way, don't have the wattage."

"You have plenty … it's me that has the serious shortage," he says, sounding surprisingly like a spud.

"Not to her," I say. His eyes warm at that – it kills me. What are we going to do with all this love?

He shakes his head in disbelief. "I got lucky. That chocolate book…"

The image assaults me: Bailey leaping off the rock the day they met when Toby returned on his board. "I knew you'd come back," she'd exclaimed, throwing the book in the air. "Just like in this story. I knew it!"

I have a feeling the same day is playing out in Toby's mind, because our polite levity has screeched to a halt – all the past tense in our words suddenly stacking up as if to crush us.

I can see the despair inching across his face as it must be across mine.

I look around our bedroom, at the singing orange paint we'd slathered over the dozy blue we'd had for years. Bailey had said, "If this doesn't change our lives, I don't know what will – this, Lennie, is *the color of extraordinary*." I remember thinking I didn't want our lives to change and didn't understand why she did. I remember thinking I'd always liked the blue.

I sigh. "I'm really glad you showed up, Toby. I'd been hiding in Bailey's closet freaking out for hours."

"Good. That you're glad, I mean, didn't know if I should bug you, but couldn't sleep either … did some stupid-ass skating that could've killed me, then ended up here, sat under the plum tree for an hour trying to decide…"

The rich timbre of Toby's voice suddenly makes me aware of the other voice in the room, the singer blaring from the speakers who sounds like he's being strangled at best. I get up to put on something more melodic, then when I sit back down, I confide, "No one gets it at school, not really, not even Sarah."

He tips his head back against the wall. "Don't know if it's possible to get it until you're in it like we are. I had no idea…"

"Me neither," I say, and suddenly I want to hug Toby because I'm just so relieved to not have to be in it by myself anymore tonight.

He's looking down at his hands, his brow furrowed, like he's struggling with how to say something. I wait.

And wait.

Still waiting here. How did Bailey brave the radio silence?

When he looks up, his face is all compassion, all cub. The words spill out of him, one on top of the next. "I've never known sisters so close. I feel so bad for you, Lennie, I'm just so sorry. I keep thinking about you without her."

"Thanks," I whisper, meaning it, and all of a sudden wanting to touch him, to run my hand over his, which rests on his thigh just inches from mine.

I glance at him sitting there so close to me that I can smell his shampoo, and I am stuck with a startling, horrifying thought: he is really good-looking, alarmingly so. How is it I never noticed before?

I'll answer that: he's Bailey's boyfriend, Lennie. What's wrong with you?

Dear Mind, I write on my jeans with my finger, *Behave*.

I'm sorry, I whisper to Bailey inside my head, I don't mean to think about Toby this way. I assure her it won't happen again.

It's just that he's the only one who understands, I add. *Oh brother*.

After a wordless while, he pulls a bottle of tequila out of his jacket pocket, uncaps it.

"Want some?" he asks. Great, that'll help.

"Sure." I hardly ever drink, but maybe it will help, maybe it'll knock this madness out of me. I reach for the bottle and our fingers graze a moment too long as I take it – I decide I imagined it, put the bottle to my lips, take a healthy sip, and then very daintily spit it out all over us. "Yuck, that's disgusting." I wipe my mouth with my sleeve. "Whoa."

He laughs, holds out his arms to show what a mess I've made of him. "It takes time to get used to it."

"Sorry," I say. "Had no idea it was so nasty."

He cheers the bottle to the air in response and takes a swig. I'm determined to try again and not projectile spew. I reach for the bottle, bring it to my lips, and let the liquid burn down my throat, then take another sip, bigger.

"Easy," Toby says, taking the tequila from me. "I need to tell you something, Len."

"Okay." I'm enjoying the warmth that has settled over me.

"I asked Bailey to marry me..." He says it so quickly it doesn't register at first. He's looking at me, trying to gage my reaction. It's stark, raving WTF!

"Marry you? Are you kidding?" Not the response he wants, I'm sure, but I'm totally blindsided; he could have just as easily told me she'd been secretly planning a career in fire-eating. Both of them were just nineteen, and Bailey a marriage-o-phobe to boot.

"What'd she say?" I'm afraid to hear the answer.

"She said yes." He says it with as much hope as hopelessness, the promise of it still alive in him. *She said yes*. I take the tequila, swig, don't even taste it or feel the burn. I'm stunned that Bailey wanted this, hurt that she wanted it, really hurt that she never told me. I have to know what she'd been thinking. I can't believe I can't ask her. Ever. I look at Toby, see the earnestness in his eyes; it's like a soft, small animal.

"I'm sorry, Toby," I say, trying to bottle my incredulity and hurt feelings, but then I can't help myself. "I don't know why she didn't tell me."

"We were going to tell you guys that very next week. I'd just asked…" His use of *we* jars me; the big *we* has always been Bailey and me, not Bailey and Toby. I suddenly feel left out of a future that isn't even going to happen.

"But what about her acting?" I say instead of: *What about me*?

"She was acting…"

"Yeah, but…" I look at him. "You know what I mean." And then I see by his expression that he doesn't know what I mean at all. Sure some girls dream of weddings, but Bailey dreamt of Juilliard: the Juilliard School in New York City. I once looked up their mission statement on the Web: *To provide the highest caliber of artistic education for gifted musicians, dancers and actors from around the world, so that they may achieve their fullest potential as artists, leaders and global citizens.* It's true after the rejection she enrolled last fall at Clover State, the only other college she applied to, but I'd been certain she'd reapply. I mean, how could she not? It was her dream.

We don't talk about it anymore. The wind's picked up and has begun rattling its way into the house. I feel a chill run through me, grab a throw blanket off the rocking chair, pull it over my legs. The tequila makes me feel like I'm melting into nothing, I want to, want to disappear. I have an impulse to write all over the orange walls – I need an alphabet of endings ripped out of books, of hands pulled off of clocks, of cold stones, of shoes filled with nothing but wind. I drop my head on Toby's shoulder. "We're the saddest people in the world."

"Yup," he says, squeezing my knee for a moment. I ignore the shivers his touch sends through me. *They were getting married.*

"How will we do this?" I say under my breath. "Day after day after day without her..."

"Oh, Len." He turns to me, smoothes the hair around my face with his hand.

I keep waiting for him to move his hand away, to turn back around, but he doesn't. He doesn't take his hand or gaze off of me. Time slows. Something shifts in the room, between us. I look into his sorrowful eyes and he into mine, and I think, *He misses her as much as I do*, and that's when he kisses me – his mouth: soft, hot, so alive, it makes me moan. I wish I could say I pull away, but I don't. I kiss him back and don't want to stop because in that moment I feel like Toby and I together have, somehow, in some way, reached across time, and pulled Bailey back.

He breaks away, springs to his feet. "I don't understand this." He's in an instant-just-add-water panic, pacing the room.

"God, I should go, I *really* should go."

But he doesn't go. He sits down on Bailey's bed, looks over at me and then sighs as if giving in to some invisible force. He says my name and his voice is so hoarse and hypnotic it pulls me up onto my feet, pulls me across miles of shame and guilt. I don't want to go to him, but I do want to too. I have no idea what to do, but still I walk across the room, wavering a bit from the tequila, to his side. He takes my hand and tugs on it gently.

"I just want to be near you," he whispers. "It's the only time I don't die missing her."

"Me too." I run my finger along the sprinkle of freckles on his cheek. He starts to well up, then I do too. I sit down next to him and then we lie down on Bailey's bed, spooning. My last thought before falling asleep in his strong, safe arms is that I hope we are not replacing our scents with the last remnants of Bailey's own that still infuse the bedding.

When I wake again, I'm facing him, our bodies pressed together, breath intermingling. He's looking at me. "You're beautiful, Len."

"No," I say. Then choke out one word. "Bailey."

"I know," he says. But he kisses me anyway. "I can't help it." He whispers it right into my mouth. I can't help it either.

I
wish
my
shadow
would
get
up
and
walk
beside
me

(Found on the back of a French exam in a flower bed, Clover High)

6

There were once two sisters who shared the same room,
the same clothes,
the same thoughts at the same moment.
These two sisters did not have a mother
but they had each other.
The older sister walked ahead of the younger
so the younger one always knew where to go.
The older one took the younger to the river
where they floated on their backs
like dead men.
The older girl would say:
Dunk your head under a few inches then open your eyes and look up at the sun
The younger girl:
I'll get water up my nose
The older:
C'mon, do it
and so the younger girl did it
and her whole world filled with light.

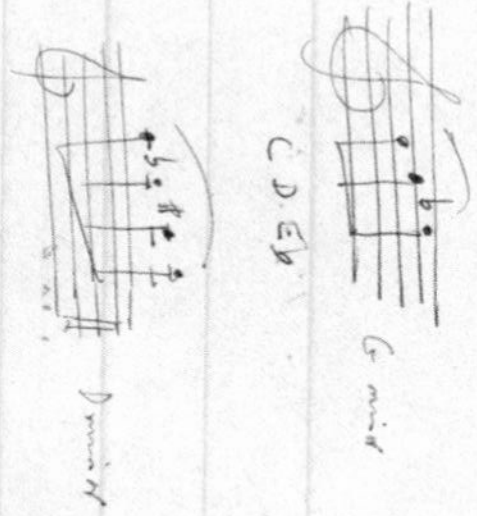

(1) Gavotte Tongue quavers in most places apart from line 3
Put in the grace notes.

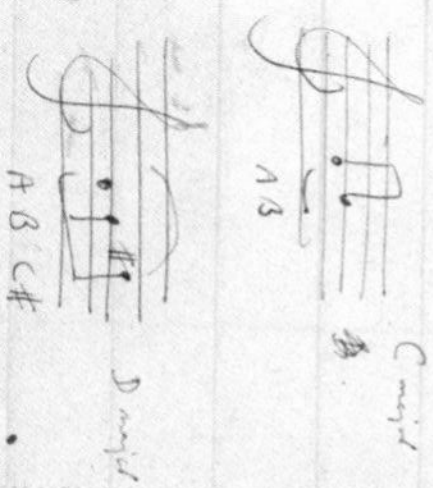

(Found on a piece of notebook paper caught in a fence up on the ridge)

Judas, Brutus, Benedict Arnold and me.

And the worst part is every time I close my eyes I see Toby's lion face again, his lips a breath away from mine, and it makes me shudder head to toe, not with guilt, like it should, but with desire – and then, just as soon as I allow myself the image of us kissing, I see Bailey's face twisting in shock and betrayal as she watches us from above: her boyfriend, her *fiancé* kissing her traitorous little sister *on her own bed*. Ugh. Shame watches me like a dog.

I'm in self-imposed exile, cradled between split branches, in my favorite tree in the woods behind school. I've been coming here every day at lunch, hiding out until the bell rings, whittling words into the branches with my pen, allowing my heart to break in private. I can't hide a thing – everyone in school sees clear to my bones.

I'm reaching into the brown bag Gram packed for me, when I hear twigs crack underneath me. Uh-oh. I look down and see Joe Fontaine. I freeze. I don't want him to see me: Lennie Walker: Mental Patient Eating Lunch in a Tree (it being decidedly out of your tree to hide out in one!). He walks in confused circles under me like he's looking for someone. I'm hardly breathing but he isn't moving on, has settled just to the right of my tree. Then I inadvertently crinkle the bag and he looks up, sees me.

"Hi," I say, like it's the most normal place to be eating lunch.

"Hey, there you are—" He stops, tries to cover. "I was wondering what was back here..." He looks around. "Perfect spot for a gingerbread house or maybe an opium den."

"You already gave yourself away," I say, surprised at my own boldness.

"Okay, guilty as charged. I followed you." He smiles at me – that same smile – wow, no wonder I'd thought—

He continues, "And I'm guessing you want to be alone. Probably don't come all the way out here and then climb a tree because you're starving for conversation." He gives me a hopeful look. He's charming me, even in my pitiful emotional state, my Toby turmoil, even though he's accounted for by Cruella de Vil.

"Want to come up?" I present him a branch and he bounds up the tree in about three seconds, finds a suitable seat right next to me, then bats his eyelashes at me. I'd forgotten about the eyelash endowment. Wow squared.

"What's to eat?" He points to the brown bag.

"You kidding? First you crash my solitude, now you want to scavenge. Where were you raised?"

"Paris," he says. "So I'm a scavenger *raffiné*."

Oh so glad *j'étudie le français*. And jeez, no wonder the school's abuzz about him, no wonder I'd wanted to kiss him. I even momentarily forgive Rachel the idiotic baguette she had sticking out of her backpack today. He goes on, "But I was born in California, lived in San Francisco until I was nine. We moved back there about a year ago and now we're here. Still want to know what's in the bag though."

"You'll never guess," I tell him. "I won't either, actually. My grandmother thinks it's really funny to put all sorts of things in our – my lunch. I never know what'll be inside: e. e. cummings, flower petals, a handful of buttons. She seems to have lost sight of the original purpose of the brown bag."

"Or maybe she thinks other forms of nourishment are more important."

"That's exactly what she thinks," I say, surprised. "Okay, you want to do the honors?" I hold up the bag.

"I'm suddenly afraid, is there ever anything alive in it?" Bat. Bat. Bat. Okay, it might take me a little time to build immunity to the eyelash bat.

"Never know..." I say, trying not to sound as swoony as I feel. And I'm going to just pretend that sitting-in-a-tree k-i-s-s-i-n-g rhyme did not just pop into my head.

He takes the bag, then reaches in with a grand gesture, and pulls out – an apple.

"An apple? How anti-climactic!" He throws it at me. "Everyone gets apples."

I urge him to continue. He reaches in, pulls out a copy of *Wuthering Heights*.

"That's my favorite book," I say. "It's like a pacifier. I've read it twenty-three times. She's always putting it in."

"*Wuthering Heights* – twenty-three times! Saddest book ever, how do you even function?"

"Do I have to remind you? I'm sitting in a tree at lunch."

"True." He reaches in again, pulls out a stemless purple peony. Its rich scent overtakes us immediately. "Wow," he says, breathing it in. "Makes me feel like I might levitate." He holds it under my nose. I close my eyes, imagine the fragrance lifting me off my feet too. I can't. But something occurs to me.

"My favorite saint of all time is a Joe," I tell him. "Joseph of Cupertino, he levitated. Whenever he thought of God, he would float into the air in a fit of ecstasy."

He tilts his head, looks at me skeptically, eyebrows raised. "Don't buy it."

I nod. "Tons of witnesses. Happened all the time. Right during Mass."

"Okay, I'm totally jealous. Guess I'm just a wannabe levitator."

"Too bad," I say. "I'd like to see you drifting over Clover playing your horn."

"Hell yeah," he exclaims. "You could come with, grab my foot or something."

We exchange a quick searching glance, both of us wondering about the other, surprised at the easy rapport – it's just a moment, barely perceptible, like a lady bug landing on your arm.

He rests the flower on my leg and I feel the brush of his fingers through my jeans. The brown bag is empty now. He hands it to me, and then we're quiet, just listening to the wind rustle around us and watching the sun filter through the redwoods in impossibly thick foggy rays just like in children's drawings.

Who is this guy? I've talked more to him in this tree than I have to anyone at school since I've been back. But how could he have read *Wuthering Heights* and still fall for Rachel Bitchzilla? Maybe it's because she's been to Fronce. Or because she pretends to like music that no one else has heard of, like the wildly popular Throat Singers of Tuva.

"I saw you the other day," he says, picking up the apple. He tosses it with one hand, catches it with the other. "By The Great Meadow. I was playing my guitar in the field. You were across the way. It looked like you were writing a note or something against a car, but then you just dropped the piece of paper—"

"Are you stalking me?" I ask, trying to keep my sudden delight at that notion out of my voice.

"Maybe a little." He stops tossing the apple. "And maybe I'm curious about something."

"Curious?" I ask. "About what?"

He doesn't answer, starts picking at moss on a branch. I notice his hands, his long fingers full of calluses from guitar strings.

"What?" I say again, dying to know what made him curious enough to follow me up a tree.

"It's the way you play the clarinet..."

The delight drains out of me. "Yeah?"

"Or the way you don't play it, actually."

"What do you mean?" I ask, knowing exactly what he means.

"I mean you've got loads of technique. Your fingering's quick, your tonguing fast, your range of tones, man ... but it's like it all stops there. I don't get it." He laughs, seemingly unaware of the bomb he just detonated. "It's like you're sleep-playing or something."

Blood rushes to my cheeks. Sleep-playing! I feel caught, a fish in a net. I wish I'd quit band altogether like I'd wanted to. I look off at the redwoods, each one rising to the sky surrounded only by its loneliness. He's staring at me, I can feel it, waiting for a response, but one is not forthcoming – this is a no trespassing zone.

"Look," he says cautiously, finally getting a clue that his charms have worn off. "I followed you out here because I wanted to see if we could play together."

"Why?" My voice is louder and more upset than I want it to be. A slow familiar panic is taking over my body.

"I want to hear John Lennon play for real, I mean, who wouldn't, right?"

His joke crashes and burns between us.

"I don't think so," I say as the bell rings.

"Look—" he starts, but I don't let him finish.

"I don't want to play with you, okay?"

"Fine." He hurls the apple into the air. Before it hits the ground and before he jumps out of the tree, he says, "It wasn't my idea anyway."

7

I wake to Ennui, Sarah's Jeep, honking down the road – it's an ambush. I roll over, look out the window, see her jump out in her favorite black vintage gown and platform combat boots, back-to-blond hair tweaked into a nest, cigarette hanging from blood red lips in a pancake of ghoulish white. I look at the clock: 7.05 a.m. She looks up at me in the window, waves like a windmill in a hurricane.

I pull the covers over my head, wait for the inevitable.

"I've come to suck your blood," she says a few moments later.

I peek out of the covers. "You really do make a stunning vampire."

"I know." She leans into the mirror over my dresser, wiping some lipstick off her teeth with her black-nail-polished finger. "It's a good look for me … Heidi goes goth." Without the accoutrements, Sarah could play Goldilocks. She's a sun-kissed beach girl who goes gothgrungepunkhippierockeremocore-metalfreakfashionistabraingeekboycrazyhiphoprastagirl to keep it under wraps. She crosses the room, stands over me, then pulls a corner of the covers down and hops into bed with me, boots and all.

"I miss you, Len." Her enormous blue eyes are shining down on me, so sincere and incongruous with her get-up. "Let's go to breakfast before school. Last day of junior year and all. It's tradition."

"Okay," I say, then add, "I'm sorry I've been so awful."

"Don't say that, I just don't know what to do for you. I can't imagine…" She doesn't finish, looks around The Sanctum. I see the dread overtake her. "It's so unbearable…" She stares at Bailey's bed. "Everything is just as she left it. God, Len."

"Yeah." My life catches in my throat. "I'll get dressed."

She bites her bottom lip, trying not to cry. "I'll wait downstairs. I promised Gram I'd talk with her." She gets out of bed and walks to the door, the leap in her from moments before now a shuffle. I pull the covers back over my head. I know the bedroom is a mausoleum. I know it upsets everyone (except Toby, who didn't even seem to notice), but I want it like this. It makes me feel like Bailey's still here or like she might come back.

On the way to town, Sarah tells me about her latest scheme to bag a babe who can talk to her about her favorite existentialist, Jean-Paul Sartre. The problem is her insane attraction to lumphead surfers who (not to be prejudicial) are not customarily the most well-versed in French literature and philosophy, and therefore must constantly be exempted from Sarah's Must-Know-Who-Sartre-Is-or-at-Least-Have-Read-Some-of-D.H. Lawrence-or-at-the-Minimum-One-of-the-Brontës-Preferably-Emily criteria of going out with her.

"There's an afternoon symposium this summer at the college in French Feminism," she tells me. "I'm going to go. Want to come?"

I laugh. "That sounds like the perfect place to meet guys."

"You'll see," she says. "The coolest guys aren't afraid to be feminists, Lennie."

I look over at her. She's trying to blow smoke rings, but

blowing smoke blobs instead.

I'm dreading telling her about Toby, but I have to, don't I? Except I'm too chicken, so I go with less damning news.

"I hung out with Joe Fontaine the other day at lunch."

"You didn't!"

"I did."

"No way."

"Yes way."

"Nah-uh."

"Uh-huh."

"Not possible.

"So possible."

We have an incredibly high tolerance for yes-no.

"You duck! You flying yellow duck! And you took this long to tell me?!" When Sarah gets excited, random animals pop into her speech like she has an Old MacDonald Had a Farm kind of Tourette's syndrome. "Well, what's he like?"

"He's okay," I say distractedly, looking out the window. I can't figure out whose idea it could've been that we play together. Mr James, maybe? But why? And argh, how freaking mortifying.

"Earth to Lennie. Did you just say Joe Fontaine is okay? The guy's holy horses *unfreakingbelievable*! And I heard he has two older brothers: holy horses to the third power, don't you think?"

"Holy horses, Batgirl," I say, which makes Sarah giggle, a sound that doesn't seem quite right coming out of her Batgoth face. She takes a last drag off her cigarette and drops it into a can of soda. I add, "He likes Rachel. What does that say about him?"

"That he has one of those Y chromosomes," Sarah says, shoving a piece of gum into her orally fixated mouth. "But really, I don't see it. I heard all he cares about is music and she plays like a screeching cat. Maybe it's those stupid Throat Singers she's always going on about and he thinks she's in the musical know or something." Great minds … then suddenly Sarah's jumping in her seat like she's on a pogo stick. "Oh Lennie, do it! Challenge her for first chair. Today! C'mon. It'll be so exciting – probably never happened in the history of honor band, a chair challenged on the last day of school!"

I shake my head. "Not going to happen."

"But why?"

I don't answer her, don't know how to.

An afternoon from last summer pops into my head. I'd just quit my lessons with Marguerite and was hanging out with Bailey and Toby at Flying Man's Gulch. He was telling us that Thoroughbred racing horses have these companion ponies that always stay by their sides, and I remember thinking, *That's me*. I'm a companion pony, and companion ponies don't solo. They don't play first chair or audition for All-State or compete nationally or seriously consider a certain performing arts conservatory in New York City like Marguerite had begun insisting.

They just don't.

Sarah sighs as she swerves into a parking spot. "Oh well,

guess I'll have to entertain myself another way on the last day of school."

"Guess so."

We jump out of Ennui, head into Cecilia's Bakery, and order up an obscene amount of pastries that Cecilia gives us for free with that same sorrowful look that follows me everywhere I go now. I think she would give me every last pastry in the store if I asked.

We land on our bench of choice by Maria's Italian Deli, where I've been chief lasagna maker every summer since I was fourteen. I start up again tomorrow. The sun has burst into millions of pieces, which have landed all over Main Street. It's a gorgeous day. Everything shines except my guilty heart.

"Sarah, I have to tell you something."

A worried look comes over her. "Sure."

"Something happened with Toby the other night." Her worry has turned into something else, which is what I was afraid of. Sarah has an ironclad girlfriend code of conduct regarding guys. The policy is sisterhood before all else.

"Something like something? Or something like *something*?" Her eyebrow has landed on Mars.

My stomach churns. "Like *something* … we kissed." Her eyes go wide and her face twists in disbelief, or perhaps it's horror. This is the face of my shame, I think, looking at her. *How could I have kissed Toby?* I ask myself for the thousandth time.

"Wow," she says, the word falling like a rock to the ground.

She's making no attempt to hold back her disdain. I bury my head in my hands, assume the crash position – I shouldn't have told her.

"It felt right in the moment, we both miss Bails so much, he just gets it, gets me, he's like the only one who does … and I was drunk." I say all this to my jeans.

"Drunk?" She can't contain her surprise. I hardly ever even have a beer at the parties she drags me to. Then in a softer voice, I hear, "Toby's the only one who gets you?"

Uh-oh.

"I didn't mean that," I say, lifting my head to meet her eyes, but it's not true, I did mean it, and I can tell from her expression she knows it. "Sarah."

She swallows, looks away from me, then quickly changes the topic back to my disgrace. "I guess it does happen. Grief sex is kind of a thing. It was in one of those books I read." I still hear the judgment in her voice, and something more now too.

"We didn't have sex," I say. "I'm still the last virgin standing."

She sighs, then puts her arm around me, awkwardly, as if she has to. I feel like I'm in a headlock. Neither of us has a clue how to deal with what's not being said, or what is.

"It's okay, Len. Bailey would understand." She sounds totally unconvincing. "And it's not like it's ever going to happen again, right?"

"Of course not," I say, and hope I'm not lying.

And hope I am.

Everyone has always said I look like Bailey,
but I don't.
I have grey eyes to her green,
an oval face to her heart-shaped one,
I'm shorter, scrawnier, paler,
flatter, plainer, tamer.
All we shared is a madhouse of curls
that I imprison in a ponytail
while she let hers rave
like madness
around her head.
I don't sing in my sleep
or eat the petals off flowers
or run into the rain instead of out of it.
I'm the unplugged-in one,
the side-kick sister,
tucked into a corner of her shadow.
Boys followed her everywhere;
they filled the booths at the restaurant
where she waitressed,
herded around her at the river.
One day, I saw a boy come up behind her
and pull a strand of her long hair.
I understood this—
I felt the same way.
In photographs of us together,
she is always looking at the camera,
and I am always looking at her.

(Found on a folded up piece of paper half buried in pine needles on the trail to the Rain River)

8

I am sitting at Bailey's desk with St Anthony: Patron of Lost Things.

He doesn't belong here. He belongs on the mantel in front of The Half Mom where I've always kept him, but Bailey must've moved him, and I don't know why. I found him tucked behind the computer in front of an old drawing of hers that's tacked to the wall – the one she made the day Gram told us our mother was an explorer (of the Christopher Columbus variety).

I've drawn the curtains, and though I want to, I won't let myself peek out the window to see if Toby is under the plum tree. I won't let myself imagine his lips lost and half wild on mine either. No. I let myself imagine igloos, nice, frigid, arctic igloos. I've promised Bailey nothing like what happened that night will ever happen again.

It's the first day of summer vacation and everyone from school is at the river. I just got a drunken call from Sarah informing me that not one, not two, but three unfreaking-believable Fontaines are supposed to be arriving momentarily at Flying Man's, that they are going to play outside, that she just found out the two older Fontaines are in a seriously awesome band in LA, where they go to college, and I better get my butt down there to witness the glory. I told her I was staying in and to revel in their Fontainely glory for me, which resurrected the bristle from yesterday: "You're not with Toby, are you, Lennie?"

Ugh.

I look over at my clarinet abandoned in its case on my

playing chair. It's in a coffin, I think, then immediately try to unthink it. I walk over to it, unlatch the lid. There never was a question what instrument I'd play. When all the other girls ran to the flutes in fifth grade music class, I beelined for a clarinet. It reminded me of me.

I reach in the pocket where I keep my cloth and reeds and feel around for the folded piece of paper. I don't know why I've kept it (for over a year!), why I fished it out of the garbage later that afternoon, after Bailey had tossed it with a cavalier "Oh well, guess you guys are stuck with me," before throwing herself into Toby's arms like it meant nothing to her. But I knew it did. How could it not? It was Juilliard.

Without reading it a final time, I crumple Bailey's rejection letter into a ball, toss it into the garbage can, and sit back down at her desk.

I'm in the exact spot where I was that night when the phone blasted through the house, through the whole unsuspecting world. I'd been doing chemistry, hating every minute of it like I always do. The thick oregano scent of Gram's chicken fricassee was wafting into our room and all I wanted was Bailey to hurry home already so we could eat because I was starving and hated isotopes. How can that be? How could I have been thinking about fricassee and carbon molecules when across town my sister had just taken her very last breath? What kind of world is this? And what do you do about it? What do you do when the worst thing that can happen actually happens? When you get *that* phone call? When you miss your sister's rollercoaster of a voice so much that you want to take apart the whole house with your fingernails?

This is what I do: I take out my phone and punch in her number. In a blind fog of a moment the other day I called to see when she'd be home and discovered her account hadn't yet been canceled.

Hey, this is Bailey, Juliet for the month, so dudes, what say'st thou? Hast thou not a word of joy? Some comfort...

I hang up at the tone, then call back, again and again, and again, and again, wanting to just pull her out of the phone. Then one time I don't hang up.

"Why didn't you tell me you were getting married?" I whisper, before snapping the phone shut and laying it on her desk. Because I don't understand. Didn't we tell each other everything? *If this doesn't change our lives, Len, I don't know what will*, she'd said when we painted the walls. Is that the change she'd wanted then? I pick up the cheesy plastic St Anthony. And what about him? Why bring him up here? I look more closely at the drawing he was leaning against. It's been up so long that the paper has yellowed and the edges have curled, so long that I haven't taken notice of it for years. Bailey drew it when she was around eleven, the time she started questioning Gram about Mom with an unrelenting ferocity.

She'd been at it for weeks.

"How do you know she'll be back?" Bailey asked for the millionth time. We were in Gram's art room, Bailey and I lay sprawled out on the floor drawing with pastels while Gram painted one of her ladies at a canvas in the corner, her back to us. She'd been skirting Bailey's questions all day, artfully changing the subject, but it wasn't working this time. I watched Gram's arm drop to her side, the brush sending droplets of a hopeful green onto the bespattered floor. She sighed, a big lonely sigh, then turned around to face us.

"I guess you're old enough, girls," she said. We perked up, immediately put down our pastels, and gave her our undivided attention. "Your mother is … well … I guess the best way to describe it … hmmm … let me think…" Bailey looked at me in shock – we'd never known Gram to be at a loss for words.

"What, Gram?" Bailey asked. "What is she?"

"Hmmm…" Gram bit her lip, then finally, hesitantly, she said, "I guess the best way to say it is … you know how some people have natural tendencies, how I paint and garden, how Big's an arborist, how you, Bailey, want to grow up and be an actress—"

"I'm going to go to Juilliard," she told us.

Gram smiled. "Yes, we know, Miss Hollywood. Or Miss Broadway, I should say."

"Our mom?" I reminded them before we ended up talking some more about that dumb school. All I'd hoped was that it was in walking distance if Bailey was going there. Or at least close enough so I could ride my bike to see her every day. I'd been too scared to ask.

Gram pursed her lips for a moment. "Okay, well, your mother, she's a little different, she's more like a … well, like an explorer."

"Like Columbus, you mean?" Bailey asked.

"Yes, like that, except without the *Niña, Pinta* and *Santa Maria*. Just a woman, a map, and the world. A solo artist." Then she left the room, her favorite and most effective way of ending a conversation.

Bailey and I stared at each other. In all our persistent musings on where Mom was and why she left, we never ever imagined anything remotely this good. I followed after Gram to try and find out more, but Bailey stayed on the floor and drew this picture.

In it, there's a woman at the top of a mountain looking off into the distance, her back to us. Gram, Big, and I – with our names beneath our feet – are waving up at the lone figure from the base of the mountain. Under the whole drawing, it says in green *Explorer*. For some reason, Bailey did not put herself in the picture.

I bring St Anthony to my chest, hold him tight. I need him now, but why did Bailey? What had she lost?

What was it she needed to find?

I put on her clothes
I button one of her frilly shirts
over my own t-shirt.
Or I wrap one, sometimes two,
sometimes all of her diva scarves around my neck.
Or I strip and slip one of her slinkier dresses over my head,
letting the fabric
fall over my skin like water.
I always feel better then,
like she's holding me.
Then I touch all the things
that haven't moved since she died:
crumpled up dollars
dredged from a sweaty pocket,
the three bottles of perfume
always with the same amount of liquid in them now,
the Sam Shepherd play
Fool for Love
where her bookmark will never move forward.
I've read it for her twice now,
always putting the bookmark back
where it was when I finish—
it kills me
she will never find out
what happens
in the end.

(Found on the inside cover of Wuthering Heights, *Clover High library)*

9

Gram spends the night
in front of The Half Mom.
I hear her weeping—
sad
endless
rain.
I sit at the top of the stairs,
know she's touching
Mom's cold flat cheek
as she says: *I'm sorry*
I'm so sorry.
I think a terrible thing.
I think: *You should be.*
I think: *How could you have*
let this happen?
How could you have let both of
them leave me?

(Found written on the wall of the bathroom at Cecilia's Bakery)

School's been out for two weeks. Gram, Big and I are certifiably out of our trees and running loose through the park – all in opposite directions.

Exhibit A: Gram's following me around the house with a teapot. The pot is full. I can see the steam coming out the spout. She has two mugs in her other hand. Tea is what Gram and I used to do together, before. We'd sit around the kitchen table in the late afternoons and drink tea and talk before the others came home. But I don't want to have tea with Gram anymore because I don't feel like talking, which she knows but still hasn't accepted. So she's followed me up the stairs and is now standing in the doorway of The Sanctum, pot in hand.

I flop onto the bed, pick up my book, pretend to read.

"I don't want any tea, Gram," I say, looking up from *Wuthering Heights,* which I note is upside down and hope she doesn't.

Her face falls. Epically.

"Fine." She puts a mug on the ground, fills the other one in her hand for herself, takes a sip. I can tell it's burned her tongue, but she pretends it hasn't. "Fine, fine, fine," she chants, taking another sip.

She's been following me around like this since school got out. Normally, summer is her busiest time as Garden Guru, but she's told all her clients she is on hiatus until the fall. So instead of guruing, she happens into Maria's while I'm at the deli, or into the library when I'm on my break, or she tails me to Flying Man's and paces on the path while I float on my back and let my tears spill into the water.

But teatime is the worst.

"Sweet pea, it's not healthy…" Her voice has melted into a familiar river of worry. I think she's talking about my remoteness, but when I glance over at her I realize it's the other thing. She's staring at Bailey's dresser, the gum wrappers strewn about, the hairbrush with a web of her black hair woven through the teeth. I watch her gaze drifting around the room to Bailey's dresses thrown over the back of her desk chair, the towel flung over her bedpost, Bailey's laundry basket still piled over with her dirty clothes…"Let's just pack up a few things."

"I told you, I'll do it," I whisper so I don't scream at the top of my lungs. "I'll do it, Gram, if you stop stalking me and leave me alone."

"Okay, Lennie," she says. I don't have to look up to know I've hurt her.

When I do look up, she's gone. Instantly, I want to run after her, take the teapot from her, pour myself a mug and join her, just spill every thought and feeling I'm having.

But I don't.

I hear the shower turn on. Gram spends an inordinate amount of time in the shower now and I know this is because she thinks she can cry under the spray without Big and me hearing. We hear.

Exhibit B: I roll onto my back and before long I'm holding my pillow in my arms and kissing the air with an embarrassing amount of passion. Not again, I think. What's wrong with me? What kind of girl wants to kiss every boy at a funeral, wants to maul a guy in a tree after making out with her sister's boyfriend the previous night? *Speaking of which, what kind of girl makes out with her sister's boyfriend, at all?*

Let me just unsubscribe to my own mind already, because I don't get any of it. I hardly ever thought about sex before, much less did anything about it. Three boys at three parties in four years: Casey Miller, who tasted like hot dogs; Dance Rosencrantz, who dug around in my shirt like he was reaching into a box of popcorn at the movies. And Jasper Stolz in eighth grade because Sarah dragged me into a game of spin the bottle. Total blobfish feeling inside each time. Nothing like Heathcliff and Cathy, like Lady Chatterley and Oliver Mellors, like Mr Darcy and Elizabeth Bennet! Sure, I've always been into the Big Bang theory of passion, but as something theoretical, something that happens in books that you can close and put back on a shelf, something that I might secretly want bad but can't imagine ever happening to me. Something that happens to the heroines like Bailey, to the commotion girls in the leading roles. But now I've gone mental, kissing everything I can get my lips on: my pillow, armchairs, doorframes, mirrors, always imagining the one person I should not be imagining, the person I promised my sister I will never ever kiss again. The one person who makes me feel just a little less afraid.

The front door slams shut, jarring me out of Toby's forbidden arms.

It's Big. Exhibit C: I hear him stomp straight into the dining room, where only two days ago, he unveiled his pyramids. This is always a bad sign. He built them years ago, based on some hidden mathematics in the geometry of the Egyptian pyramids. (Who knows? The guy also talks to trees.) According to Big, his pyramids, like the ones in the Middle East, have extraordinary properties. He's always believed his replicas would be able to prolong the life of cut flowers and fruit, even revive bugs, all of which he would place under them for ongoing study. During his pyramid spells, Big, Bails and I would spend hours searching the house for dead spiders or flies, and then each morning we'd run to the pyramids hoping to witness a resurrection. We never did. But whenever Big's really upset, the necromancer in him comes out, and with it, the pyramids. This time, he's at it with a fervor, sure it will work, certain that he only failed before because he forgot a key element: an electrically charged coil, which he's now placed under each pyramid.

A little while later, a stoned Big drifts past my open door. He's been smoking so much weed that when he's home he seems to hover above Gram and me like an enormous balloon – every time I come upon him, I want to tie him to a chair.

He backtracks, lingers in my doorway for a moment.

"I'm going to add a few dead moths tomorrow," he says, as if picking up on a conversation we'd been having.

I nod. "Good idea."

He nods back, then floats off to his room, and most likely, right out the window.

This is us. Two months and counting. Booby Hatch Central.

The next morning, a showered and betoweled Gram is fixing breakfast ashes, Big is sweeping the rafters for dead moths to put under the pyramids, and I am trying not to make out with my spoon, when there's a knock at the door. We freeze, all of us suddenly panicked that someone might witness the silent sideshow of our grief. I walk to the front door on tiptoe, so as not to let on that we are indeed home, and peek through the peephole. It's Joe Fontaine, looking as animated as ever, like the front door is telling him jokes. He has a guitar in his hand.

"Everybody hide," I whisper. I prefer all boys safe in the recesses of my sex-crazed mind, not standing outside the front door of our capsizing house. Especially this minstrel. I haven't even taken my clarinet out of its case since school ended. I have no intention of going to summer band practice.

"Nonsense," Gram says, making her way to the front of the house in her bright purple towel muumuu and pink towel turban ensemble. "Who is it?" she asks me in a whisper hundreds of decibels louder than her normal speaking voice.

"It's that new kid from band, Gram, I can't deal." I swing my arms back and forth trying to shoo her into the kitchen.

I've forgotten how to do anything with my lips but kiss furniture. I have no conversation in me. I haven't seen anyone from school, don't want to, haven't called back Sarah, who's taken to writing me long e-mails (essays) about how she's not judging me at all about what happened with Toby, which just lets me know how much she's judging me about what happened with Toby. I duck into the kitchen, back into a corner, pray for invisibility.

"Well, well, a troubadour," Gram says, opening the door. She has obviously noticed the mesmery that is Joe's face and has already begun flirting. "Here I thought we were in the twenty-first century..." She is starting to purr. I have to save him.

I reluctantly come out of hiding and join swami seductress Gram. I get a good look at him. I've forgotten quite how luminous he is, like another species of human that doesn't have blood but light running through their veins. He's spinning his guitar case like a top while he talks to Gram. He doesn't look like he needs saving, he looks amused.

"Hi, John Lennon." He's beaming at me like our tree-spat never happened.

What are you doing here? I think so loudly my head might explode.

"Haven't seen you around," he says. Shyness overtakes his face for a quick moment – it makes my stomach flutter. Uh, I think I need to get a restraining order for all boys until I can get a handle on this newfound body buzz.

"Do come in," Gram says, as if talking to a knight. "I was just preparing breakfast." He looks at me, asking if it's okay with his eyes. Gram's still talking as she walks back into the kitchen. "You can play us a song, cheer us up a bit." I smile at him, it's impossible not to, and motion a welcome with my arm. As we enter the kitchen, I hear Gram whisper to Big, still in knight parlance, "I daresay, the young gentleman batted his extraordinarily long eyelashes at me."

We haven't had a real visitor since the weeks following the funeral and so don't know how to behave. Uncle Big has seemingly floated to the floor and is leaning on the broom he had been using to sweep up the dead. Gram stands, spatula in hand, in the middle of the kitchen with an enormous smile on her face. I'm certain she's forgotten what she's wearing. And I sit upright in my chair at the table. No one says anything and all of us stare at Joe like he's a television we're hoping will just turn itself on. .

It does.

"That garden is wild, never seen flowers like that, thought some of those roses might chop off *my* head and put me in a vase." He shakes his head in amazement and his hair falls too adorably into his eyes. "It's like Eden or something."

"Better be careful in Eden, all that temptation." The thunder of Big's God voice surprises me – he's been my partner in muteness lately, much to Gram's displeasure. "Smelling Gram's flowers has been known to cause all sorts of maladies of the heart."

"Really?" Joe says. "Like what?"

"Many things. For instance, the scent of her roses causes a mad love to flourish." At that, Joe's gaze ever so subtlety shifts to me – whoa, or did I imagine it? Because now his eyes are back on Big, who's still talking. "I believe this to be the case from personal experience and five marriages." He grins at Joe. "Name's Big, by the way, I'm Lennie's uncle. Guess you're new around here or you'd already know all this."

What he would know is that Big is the town lothario. Rumors have it that at lunchtime women from all over pack a picnic and set out to find which tree that arborist is in, hoping for an invitation to lunch with him in his barrel high in the canopy. The stories go that shortly after they dine, their clothes flutter down like leaves.

I watch Joe taking in my uncle's gigantism, his wacked-out mustache. He must like what he sees, because his smile immediately brightens the room a few shades.

"Yup, we moved here just a couple months ago from the city, before that we were in Paris—" Hmm. He must not have read the warning on the door about saying the word *Paris* within a mile radius of Gram. It's too late. She's already off on a Francophiliac rhapsody, but Joe seems to share her fanaticism.

He laments, "Man, *if only* we still lived—"

"Now, now," she interrupts, wagging her finger like she's scolding him. Oh no. Her hands have found her hips. Here it comes: she singsongs, "*If only* I had wheels on my ass, I'd be a trolley cart." A Gram standard to forestall wallowing. I'm appalled, but Joe cracks up.

Gram's in love. I don't blame her. She's taken him by the hand and is now escorting him on a docent walk through the house, showing off her willowy women, with whom he seems duly and truly impressed, from the exclamations he's making, in French, I might add. This leaves Big to resume his scaven-ging for bugs and me to replace fantasies of my spoon with Joe Fontaine's mouth. I can hear them in the living room, know they are standing in front of The Half Mom because everyone who comes in the house has the same reaction to it.

"It's so haunting," Joe says.

"Hmm, yes … that's my daughter, Paige. Lennie and Bailey's mom, she's been away for a long, long time…" I'm shocked. Gram hardly ever talks about Mom voluntarily. "One day I'll finish this painting, it's not done…" Gram has always said she'll finish it when Mom comes back and can pose for her.

"Come now, let's eat." I can hear the heartache in Gram's voice through three walls. Mom's absence has grown way more pronounced for her since Bailey's death. I keep catching her and Big staring at The Half Mom with a fresh, almost desperate kind of longing. It's become more pronounced for me too.

Mom was what Bails and I did together before bed when we'd imagine where she was and what she was doing. I don't know how to think about Mom without her.

I'm jotting down a poem on the sole of my shoe when they come back in.

"Run out of paper?" Joe asks.

I put my foot down. Ugh. What's your major, Lennie? Oh yeah: Dorkology.

Joe sits down at the table, all limbs and graceful motion, an octopus.

We are staring at him again, still not certain what to make

of the stranger in our midst. The stranger, however, appears quite comfortable with us.

"What's up with the plant?" He points to the despairing Lennie houseplant in the middle of the table. It looks like it has leprosy. We all go silent, because what do we say about my doppelgänger houseplant?

"It's Lennie, it's dying, and frankly, we don't know what to do about it," Big booms with finality. It's as if the room itself takes a long awkward breath, and then at the same moment Gram, Big and I lose it – Big slapping the table and barking laughter like a drunk seal, Gram leaning back against the counter wheezing and gasping for breath, and me doubled over trying to breathe in between my own uncontrolled gasping and snorting, all of us lost in a fit of hysterics the likes of which we haven't had in months.

"Aunt Gooch! Aunt Gooch!" Gram is shrieking in between peals of laugher. Aunt Gooch is the name Bailey and I gave to Gram's laugh because it would arrive without notice like a crazy relative who shows up at the door with pink hair, a suitcase full of balloons, and no intention of leaving.

Gram gasps, "Oh my, oh my, I thought she was gone for good."

Joe seems to be taking the outburst quite well. He's leaned back in his chair, is balancing on its two back legs; he looks entertained, like he's watching, well, like he's watching three heartbroken people lose their marbles. I finally settle enough to explain to Joe, amidst tears and residual giggles, the story of the plant. If he hadn't already thought he'd gained entry to the local loony bin, he was sure to now. To my amazement, he doesn't make an excuse and fly out the door, but takes the predicament quite seriously, like he actually cares about the fate of the plain, sickly plant that will not revive.

After breakfast, Joe and I go onto the porch, which is still eerily cloaked in morning fog. The moment the screen door closes behind us, he says, "One song," as if no time has elapsed since we were in the tree.

I walk over to the railing, lean against it, and cross my arms in front of my chest. "You play. I'll listen."

"I don't get it," he says. "What the deal?"

"The deal is I don't want to."

"But why? Your pick, I don't care what."

"I told you, I don't—"

He starts to laugh. "God, I feel like I'm pressuring you to have sex or something." Every ounce of blood in a ten-mile radius rushes to my cheeks. "C'mon. I know you want to..." he jokes, raising his eyebrows like a total dork. What I want is to hide under the porch, but his giant loopy grin makes me laugh. "Bet you like Mozart," he says, squatting to open his case. "All clarinettists do. Or maybe you're a Bach's Sacred Music devotee?" He squints up at me. "Nah, don't seem like one of those." He takes the guitar out, then sits on the edge of the coffee table, swinging it over his knee. "I've got it. No clarinet player with blood in her veins can resist Gypsy jazz." He plays a few sizzling chords. "Am I right? Or ... I know!" He starts beating a rhythm on his guitar with his hand, his foot pounding the floor. "Dixieland!"

The guy's life-drunk, I think, makes Candide look like a sourpuss. Does he even know that death exists?

"So, whose idea was it?" I ask him.

He stops finger-drumming. "What idea?"

"That we play together. You said—"

"Oh, that. Marguerite St Denis is an old friend of the family – the one I blame actually for my exile up here. She might've mentioned something about how Lennie Walker *joue de la clarinette comme un rêve*." He twirls his hand in the air like Marguerite. *"Elle joue à ravir, de merveille."*

I feel a rush of something, everything, panic, pride, guilt, nausea – it's so strong I have to hold on to the railing. I wonder what else she told him.

"*Quelle catastrophe*," he continues. "You see, I thought *I* was her only student who played like a dream." I must look confused, because he explains, "In France. She taught at the conservatory, most summers."

As I take in the fact that my Marguerite is also Joe's Marguerite, I see Big barreling past the window, back at it, broom over head, looking for creatures to resurrect. Joe doesn't seem to notice, probably a good thing. He adds, "I'm joking, about me, clarinet's never been my thing."

"Not what I heard," I say. "Heard you were *fabulous*."

"Rachel doesn't have much of an ear," he replies matter-of-factly, without insult. Her name falls too easily from his lips, like he says it all the time, probably right before he kisses her. I feel my face flush again. I look down, start examining my shoes. What's with me? I mean really. He just wants to play music together like normal musicians do.

Then I hear, "I thought about you…"

I don't dare look up for fear I imagined the words, the sweet tentative tone. But if I did, I'm imagining more of them. "I thought about how crazy sad you are, and…"

He's stopped talking. *And what?* I lift my head to see that he's examining my shoes too. "Okay," he says, meeting my gaze. "I had this image of us holding hands, like up at The Great Meadow or somewhere, and then taking off into the air."

Whoa – I wasn't expecting that, but I like it. "*A la* St Joseph?"

He nods. "Got into the idea."

"What kind of launch?" I ask. "Like rockets?"

"No way, an effortless take-off, Superman-style." He raises one arm up and crosses his guitar with the other to demonstrate. "You know."

I do know. I know I'm smiling just to look at him. I know that what he just said is making something unfurl inside. I know that all around the porch, a thick curtain of fog hides us from the world.

I want to tell him.

"It's not that I don't want to play with you," I say quickly so I don't lose my nerve. "It's that, I don't know, it's different, playing is." I force out the rest. "I didn't want to play first chair, didn't want to do the solos, didn't want to do any of it. I blew it, the chair audition … on purpose." It's the first time I've said it aloud, to anyone, and the relief is the size of a planet. I go on. "I hate soloing, not that you'd understand that. It's just so…" I'm waving my arm around, unable to find the words. But then I point my hand in the direction of Flying Man's. "So like jumping from rock to rock in the river, but in this kind of thick fog, and you're all alone, and every single step is…"

"Is what?"

I suddenly realize how ridiculous I must sound. I have no clue what I'm talking about, no clue. "It doesn't matter," I say.

He shrugs. "Tons of musicians are afraid to fall on their faces."

I can hear the steady whoosh of the river as if the fog's parted to let the sound through.

It's not just performance anxiety though. That's what Marguerite thought too. It's why she thought I quit – *You must work on the nerves, Lennie, the nerves* – but it's more than that, way more. When I play, it's like I'm all shoved and crammed and scared inside myself, like a jack-in-the-box, except one without a spring. And it's been like that for over a year now.

Joe bends down and starts flipping through the sheet music in his case; lots of it is handwritten. He says, "Let's just try. Guitar and clarinet's a cool duet, untapped."

He's certainly not taking my big admission too seriously. It's like finally going to confession only to find out the priest has earplugs in.

I tell him, "Maybe sometime," so he'll drop it.

"Wow." He grins. "Encouraging."

And then it's as if I've vanished. He's bent over the strings, tuning his guitar with such passionate attention I almost feel like I should look away, but I can't. In fact, I'm full on gawking, wondering what it would be like to be cool and casual and fearless and passionate and so freaking alive, just like he is – and for a split second, I want to play with him. I want to disturb the birds.

Later, as he plays and plays, as all the fog burns away, I think, he's right. That's exactly it – I am crazy sad and, somewhere deep inside, all I want is to fly.

10

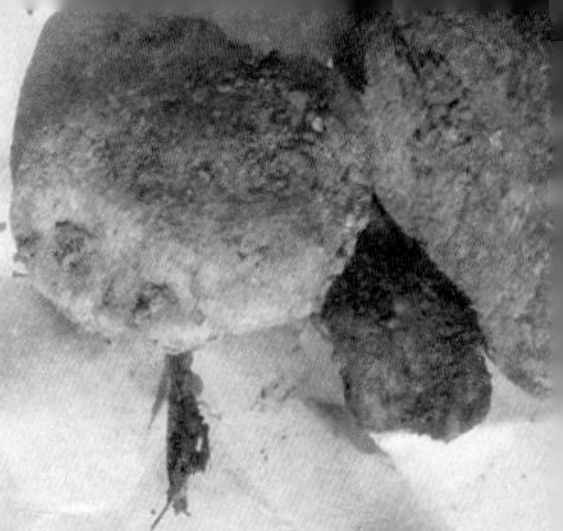

Grief is a house
where the chairs
have forgotten how to hold us
the mirrors how to reflect us
the walls how to contain us
Grief is a house that disappears
each time someone knocks at the door
or rings the bell
a house that blows into the air
at the slightest gust
that buries itself deep in the ground
while everyone is sleeping
Grief is a house where no one can protect you
where the younger sister ~~will grow~~
will grow older than the older one
where the doors
no longer let you in
or out

(Found under a stone in Gram's garden)

As usual I can't sleep and am sitting at Bailey's desk, holding St Anthony, in a state of dread about packing up her things. Today, when I got home from lasagna duty at the deli, there were cardboard boxes opened by her desk. I've yet to crack a drawer. I can't. Each time I touch the wooden knobs, I think about her never thumbing through her desk for a notebook, an address, a pen, and all the breath races out of my body with one thought: *Bailey's in that airless box—*

No. I shove the image into a closet in my mind, kick the door shut. I close my eyes, take one, two, three breaths, and when I open them, I find myself staring again at the picture of Explorer Mom. I touch the brittle paper, feel the wax of the crayon as I glide my finger across the fading figure. Does her human counterpart have any idea one of her daughters has died at nineteen years old? Did she feel a cold wind or a hot flash or was she just eating breakfast or tying her shoe like it was any other ordinary moment in her extraordinary itinerant life?

Gram told us our mom was an explorer because she didn't know how else to explain to us that Mom had what generations of Walkers call the "restless gene." According to Gram, this restlessness has always plagued our family, mostly the women. Those afflicted keep moving, they go from town to town, continent to continent, love to love – this is why, Gram explained, Mom had no idea who either of our fathers were, and so neither did we – until they wear themselves out and return home. Gram told us her Aunt Sylvie and a distant cousin, Virginia, also had the affliction, and after many years adventuring across the globe, they, like all the others before them, found their way back. It's their destiny to leave, she told us, and their destiny to return, as well.

"Don't boys get it?" I asked Gram when I was ten years old and "the condition" was becoming more understandable to me. We were walking to the river for a swim.

"Of course they do, sweet pea." But then, she stopped in her tracks, took my hands in hers, and spoke in a rare solemn tone. "I don't know if at your mature age you can understand this, Len, but this is the way it is: when men have it, no one seems to notice, they become astronauts or pilots or cartographers or criminals or poets. They don't stay around long enough to know if they've fathered children or not. When women get it, well, it's complicated, it's just different."

"How?" I asked. "How is it different?"

"Well, for instance, it's not customary for a mother to not see her own girls for this many years, is it?"

She had a point there.

"Your mom was born like this, practically flew out of my womb and into the world. From day one, she was running, running, running."

"Running away?"

"Nope, sweet pea, never *away*, know that." She squeezed my hand. "She was always running toward."

Toward what? I think, getting up from Bailey's desk. What was my mother running toward then? What is she running toward now? What was Bailey? What am I?

I walk over to the window, open the curtain a crack and see Toby, sitting under the plum tree, under the bright stars, on the green grass, in the world. Lucy and Ethel are draped over his legs – it's amazing how those dogs only come around when he does.

I know I should turn off the light, get into bed, and moon about Joe Fontaine, but that is not what I do.

I meet Toby under the tree and we duck into the woods to the river, wordlessly, as if we've had a plan to do this for days. Lucy and Ethel follow on our heels a few paces, then turn back around and go home after Toby has an indecipherable talk with them.

I'm leading a double life: Lennie Walker by day, Hester Prynne of *The Scarlet Letter* fame by night.

I tell myself, I will not kiss him, no matter what.

It's a warm, windless night and the forest is still and lonely. We walk side by side in the quiet, listening to the fluted song of the thrush. Even in the moonlit stillness, Toby looks sun-drenched and windswept, like he's on a sailboat.

"I know I shouldn't have come, Len."

"Probably not."

"Was worried about you," he says quietly.

"Thanks," I say, and the cloak of being fine that I wear with everyone else slips right off my shoulders.

Sadness pulses out of us as we walk. I almost expect the trees to lower their branches when we pass, the stars to hand down some light. I breathe in the horsy scent of eucalyptus, the thick sugary pine, aware of each breath I take, how each one keeps me in the world a few seconds longer. I taste the sweetness of the summer air on my tongue and want to just gulp and gulp and gulp it into my body – this living, breathing, heart-beating body of mine.

"Toby?"

"Hmm?"

"Do you feel more alive since…" I'm afraid to ask this, like I'm revealing something shameful, but I want to know if he feels it too.

He doesn't hesitate. "I feel more *everything* since."

Yeah, I think, more everything. Like someone flipped on the switch of the world and everything is just on now, including me, and everything in me, bad and good, all cranking up to the max.

He grabs a twig off a branch, snaps it between his fingers. "I keep doing this stupid stuff at night on my board," he says, "gnarly-ass tricks only show-off dip-shits do, and I've been doing it alone … and a couple times totally wasted."

Toby is one of a handful of skaters in town who regularly and spectacularly defy gravity. If *he* thinks he's putting himself in danger he's going full-on kamikaze.

"She wouldn't want that, Toby." I can't keep the pleading out of my voice.

He sighs, frustrated. "I know that, I know." He picks up his pace as if to leave behind what he just told me.

"She'd kill me." He says it so definitively and passionately that I wonder if he's really talking about skating or what happened between us.

"I won't do it anymore," he insists.

"Good," I say, still not totally sure what he's referring to, but if it's us, he doesn't have to worry, right? I've kept the curtains drawn. I've promised Bailey nothing will ever happen again.

Though even as I think this, I find my eyes drinking him in, his broad chest and strong arms, his freckles. I remember his mouth hungrily on mine, his big hands in my hair, the heat coursing through me, how it made me feel—

"It's just so reckless…" he says.

"Yeah." It comes out a little too breathy.

"Len?"

I need smelling salts.

He looks at me funny, but then I think he reads in my eyes what has been going on in my head, because his eyes kind of widen and spark, before he quickly looks away.

GET A GRIP, LENNIE.

We walk in silence then through the woods and it snaps me back into my senses. The stars and moon are mostly hidden over the thick tree cover, and I feel like I'm swimming through darkness, my body breaking the air as if it were water. I can hear the rush of the river getting louder with every step I take, and it reminds me of Bailey, day after day, year after year, the two of us on this path, lost in talk, the plunge into the pool, and then the endless splaying on the rocks in the sun—

I whisper, "I'm left behind."

"Me too..." His voice catches. He doesn't say anything else, doesn't look at me; he just takes my hand and holds it and doesn't let it go as the cover above us gets thicker and we push together farther into the deepening dark.

I say softly, "I feel so guilty," almost hoping the night will suck my words away before Toby hears.

"I do too," he whispers back.

"But about something else too, Toby..."

"What?"

With all the darkness around me, with my hand in Toby's, I feel like I can say it. "I feel guilty that I'm still here..."

"Don't. Please, Len."

"But she was always so much ... more—"

"No." He doesn't let me finish. "She'd hate for you to feel that way."

"I know."

And then I blurt out what I've forbidden myself to think, let alone say: "She's in a coffin, Toby." I say it so loud, practically shriek it – the words make me dizzy, claustrophobic, like I need to leap out of my body.

I hear him suck in air. When he speaks, his voice is so weak I barely hear it over our footsteps. "No, she isn't."

I know this too. I know both things at once.

Toby tightens his grip around my hand.

Once at Flying Man's, the sky floods through the opening in the canopy. We sit on a flat rock and the full moon shines so brightly on the river, the water looks like pure rushing light.

“How can the world continue to shimmer like this?” I say as I lie down under a sky drunk with stars.

Toby doesn’t answer, just shakes his head and lies down next to me, close enough for him to put his arm around me, close enough for me to put my head on his chest if he did so. But he doesn’t, and I don’t.

He starts talking then, his soft words dissipating into the night like smoke. He talks about how Bailey wanted to have the wedding ceremony here at Flying Man’s so they could jump into the pool after saying their vows. I lean up on my elbows and can see it as clearly in the moonlight as if I were watching a movie, can see Bailey in a drenched bright orange wedding dress laughing and leading the party down the path back to the house, her careless beauty so huge it had to walk a few paces ahead of her, announcing itself. I see in the movie of Toby’s words how happy she would have been, and suddenly, I just don’t know where all that happiness, her happiness, and ours, will go now, and I start to cry, and then Toby’s face is above mine and his tears are falling onto my cheeks until I don’t know whose are whose, just know that all that happiness is gone, and that we are kissing again.

When I'm with him,
there is someone with me
in my house of grief,
someone who knows
its architecture as I do,
who can walk with me,
from room to sorrowful room,
making the whole rambling structure
of wind and emptiness
not quite as scary, as lonely
as it was before.

(Found on a branch of a tree outside Clover High)

11

Joe Fontaine's knocking. I'm lying awake in bed, thinking about moving to Antarctica to get away from this mess with Toby. I prop myself up on an elbow to look out the window at the early, bony light.

Joe's our rooster. Each morning since his first visit, a week and a half ago, he arrives at dawn with his guitar, a bag of chocolate croissants from the bakery and a few dead bugs for Big. If we aren't up, he lets himself in, makes a pot of coffee thick as tar and sits at the kitchen table strumming melancholy chords on his guitar. Every so often he asks me if I feel like playing, to which I reply *no,* to which he replies *fine*. A polite stand-off. He hasn't mentioned Rachel again, which is okay by me.

The strangest part about all this is that it's not strange at all, for any of us. Even Big, who is not a morning person, pads down the stairs in his slippers, greets Joe with a boisterous back slap, and after checking the pyramids (which Joe has already checked), he jumps right back into their conversation from the previous morning about his obsession *du jour*: exploding cakes.

Big heard that a woman in Idaho was making a birthday cake for her husband when the flour ignited. They were having a dry spell, so there was lots of static electricity in the air. A cloud of flour dust surrounded her and due to a spark from a static charge in her hand, it exploded: an inadvertent flour bomb. Now Big is trying to enlist Joe to re-enact the event with him for the sake of science. Gram and I have been adamantly opposed to this for obvious reasons. "We've had enough catastrophe, Big," Gram said yesterday, putting her foot down. I think the amount of pot Big's been smoking has made the idea of the exploding cake much funnier and more fascinating than it really is, but somehow Joe is equally enthralled with the concept.

It's Sunday and I have to be at the deli in a few hours. The kitchen's bustling when I stumble in.

"Morning, John Lennon," Joe says, looking up from his guitar strings and throwing me a jaw-dropping grin – what am I doing making out with Toby, *Bailey's* Toby, I think as I smile back at the holy horses unfreakingbelievable Joe Fontaine, who has seemingly moved into our kitchen. Things are so mixed up – the boy who should kiss me acts like a brother and the boy who should act like a brother keeps kissing me. Sheesh.

"Hey, John Lennon," Gram echoes.

Unbelievable. This can't be catching on. "Only Joe's allowed to call me that," I grumble at her.

"John Lennon!" Big whisks into the kitchen and me into his arms, dancing me around the room. "How's my girl today?"

"Why's everyone in such a good mood?" I feel like Scrooge.

"I'm not in a good mood," Gram says, beaming ear to ear, looking akin to Joe. I notice her hair is dry too. No grief-shower this morning. A first. "I just got an idea last night. It's a surprise." Joe and Big glance at me and shrug. Gram's ideas often rival Big's on the bizarre scale, but I doubt this one involves explosions or necromancy.

"We don't know what it is either, honey," Big bellows in a

baritone unfit for 8 a.m. "In other breaking news, Joe had an epiphany this morning: He put the Lennie houseplant under one of the pyramids – I can't believe I never thought of that." Big can't contain his excitement, he's smiling down on Joe like a proud father. I wonder how Joe slipped in like this, wonder if it's somehow because he never knew her, doesn't have one single memory of her, he's like the world without our heartbreak—

My cell phone goes off. I glance at the screen. It's Toby. I let it go to voicemail, feeling like the worst person in the world because just seeing his name recalls last night, and my stomach flies into a sequence of contortions. How could I have let this happen?

I look up, all eyes are on me, wondering why I didn't pick up the phone. I have to get out of the kitchen.

"Want to play, Joe?" I say, heading upstairs for my clarinet.

"Holy shit," I hear, then apologies to Gram and Big.

Back on the porch, I say, "You start, I'll follow."

He nods and starts playing some sweet soft chords in G minor. But I feel too unnerved for sweet, too unnerved for soft. I can't shake off Toby's call, his kisses. I can't shake off cardboard boxes, perfume that never gets used, bookmarks that don't move, St Anthony statues that do. I can't shake off the fact that Bailey at eleven years old did not put herself in the drawing of our family, and suddenly, I am so upset I forget I'm playing music, forget Joe's even there beside me.

I start to think about all the things I haven't said since

Bailey died, all the words stowed deep in my heart, in our orange bedroom, all the words in the whole world that aren't said after someone dies because they are too sad, too enraged, too devastated, too guilty to come out – all of them begin to course inside me like a lunatic river. I suck in all the air I can, until there's probably no air left in Clover for anyone else, and then I blast it all out my clarinet in one mad bleating typhoon of a note. I don't know if a clarinet has ever made such a terrible sound, but I can't stop, all the years come tumbling out now – Bailey and me in the river, the ocean, tucked so snug into our room, the backseat of cars, bathtubs, running through the trees, through days and nights and months and years without Mom – I am breaking windows, busting through walls, burning up the past, pushing Toby off me, taking the dumb-ass Lennie houseplant and hurling it into the sea—

I open my eyes. Joe's staring at me, astonished. The dogs next door are barking.

"Wow, I think I'll follow next time," he says.

I'd been making decisions for days.
I picked out the dress Bailey would wear **forever**—
a black slinky one—inappropriate—that she loved.
I chose a sweater to go over it, earrings, bracelet, necklace,
her most beloved strappy sandals.
I collected her make-up to give to the funeral director
with a recent photo—
I thought it would be me that would dress her;
I didn't think a strange man should see her naked
touch her body
shave her legs
apply her lipstick
but that's what happened all the same.
I helped Gram pick out the casket, the plot at the cemetery.
I changed a few lines in the obituary that Big composed.
I wrote on a piece of paper what I thought
should go on the headstone.
I did all this without uttering a word.
Not one word, for days,
until I saw Bailey before the funeral
and lost my mind.
I hadn't realized that when people say so-and-so
snapped
that's actually what happens—
I started shaking her—
I thought I could wake her up
and get her the hell out of that box.
When she didn't wake,
I screamed: **TALK TO ME.**
Big swooped me up into his arms,
carried me out of the room, the church,
into the slamming rain,
and down to the creek
where we sobbed together
under the black coat he held over our heads
to protect us from the weather.

(Found on a piece of music paper crumpled up by the trailhead)

12

I wish I had my clarinet, I think as I walk home from the deli. If I did, I'd head straight into the woods where no one could hear me and fall on my face like I did on the porch this morning. *Play the music, not the instrument*, Marguerite always said. And Mr James: *Let the instrument play you.* I never got either instruction until today. I always imagined music trapped inside my clarinet, not trapped inside of me. But what if music is what escapes when a heart breaks?

I turn onto our street and see Uncle Big road-reading, tripping over his massive feet, greeting his favorite trees as he passes them. Nothing too unusual, but for the flying fruit. There are a few weeks every year when if circumstances permit, like the winds are just so and the plums particularly heavy, the plum trees around our house become hostile to humans and begin using us for target practice.

Big waves his arm east to west in enthusiastic greeting, narrowly escaping a plum to the head.

I salute him, then when he's close enough, I give a hello twirl to his mustache, which is waxed and styled to the hilt, the fanciest (i.e. freakiest) I've seen it in some time.

"Your friend is over," he says, winking at me. Then he puts his nose back into his book and resumes his promenade. I know he means Joe, but I think of Sarah and my stomach twists a little. She sent me a text today: *Sending out a search party for our friendship.* I haven't responded. I don't know where it is either.

A moment later, I hear Big say, "Oh, Len, Toby called for you, wants you to ring him right away."

He called me on my cell again too while I was at work. I didn't listen to the voicemail. I reiterate the oath I've been swearing all day, that I will never see Toby Shaw again, then I beg my sister for a sign of forgiveness – *no need for subtlety either, Bails, an earthquake will do.*

As I get closer, I see that the house is inside out – in the front yard are stacks of books, furniture, masks, pots and pans, boxes, antiques, paintings, dishes, knickknacks – then I see Joe and someone who looks just like him but broader and even taller coming out of the house with our sofa.

"Where do you want this, Gram?" Joe says, like it's the most natural thing in the world to be moving the couch outside. This must be Gram's surprise. We're moving into the yard. Great.

"Anywhere's fine, boys," Gram says, then sees me. "Lennie." She glides over. "I'm going to figure out what's causing the terrible luck," she says. "This is what came to me in the middle of the night. We'll move anything suspicious out of the house, do a ritual, burn sage, then make sure not to put anything unlucky back inside. Joe was nice enough to go get his brother to help."

"Hmmm," I say, not knowing what else to say, wishing I could've seen Joe's face as Gram very sanely explained this INSANE idea to him. When I break away from her, Joe practically gallops over. He's such a downer.

"Just another day at the psych ward, huh?" I say.

"What's quite perplexing…" he says, pointing a finger professorially at his brow, "is just how Gram is making the lucky or unlucky determination. I've yet to crack the code." I'm impressed at how quickly he's caught on that there is nothing to do but grab a wing when Gram's aflight with fancy.

His brother comes up then, rests his hand carelessly on Joe's shoulder, and it instantly transforms Joe into a little brother – the slice into my heart is sharp and sudden – *I'm no longer a little sister*. No longer a sister, period.

Joe can barely mask his adulation and it topples me. I was just the same – when I introduced Bailey I felt like I was presenting the world's most badass work of art.

"Marcus is here for the summer, goes to UCLA. He and my oldest brother are in a band down there." Brothers and brothers and brothers.

"Hi," I say to another beaming guy. Definitely no need for lightbulbs Chez Fontaine.

"I heard you play a mean clarinet," Marcus says. This makes me blush, which makes Joe blush, which makes Marcus laugh and punch his brother's arm. I hear him whisper, "Oh Joe, you've got it so bad." Then Joe blushes even more, if that's possible, and heads into the house for a lamp.

I wonder why though if Joe's got it so bad he doesn't make a move, even a suggestion of one. I know, I know, I'm a feminist, I could make a move, but a) I've never made a move on anyone in my life and therefore have no moves to make, b) I've been a wee bit preoccupied with the bat in my belfry who doesn't belong there, and c) Rachel – I mean, I know he spends mornings at our house, but how do I know he doesn't spend evenings at hers?

Gram's taken a shine to the Fontaine boys. She's flitting around the yard, telling them over and over again how handsome they are, asking if their parents ever thought about selling them. "Bet they'd make a bundle on you boys. Shame to give boys eyelashes like yours. Don't you think so, Lennie? Wouldn't you kill for eyelashes like that?" God, I'm embarrassed, though she's right about the eyelashes. Marcus doesn't blink either, they both bat.

She sends Joe and Marcus home to get their third brother, convinced that all Fontaine brothers have to be here for the ritual. It's clear both Marcus and Joe have fallen under her spell. She probably could get them to rob a bank for her.

"Bring your instruments," she yells after them. "You too, Lennie."

I do as I'm told and get my clarinet from the tree it's resting in with an assortment of my worldly possessions. Then Gram and I take some of the pots and pans she has deemed lucky back into the kitchen to cook dinner. She prepares the chicken while I quarter the potatoes and spice them with garlic and rosemary. When everything is roasting in the oven, we go outside to gather some strewn plums to make a tart. She is rolling out the dough for the crust while I slice tomatoes and avocados for the salad. Every time she passes me, she pats my head or squeezes my arm.

"This is nice, cooking together again, isn't it, sweet pea?"

I smile at her. "It is, Gram." Well, it was, because now she's looking at me in her talk-to-me-Lennie way. The

Gramouncements are about to begin.

"Lennie, I'm worried about you." Here goes.

"I'm all right."

"It's really time. At the least, tidy up, do her laundry or allow me to. I can do it while you're at work."

"I'll do it," I say, like always. And I will, I just don't know when.

She slumps her shoulders dramatically. "I was thinking you and I could go to the city for the day next week, go to lunch—"

"That's okay."

I drop my eyes back to my task. I don't want to see her disappointment.

She sighs in her big, loud, lonely way and goes back to the crust. Telepathically, I tell her I'm sorry. I tell her I just can't confide in her right now, tell her the three feet between us feels like three light-years to me and I don't know how to bridge it.

Telepathically, she tells me back that I'm breaking her broken heart.

When the boys come back they introduce the oldest Fontaine, who is also in town for the summer from LA.

"This is Doug," Marcus says just as Joe says, "This is Fred."

"Parents couldn't make up their mind," the newest Fontaine offers. This one looks positively deranged with glee. Gram's right, we should sell them.

"He's lying," Marcus pipes in. "In high school, Fred wanted to be sophisticated so he could hook up with lots of French girls. He thought Fred was way too uncivilized and Flintstone-ish so decided to use his middle name, Doug. But Joe and I couldn't get used to it."

"So now everyone calls him DougFred on two continents." Joe hand-butts his brother's chest, which provokes a counter-attack of several jabs to the ribs. The Fontaine boys are like a litter of enormous puppies, rushing and swiping at each other, stumbling all around, a whirl of perpetual motion and violent affection.

I know it's ungenerous, but watching them, their camaraderie, makes me feel lonely as the moon. I think about Toby and me holding hands in the dark last night, kissing by the river, how with him, I'd felt like my sadness had a place to be.

We eat sprawled out on what is now our lawn furniture. The wind has died down a bit, so we can sit without being pelted by fruit. The chicken tastes like chicken, the plum tart like plum tart. It's too soon for there not to be one bite of ash.

Dusk splatters pink and orange across the sky, beginning its languorous summer stroll. I hear the river through the trees sounding like possibility—

She will never know the Fontaines.

She will never hear about this dinner on a walk to the river.

She will not come back in the morning or Tuesday or in three months.

She will not come back ever.

She's gone and the world is ambling on without her—

I can't breathe or think or sit for another minute.

I try to say "I'll be right back," but nothing comes out, so I just turn my back on the yard full of concerned faces and hurry toward the tree line. When I get to the path, I take off, trying to outrun the heartache that is chasing me down.

I'm certain Gram or Big will follow me, but they don't, Joe does. I'm out of breath and writing on a piece of paper I found on the path when he comes up to me. I ditch the note behind a rock, try to brush away my tears.

This is the first time I've seen him without a smile hidden somewhere on his face.

"You okay?" he asks.

"You didn't even know her." It's out of my mouth, sharp and accusatory, before I can stop it. I see the surprise cross his face.

"No."

He doesn't say anything more, but I can't seem to shut my insane self up. "And you have all these brothers." As if it were a crime, I say this.

"I do."

"I just don't know why you're hanging out with us all the time." I feel my face get hot as embarrassment snakes its way through my body – the real question is why I am persisting like a full-fledged maniac.

"You don't?" His eyes rove my face, then the corners of his mouth begin to curl upward. "I like you, Lennie, duh." He looks at me incredulously. "I think you're amazing…" Why would he think this? Bailey is amazing and Gram and Big, and of course Mom, but not me, I am the two-dimensional one in a 3-D family.

He's grinning now. "Also I think you're really pretty and I'm incredibly shallow."

I have a horrible thought: *He only thinks I'm pretty, only thinks I'm amazing, because he never met Bailey*, followed by a really terrible, horrible thought: *I'm glad he never met her*. I shake my head, try to erase my mind, like an Etch A Sketch.

"What?" He reaches his hand to my face, brushes his thumb slowly across my cheek. His touch is so tender, it startles me. No one has ever touched me like this before, looked at me the way he's looking at me right now, deep into me. I want to hide from him and kiss him all at the same time.

And then: Bat. Bat. Bat.

I'm sunk.

I think his acting-like-a-brother stint is over.

"Can I?" he says, reaching for the rubber band on my ponytail.

I nod. Very slowly, he slides it off, the whole time holding my eyes in his. I'm hypnotized. It's like he's unbuttoning my shirt. When he's done, I shake my head a little and my hair springs into its habitual frenzy.

"Wow," he says softly. "I've wanted to do that…"

I can hear our breathing. I think they can hear it in New York.

"What about Rachel?" I say.

"What about her?"

"You and her?"

"You," he answers. Me!

I say, "I'm sorry I said all that, before…"

He shakes his head like it doesn't matter, and then to my surprise he doesn't kiss me but wraps his arms around me instead. For a moment, in his arms, with my mind so close to his heart, I listen to the wind pick up and think it just might lift us off our feet and take us with it.

13

The dry trunks of the old growth redwoods creak and squeak eerily over our heads.

"Whoa. What is *that*?" Joe asks, all of a sudden pulling away as he glances up, then over his shoulder.

"What?" I ask, embarrassed how much I still want his arms around me. I try to joke it off. "Sheesh, how to ruin a moment. Don't you remember? I'm having a crisis?"

"I think you've had enough freak-outs for one day," he says, smiling now, and twirling his finger by his ear to signify what a wack-job I am. This makes me laugh out loud. He's looking all around again in a mild panic. "Seriously, what was that?"

"Are you scared of the deep dark forest, city boy?"

"Of course I am, like most sane people, remember lions and tigers and bears, oh my?" He curls his finger around my belt loop, starts veering me back to the house, then stops suddenly. "That, right then. That creepy horror movie noise that happens right before the ax murderer jumps out and gets us."

"It's the old growths creaking. When it's really windy, it sounds like hundreds of doors squeaking open and shut back here, all at the same time, it's beyond spooky. Don't think you could handle it."

He puts his arm around me. "A dare? Next windy day then." He points to himself – "Hansel" – then at me – "Gretel."

Right before we break from the trees, I say, "Thanks, for following me, and…" I want to thank him for spending all day moving furniture for Gram, for coming every morning with dead bugs for Big, for somehow being there for them when

I can't be. Instead, I say, "I really love the way you play." Also true.

"Likewise."

"C'mon," I say. "That wasn't playing. It was honking. Total face-plant."

He laughs. "No way. Worth the wait. Testament to why if given the choice I'd rather lose the ability to talk than play. By far the superior communication."

This I agree with, face-plant or not. Playing today was like finding an alphabet – it was like being sprung. He pulls me even closer to him and something starts to swell inside, something that feels quite a bit like joy.

I try to ignore the insistent voice inside: *How dare you, Lennie? How dare you feel joy this soon?*

When we emerge from the woods, I see Toby's truck parked in front of the house and it has an immediate bone-liquefying effect on my body. I slow my pace, disengage from Joe, who looks quizzically over at me. Gram must have invited Toby to be part of her ritual. I consider staging another freak-out and running back into the woods so I don't have to be in a room with Toby and Joe, but I am not the actress and know I couldn't pull it off. My stomach churns as we walk up the steps, past Lucy and Ethel, who are, of course, sprawled out on the porch awaiting Toby's exit, and who, of course, don't move a muscle as we pass. We push through the door and then cross the hall into the living room. The room is aglow with candles, the air thick with the sweet scent of sage.

DougFred and Marcus sit on two of the remaining chairs in the center of the room playing flamenco guitar. The Half Mom hovers above them as if she's listening to the course, fiery chords that are overtaking the house. Uncle Big towers over the mantel clapping his hand on his thigh to the feverish beat. And Toby stands on the other side of the room, apart from everyone, looking as lonely as I felt earlier – my heart immediately lurches toward him. He leans against the window, his golden hair and skin gleaming in the flickery light. He watches us enter the room with an inappropriate hawkish intensity that is not lost on Joe and sends shivers through me. I can feel Joe's bewilderment without even looking to my side.

Meanwhile, I am now imagining roots growing out of my feet so I don't fly across the room into Toby's arms because I have a big problem: even in this house, on this night, with all these people, with Joe Fabulous Fontaine, who is no longer acting like my brother, right beside me, I still feel this invisible rope pulling me across the room toward Toby and there doesn't seem to be anything I can do about it.

I turn to Joe, who looks like I've never seen him: unhappy, his body stiff with confusion, his gaze shifting from Toby to me and back again. It's as if all the moments between Toby and me that never should have happened are spilling out of us in front of Joe.

"Who's that guy?" Joe asks, with none of his usual equanimity.

"Toby." It comes out oddly robotic.

Joe looks at me like: *Well, who's Toby, retard?*

"I'll introduce you," I say, because I have no choice and cannot just keep standing here like I've had a stroke.

There's no other way to put it: THIS BLOWS.

And on top of everything, the flamenco has begun to crescendo all around us, whipping fire and sex and passion every which way. Perfect. Couldn't they have chosen some sleepy sonata? Waltzes are lovely too, boys. With me on his heels, Joe crosses the room toward Toby: the sun on a collision course with the moon.

The dusky sky pours through the window, framing Toby. Joe and I stop a few paces in front of him, all of us now caught in the uncertainty between day and night. The music continues its fiery revolution all around us and there is a girl inside of me that wants to give in to the fanatical beat – she wants to dance wild and free all around the thumping room, but unfortunately, that girl's in me, not me. Me would like an invisibility cloak to get the hell out of this mess.

I look over at Joe and am relieved to see that the fevered chords have momentarily hijacked his attention. His one hand plays his thigh, his foot drums the ground, and his head bobs around, which flops his hair into his eyes. He can't stop smiling at his brothers, who are pounding their guitars into notes so ferocious they probably could overthrow the government. I realize I'm smiling like a Fontaine as I watch the music riot through Joe. I can feel how intensely he wants his guitar, just as, all of a sudden, I can feel how intensely Toby wants me.

I steal a glance at him, and as I suspected, he's watching me watch Joe, his eyes clamped on me. How did we get ourselves into this? It doesn't feel like solace in this moment at all, but something else. I look down, write *help* on my jeans with my finger, and when I look back up I see that Toby's and Joe's eyes have locked. Something passes silently between them that has everything to do with me, because as if on cue they look from each other to me, both saying with their eyes: *What's going on, Lennie?*

Every organ in my body switches places.

Joe puts his hand gently on my arm as if it will remind me to open my mouth and form words. At the contact, Toby's eyes flare. What's going on with him tonight? He's acting like my boyfriend, not my sister's, not someone I made out with twice under very extenuating circumstances. And what about me and this inexplicable and seemingly inescapable pull to him despite everything?

I say, "Joe just moved to town." Toby nods civilly and I sound human, a good start. I'm about to say "Toby was Bailey's boyfriend," which I loathe saying for the *was* and for how it will make me feel like the traitorous person that I am.

But then Toby looks right at me and says, "Your hair, it's down." Hello? This is not the right thing to say. The right thing to say is "Oh, where'd you move from, dude?" or "Clover's pretty cool." Or "Do you skate?" Or basically anything but "Your hair, it's down."

Joe seems unperturbed by the comment. He's smiling at

me like he's proud that he was the one that let my hair out of its bondage.

Just then, I notice Gram in the doorway, looking at us. She blows over, holding her burning stick of sage like a magic wand. She gives me a quick once-over, seems to decide I've recovered, then points her wand at Toby and says, "Let me introduce you boys. Joe Fontaine, this is Toby Shaw, Bailey's boyfriend."

Whoosh – I see it: a waterfall of relief pours over Joe. I see the case close in his mind, as he probably thinks there couldn't be anything going on – because what kind of sister would ever cross that kind of line?

"Hey, I'm so sorry," he tells Toby.

"Thanks." Toby tries to smile, but it comes out all wrong and homicidal. Joe, however, so unburdened by Gram's revelation, doesn't even notice, just turns around buoyant as ever, and goes to join his brothers, followed by Gram.

"I'm going to go, Lennie." Toby's voice is barely audible over the music. I turn around, see that Joe is now bent over his guitar, oblivious to everything but the sound his fingers are making.

"I'll walk you out," I say.

Toby says good-bye to Gram, Big and the Fontaines, all of whom are surprised he's leaving so soon, especially Gram, who I can tell is adding some things up.

I follow him to his truck – Lucy, Ethel and I, all yapping at his feet. He opens the door, doesn't get in, leans against the cab. We are facing each other and there's not a trace of the calm or gentleness I've become so accustomed to seeing in his expression, but something fierce and unhinged in its place. He's in total tough-skater-dude mode, and though I don't want to, I'm finding it arresting. I feel a current coursing between us, feel it begin to rip out of control inside of me. *What is it?* I think as he looks into my eyes, then at my mouth, then sweeps his gaze slowly, proprietarily over my body. *Why can't we stop this?* I feel so reckless – like I'm reeling with him into the air on his board with no regard for safety or consequence, with no regard for anything but speed and daring and being hungrily, greedily alive – but I tell him, "No. Not now."

"When?"

"Tomorrow. After work," I say, against my better judgment, against any judgment.

What do you girls want for dinner?
What do you girls think about my new painting?
What do the girls want to do this weekend?
Did the girls leave for school yet?
I haven't seen the girls yet today.
I told those girls to hurry up!
Where are those girls?
Girls, don't forget your lunches.
Girls, be home by 11 PM.
Girls, don't even think of swimming – it's freezing out.
Are the Walker Girls coming to the party?
The Walker Girls were at the river last night.
Let's see if the Walker Girls are home.

(Found written on the wall of Bailey's closet)

14

I find Gram, who is twirling around the living room with her sage wand like an overgrown fairy. I tell her that I'm sorry, but I don't feel well and need to go upstairs.

She stops mid-whirl. I know she senses trouble, but she says, "Okay, sweet pea." I apologize to everyone and say good night as nonchalantly as possible.

Joe follows me out of the room, and I decide it might be time to join a convent, just cloister up with the Sisters for a while.

He touches my shoulder and I turn around to face him. "I hope what I said in the woods didn't freak you out or something … hope that's not why you're crashing…"

"No, no." His eyes are wide with worry. I add, "It made me pretty happy, actually." Which of course is true except for the slight problem that immediately after hearing his declaration, I made a date with my dead sister's boyfriend to do *God knows what!*

"Good." He brushes his thumb on my cheek, and again his tenderness startles me. "Because I'm going crazy, Lennie." Bat. Bat. Bat. And just like that, I'm going crazy too because I'm thinking Joe Fontaine is about to kiss me. Finally.

Forget the convent.

Let's get this out of the way: my previously non-existent floozy-factor is blowing right off the charts.

"I didn't know you knew my name," I say.

"So much you don't know about me, *Lennie*." He smiles and takes his index finger and presses it to my lips, leaves it there until my heart lands on Jupiter: three seconds, then removes it, turns around, and heads back into the living room. Whoa – well, that was either the dorkiest or sexiest moment of my life, and I'm voting for sexy on account of my standing here dumbstruck and giddy, wondering if he did kiss me after all.

I am totally out of control.

I do not think this is how normal people mourn.

When I can move my legs one in front of the other, I make my way up to The Sanctum. Thankfully, it has been deemed fairly lucky by Gram so is mostly untouched, especially Bailey's things, which she mercifully didn't touch at all. I go straight over to her desk and start talking to the explorer picture like we sometimes talk to The Half Mom.

Tonight, the woman on the mountaintop will have to be Bailey.

I sit down and tell her how sorry I am, that I don't know what's wrong with me and that I'll call Toby and cancel the date first thing in the morning. I also tell her I didn't mean to think what I thought in the woods and I would do anything for her to be able to meet Joe Fontaine. Anything. And then I ask her again to please give me a sign that she forgives me before the list of unpardonable things I think and do gets too long and I become a lost cause.

I look over at the boxes. I know I'm going to have to start eventually. I take a deep breath, banish all morbid thoughts from my mind, and put my hands on the wooden knobs of the top desk drawer. Only to immediately think about Bailey and my anti-snooping pact. I never broke it, not once, despite a natural propensity for nosing around. At people's houses, I open medicine cabinets, peek behind shower curtains, open drawers and closet doors whenever possible. But with Bailey, I adhered to the pact—

Pacts. So many between us, breaking now. And what about the unspoken ones, those entered into without words, without pinky swears, without even realizing it? A squall of emotion lands in my chest. Forget talking to the picture, I take out my phone, punch in Bailey's number, listen impatiently to her as Juliet, heat filling my head, then over the tone, I hear myself say, "What happens to a stupid companion pony when the racehorse dies?" There's both anger and despair in my voice and immediately and illogically I wish I could erase the message so she won't hear it.

I slowly open the desk drawer, afraid of what I might find, afraid of what else she might not have told me, afraid of this rollicking bananas pact-breaking me. But there are just things, inconsequential things of hers, some pens, a few playbills from shows at Clover Repertory, concert tickets, an address book, an old cell phone, a couple of business cards, one from our dentist reminding her of her next appointment, and one from Paul Booth, Private Investigator with a San Francisco address.

WTF?

I pick it up. On the back in Bailey's writing it says *April 25 4 p.m., Suite 2B*. The only reason I can think of that she would go see a private investigator would be to find Mom. But why would she do that? We both knew that Big already tried, just a few years ago in fact, and that the PI had said it would be impossible to find her.

The day Big told us about the detective, Bailey had been furious, torpedoing around the kitchen while Gram and I snapped peas from the garden for dinner.

Bailey said, "I know you know where she is, Gram."

"How could I know, Bails?" Gram replied.

"Yeah, how could she know, Bails?" I repeated. I hated when Gram and Bailey fought, and sensed things were about to blow.

Bailey said, "I could go after her. I could find her. I could bring her back." She grabbed a pod, putting the whole thing, shell and all, into her mouth.

"You couldn't find her, and you couldn't bring her back either." Big stood in the doorway, his words filled the room like gospel. I had no idea how long he'd been listening.

Bailey went to him. "How do you know that?"

"Because I've tried, Bailey."

Gram and I stopped snapping and looked up at Big. He hulked over to the table and sat in a kitchen chair, looking like a giant in a kindergarten classroom. "I hired a detective a few years back, a good one, figured I would tell you all if he came up with something, but he didn't. He said it's the easiest thing to be lost if you don't want to be found. He thinks Paige changed her name and probably changes her social security number if she moves..." Big strummed his fingers on the table – it sounded like little claps of thunder.

"How do we even know she's alive?" Big said under his breath, but we all heard it as if he hollered it from the mountaintop. Strangely, this had never occurred to me and I don't think it had ever occurred to Bailey either. We were always told she would be back and we believed it, deeply.

"She's alive, she's most certainly alive," Gram said to Big. "And she will be back."

I saw suspicion dawn again on Bailey's face.

"How do you know, Gram? You must know something if you're so sure."

"A mother knows, okay? She just does." With that, Gram left the room.

I put the card back in the desk drawer, take St Anthony with me, and get into bed. I put him on the nightstand. Why was she keeping so many secrets from me? And how in the world can I possibly be mad at her about it now? About anything. Even for a moment.

Bailey and I didnt talk too much
about Gram's spells,
what she called her Private Times
days spent in the art room
without break.
It was just a part of things,
like green summer leaves,
burning up in fall.
I'd peek through the crack in the door,
see her surrounded by easels
of green women, half-formed—
the paint still wet and hungry.
She'd work on them all at once,
and soon, she'd begin
to look like one of them, too,
all that green spattered on her clothes,
her hands, her face.
Bails and I would pack
our own brown bags those days,
would pull out our sandwiches at noon,
hating the disappointment of a world
where polka dotted scarves,
sheets of music, blue feathers,
didn't surprise us at lunch.
After school, we'd bring her tea
or a sliced apple with cheese,
but it'd just sit on the table, untouched.
Big would tell us to ride it out—
that everyone needs a break
from the routine now and then.
So we did—
it was like Gram would go
on vacation with her ladies
and like them
would get caught somewhere
between here and there.

(Found on a piece of paper in Lennie's clarinet case)

15

Len, you awake?
Yeah.
Let's do Mom.
Okay, I'll start. She's in Rome—
She's always in Rome lately—
Well, now she's a famous Roman pizza chef and it's late at night, the restaurant just closed and
she's drinking a glass of wine with—
With Luigi, the drop dead gorgeous waiter, they just grabbed the bottle of wine and are walking
through the moonlit streets, it's hot, and when they come to a fountain she takes off her shoes
and jumps in…
Luigi doesn't even take off his shoes, just jumps in and splashes her, they're laughing…
But standing in the fountain under the big, bright moon makes her think of Flying Man's, how
she used to swim at night with Big…
You really think so, Bails? You really think she's in a fountain in Rome on a hot summer night
with gorgeous Luigi and thinking about us? About Big?
Sure.
No way.
We're thinking about her.
That's different.
Why?
Because we're not in a fountain in Rome on a hot summer night with gorgeous Luigi.
True.
Night, Bails.

(Found on a piece of notebook paper balled up in a shoe in Lennie's closet)

The day everything happens begins like all others lately with Joe's soft knock. I roll over, peek out the window, and see only the lawn through the morning fog. Everything must have been moved back into the house after I'd gone to sleep.

I go downstairs, find Gram sitting at her seat at the kitchen table, her hair wrapped in a towel. She has her hands around a mug of coffee and is staring at Bailey's chair. I sit down next to her. "I'm really sorry about last night," I say. "I know how much you wanted to do a ritual for Bailey, for us."

"It's okay, Len, we'll do one. We have plenty of time." She takes my hand with one of hers, rubs it absent-mindedly with the other. "And anyway, I think I figured out what was causing the bad luck."

"Yeah?" I say. "What?"

"You know that mask Big brought back from South America when he was studying those trees. I think that it might have a curse on it."

I've always hated that mask. It has fake hair all over it, eyebrows that arch in astonishment, and a mouth baring shiny, wolfish teeth. "It always gave me the creeps," I tell her. "Bailey too."

Gram nods but she seems distracted. I don't think she's really listening to me, which couldn't be more unlike her lately.

"Lennie," she says tentatively. "Is everything okay between you and Toby?"

My stomach clenches. "Of course," I say, swallowing hard, trying to make my voice sound casual. "Why?" She owl-eyes me.

"Don't know, you both seemed funny last night around each other." Ugh. Ugh. Ugh.

"And I keep wondering why Sarah isn't coming around. Did you get in a fight?" she says to further send me into a guilt spiral.

Just then, Big and Joe come in, saving me. Big says, "We thought we saw life in spider number six today."

Joe says, "I swear I saw a flutter."

"Almost had a heart attack, Joe here, practically launched through the roof, but it must have been a breeze, little guy's still dead as a doornail. The Lennie plant's still languishing too. I might have to rethink things, maybe add a UV light."

"Hey," Joe says, coming behind me, dropping a hand to my shoulder. I look up at the warmth in his face and smile at him. I think he could make me smile even while I was hanging at the gallows, which I'm quite certain I'm headed for. I put my hand over his for a second, see Gram notice this as she gets up to make us breakfast.

I feel somehow responsible for the scrambled ashes that we are all shoveling into our mouths, as if I've somehow derailed the path to healing that our household was on yesterday morning. Joe and Big banter on about resurrecting bugs and exploding cakes – the conversation that would not die – while I actively avoid Gram's suspicious gaze.

"I need to get to work early today, we're catering the Dwyers' party tonight." I say this to my plate but can see Gram nodding in my periphery. She knows because she's been asked to help with the flower arrangements. She's asked all the time to oversee flower arrangements for parties and weddings but rarely says yes because she hates cut flowers. We all knew not to prune her bushes or cut her blooms under penalty of death. She probably said yes this time just to get out of the house for an afternoon. Sometimes I imagine the poor gardeners all over town this summer without Gram, standing in their yards, scratching their heads at their listless wisteria, their forlorn fuchsias.

Joe says, "I'll walk you to work. I need to go to the music store anyway." All the Fontaine boys are supposedly working for their parents this summer, who've converted a barn into a workshop where his dad makes specialty guitars, but I get the impression they spend all day working on new songs for their band Dive.

We embark on the seven-block walk to town, which looks like it's going to take two hours because Joe comes to a standstill every time he has something to say, which is every three seconds.

"You can't walk and talk at the same time, can you?" I ask.

He stops in his tracks, says "Nope." Then continues on for a minute in silence until he can't take it anymore and stops, turns to me, takes my arm, forcing me to stop, while he tells me how I have to go to Paris, how we'll play music in the metro, make tons of money, eat only chocolate croissants, drink red wine, and stay up all night every night because no one ever sleeps in Paris. I can hear his heart beating the whole time and I'm thinking, *Why not?* I could step out of this sad life like it's an old sorry dress, and go to Paris with Joe – we could get on a plane and fly over the ocean and land in *France*. We could do it today even. I have money saved. I have a beret. A hot black bra. I know how to say *Je t'aime*. I love coffee and chocolate and Baudelaire. And I've watched Bailey enough to know how to wrap a scarf. We could really do it, and the possibility makes me feel so giddy I think I might catapult into the air. I tell him so. He takes my hand and puts his other arm up Superman-style.

"You see, I was right," he says with a smile that could power the state of California.

"God, you're gorgeous," I blurt out and want to die because I can't believe I said it aloud and neither can he – his smile, so huge now, he can't even get any words past it.

He stops again. I think he's going to go on about Paris some more – but he doesn't. I look up at him. His face is serious like it was last night in the woods.

"Lennie," he whispers.

I look into his sorrowless eyes and a door in my heart blows open.

And when we kiss, I see that on the other side of that door is sky.

16

I
CAN'T
SHOVE
THE
DARK
OUT
OF
MY
WAY

(Found scrawled on the bench outside of Maria's Italian Deli)

I make a million lasagnas in the window at the deli, listening to Maria gossip with customer after customer, then come home to find Toby lying on my bed. The house is still as stone with Gram at the Dwyers' and Big at work. I punched Toby's number into my phone ten times today, but stopped each time before pressing send. I was going to tell him I couldn't see him. Not after promising Bailey. Not after kissing Joe. Not after Gram's inquisition. Not after reaching into myself and finding some semblance of conscience. I was going to tell him that we had to stop this, had to think how it would make Bailey feel, how bad it makes us feel. I was going to tell him all these things, but didn't because each time I was about to complete the call, I got transported back to the moment by his truck last night and that same inexplicable recklessness and hunger would overtake me until the phone was closed and lying silent on the counter before me.

"Hi, you." His voice is deep and dark and unglues me instantly.

I'm moving toward him, unable not to, the pull, unavoidable, tidal. He gets up quickly, meets me halfway across the room. For one split second we face each other; it's like diving into a mirror. And then I feel his mouth crushing into mine, teeth and tongue and lips and all his raging sorrow crashing right into mine, all our raging sorrow together now crashing into the world that did this to us. I'm frantic as my fingers unbutton his shirt, slip it off his shoulders, then my hands are on his chest, his back, his neck, and I think he must have eight hands because one is taking off my shirt, another two are holding my face while he kisses me, one is running through my hair, another two are on my breasts, a few are pulling my hips to his and then the last undoes the button on my jeans, unzips the fly and we are on the bed, his hand edging its way between my legs, and that is when I hear the front door slam shut—

We freeze and our eyes meet – a mid-air collision of shame: all the wreckage explodes inside me. I can't bear it. I cover my face with my hands, hear myself groan. What am I doing? What did we almost do? I want to press the rewind button. Press it and press it and press it. But I can't think about that now, can only think about not getting caught in this bed with Toby.

"Hurry," I say, and it unfreezes and de-panics both of us.

He springs to his feet and I scramble across the floor like a crazed crab, put on my shirt, throw Toby his. We're both dressing at warp speed—

"No more," I say, fumbling with the buttons on my shirt, feeling criminal and wrong, full of ick and shame. "Please."

He's straightening the bedding, frenetically puffing pillows, his face flushed and wild, blond hair flying in every direction. "I'm sorry, Len—"

"It doesn't make me miss her less, not anymore." I sound half resolute, half frantic. "It makes it worse."

He stops what he's doing, nods, his face a wrestling match of competing emotions, but it looks like hurt is winning out. God, I don't want to hurt him, but I don't want to do this anymore either. I can't. And what is *this* anyway? Being with him just now didn't feel like the safe harbor it did before – it was different, desperate, like two people struggling for breath.

"John Lennon," I hear from downstairs. "You home?"

This can't be happening, it can't. Nothing used to happen to me, nothing at all for seventeen years and now everything at once. Joe is practically singing my name, he sounds so elated, probably still riding high from that kiss, that sublime kiss that could make stars fall into your open hands, a kiss like Cathy and Heathcliff must have had on the moors with the sun beating on their backs and the world streaming with wind and possibility. A kiss so unlike the fearsome tornado that moments before ripped through Toby and me.

Toby is dressed and sitting on my bed, his shirt hanging over his lap. I wonder why he doesn't tuck it in, then realize he's trying to cover a freaking hard-on – oh God, who am I? How could I have let this get so out of hand? And why doesn't my family do anything normal like carry house keys and lock front doors?

I make sure I'm buttoned and zipped. I smooth my hair and wipe my lips before I swing open the bedroom door and stick my head out just as Joe is barreling down the hallway. He smiles wildly, looks like love itself stuffed into a pair of jeans, black T-shirt, and backward baseball cap.

"Come over tonight. They're all going to the city for some jazz show." He's out of breath – I bet he ran all the way here. "Couldn't wait..." He reaches for my hand, takes it in his, then sees Toby sitting on the bed behind me. First he drops my hand, and then the impossible happens: Joe Fontaine's face shuts like a door.

"Hey," he says to Toby, but his voice is pinched and wary.

"Toby and I were just going through some of Bailey's things," I blurt out. I can't believe I'm using Bailey to lie to Joe to cover up fooling around with her boyfriend. A new low even for the immoral girl I've become. I'm a Gila monster of a girl. Loch Ness Lennie. No convent would even take me.

Joe nods, mollified by that, but he's still looking at me and Toby and back again with suspicion. It's as if someone hit the dimmer switch and turned down his whole being.

Toby stands up. "I need to get home." He crosses the room, his carriage slumped, his gait awkward, uncertain. "Good seeing you again," he mumbles at Joe. "I'll see you soon, Len." He slips past us, sad as rain, and I feel terrible. My heart follows after him a few paces, but then it ricochets back to Joe, who stands before me without a trace of death anywhere on him.

"Lennie, is there—"

I have a pretty good idea what Joe is about to ask and so I do the only thing I can think of to stop the question from coming out of his mouth: I kiss him. I mean *really* kiss him, like I've wanted to do since that very first day in band. No sweet soft peck about it. With the same lips that just kissed someone else, I kiss away his question, his suspicion, and after a while, I kiss away the someone else too, the something else that almost just happened, until it is only the two of us, Joe and me, in the room, in the world, in my crazy swelling heart.

Holy horses.

I put aside for a moment the fact that I've turned into a total strumpet-harlot-trollop-wench-jezebel-tart-harridan-chippy-nymphet because I've just realized something incredible. *This is it* – what all the hoopla is about, what *Wuthering Heights* is about – it all boils down to this feeling rushing through me in this moment with Joe as our mouths refuse to part. Who knew all this time I was one kiss away from being Cathy and Juliet and Elizabeth Bennet and Lady Chatterley!?

Years ago, I was crashed in Gram's garden and Big asked me what I was doing. I told him I was looking up at the sky. He said, "That's a misconception, Lennie, the sky is everywhere, it begins at your feet."

Kissing Joe, I believe this, for the first time in my life.

I feel delirious, Joelirious, I think as I pull away for a moment, and open my eyes to see that the Joe Fontaine dimmer switch has been cranked back up again and that he is Joelirious too.

"That was—" I can hardly form words.

"Incredible," he interrupts. "Totally *incroyable*."

We're staring at each other, stunned.

"Sure," I say, suddenly remembering he invited me over tonight.

"Sure what?" He looks at me like I'm speaking Swahili, then smiles and puts his arms around me, says, "Ready?" He lifts me off my feet and spins me around and I am suddenly in the dorkiest movie ever, laughing and feeling a happiness so huge I am ashamed to be feeling it in a world without my sister.

"Sure, I'll come over tonight," I say as everything stops spinning and I land back on my own two feet.

17

What's wrong, Lennie?

Nothing.

Tell me.

No.

C'mon, spill it.

Okay. It's just that you're different now.

How?

Like Zombieville.

I'm in love, Len – I've never felt like this before.

Like what?

Like forever.

Forever?

Yeah. This is it. He's it.

How do you know?

My toes told me. The toes knows.

(Found on a napkin stuffed in a mug, Cecilia's Bakery)

I'm going over to Joe's," I say to Gram and Big, who are both home now, camped out in the kitchen, listening to a baseball game on the radio, circa 1930.

"That sounds like a plan," Gram says. She's taken the still despairing Lennie houseplant out from under the pyramid and is sitting beside it at the table, singing to it softly, something about greener pastures. "I'll just freshen up and get my bag, sweet pea."

She can't be serious.

"I'll go too," says Big, who is hunched over a crossword puzzle. He's the fastest puzzler in all Christendom. I look over and note, however, that this time he's putting numbers in the boxes instead of letters. "As soon as I finish this, we can all head up to the Fontaines'."

"Uh, I don't think so," I say.

They both look up at me, incredulous.

Big says, "What do you mean, Len, he's here every single morning, it's only fair that—"

And then he can't keep it up anymore and bursts out laughing, as does Gram. I'm relieved. I had actually started to imagine trucking up the hill with Gram and Big in tow: the Munsters follow Marilyn on a date.

"Why, Big, she's all dressed up. And her hair's down. Look at her." This is a problem. I was going for the short flowery dress and heels and lipstick and wild hair look that no one would notice is any different from the jeans, ponytail, and no makeup look I've mastered every other day of my life. I know I'm blushing, also know I better get out of the house before I run back upstairs and challenge Bailey's Guinness-Book-of-Changing-Clothes-Before-a-Date record of thirty-seven outfits. This was only my eighteenth, but clothes-changing is an exponential activity, the frenzy only builds, it's a law of nature. Even St Anthony peering at me from the nightstand, reminding me of what I'd found in the drawer last night, couldn't snap me out of it. I'd remembered something about him though. He was like Bailey, charismatic as anything. He had to give his sermons in marketplaces because he overflowed even the largest of churches. When he died all the church bells in Padua rang of their own accord. Everyone thought angels had come to earth.

"Goodbye, you guys," I say to Gram and Big, and head for the door.

"Have fun, Len … and not too late, okay?"

I nod, and am off on the first real date of my life. The other nights I've had with boys don't count, not the ones with Toby I'm actively trying not to think about, and definitely not the parties, after which I'd spent the next day, week, month, year thinking of ways to get my kisses back. Nothing has been like this, nothing has made me feel like I do right now walking up the hill to Joe's, like I have a window in my chest where sunlight is pouring in.

18

When
Joe
plays
his
horn
I
fall
out
of
my
chair
and
onto
my
knees
When
he
plays
all
the
flowers
swap
colors
and
years
and
decades
and
centuries
of
rain
pour
back
into
the
sky

(Found on the bathroom wall, music room, Clover High)

The feeling I had earlier today with Joe in The Sanctum overwhelms me the moment I see him sitting on the stoop of the big white house playing his guitar. He's bent over it, singing softly, and the wind is carrying his words through the air like fluttering leaves.

"Hey, John Lennon," he says, putting aside his guitar, standing up and jumping off the front step. "Uh-oh. You look *vachement* amazing. Too good to be alone with me all night long."

He's practically leaping over. His delight quotient mesmerizes me. At the human factory, someone must have messed up and just slipped him more than the rest of us. "I've been thinking about a duet we could do. I just need to rearrange—"

I'm not listening anymore. I hope he just keeps talking up a storm, because I can't utter a word. I know the expression *love bloomed* is metaphorical, but in my heart in this moment, there is one badass flower, captured in time-lapse photography, going from bud to wild radiant blossom in ten seconds flat.

"You okay?" he asks. His hands are on either side of my arms and he's peering into my face.

"Yes." I'm wondering how people breathe in these situations. "I'm fine."

"You are *fine*," he says, looking me over like a major dork, which immediately snaps me out of my love spell.

"Ugh, *quel dork*," I say, pushing him away.

He laughs and slips his arm around my shoulders. "C'mon, you enter Maison Fontaine at your own risk."

The first thing I notice about Maison Fontaine is that the

phone is ringing and Joe doesn't seem to notice. I hear a girl's voice on an answering machine far away in another room and think for a minute it sounds like Rachel before deciding it doesn't. The second thing I notice is how opposite this house is to Maison Walker. Our house looks like Hobbits live there. The ceilings are low, the wood is dark and gnarly, colorful rag rugs line the floors, paintings, the walls, whereas Joe's house floats high in the sky with the clouds. There are windows everywhere that reveal sunburned fields swimming in the wind, dark green woods that cloister the river and the river itself as it wends from town to town in the distance. There are no tables piled with weeks of mail, shoes kicked around under furniture, books open on every surface. Joe lives in a museum. Hanging all over the walls are gorgeous guitars of every color, shape and size. They look so animate, like they could make music all by themselves.

"Pretty cool, huh? My dad makes amazing instruments. Not just guitars either. Mandolins, lutes, dulcimers," he says as I ogle one and then the next.

And now for something completely different: Joe's room. The physical manifestation of chaos theory. It's overflowing with instruments I've never seen before and can't even imagine what kind of sound they'd make, CDs, music magazines, library books in French and English, concert posters of French bands I've never heard of, comic books, notebooks with tiny boxlike weirdo boy writing in them, sheets of music, stereo equipment unplugged and plugged, broken-open amps and other sound equipment I don't recognize, odd rubber animals, bowls of blue marbles, decks of cards, piles of clothes as high as my knee, not to mention the dishes, bottles, glasses … and over his desk a small poster of John Lennon.

"Hmm," I say, pointing to the poster. I look around, taking it all in. "I think your room is giving me new insight into Joe Fontaine aka freaking madman."

"Yeah, thought it best to wait to show you the bombroom until…"

"Until what?"

"I don't know, until you realized…"

"Realized what?"

"I don't know, Lennie." I can see he's embarrassed. Somehow things have turned uncomfortable.

"Tell me," I say. "Wait until I realized what?"

"Nothing, it's stupid." He looks down at his feet, then back up at me. Bat. Bat. Bat.

"I want to know," I say.

"Okay, I'll say it: wait until you realized that maybe you liked me too."

The flower is blooming again in my chest, this time three seconds from bud to showstopper.

"I do," I say, and then without thinking, add, "A lot." What's gotten into me? Now I really can't breathe. A situation made worse by the lips that are suddenly pressing into mine.

Our tongues have fallen madly in love and gotten married and moved to Paris.

After I'm sure I've made up for all my former years of kisslessness, I say, "I think if we don't stop kissing, the world is going to explode."

"Seems like it," he whispers. He's staring dreamily into my eyes. Heathcliff and Cathy have nothing on us. "We can do something else for a while," he says. "If you want…" He smiles. And then: Bat. Bat. Bat. I wonder if I am going to survive the night.

"Want to play?" he asks.

"I do," I tell him, "but I didn't bring my instrument."

"I'll get one." He leaves the room, which gives me a chance to recover, and unfortunately, to think about what happened with Toby earlier. How scary and out of control it was today, like we were trying to break each other apart. But why? To find Bailey? To wrench her from the other's heart? The other's body? Or was it something worse? Were we trying to forget her, to wipe out her memory for one passionate moment? But no, it's not that, it can't be, can it? When we're together, Bailey's all around us like air we can breathe; that's been the comfort until today, until it got so out of hand. I don't know. The only thing I do know is that it's all about her, because even now if I imagine Toby alone with his heartache while I am here with Joe obliterating my own, I feel guilty, like I've abandoned him, and with him, my grief, and with my grief, my sister.

The phone rings again and it mercifully ejects me from these thoughts, and crash-lands me back into the bombroom – this room where Joe sleeps in this unmade bed and reads these books strewn everywhere and drinks out of these five hundred half-full glasses seemingly at once. I feel giddy with the intimacy of being where he thinks and dreams, where he changes his clothes and flings them absolutely all over the place, where he's naked. *Joe, naked*. The thought of it, him, all of him – *guh*. I've never even seen a real live guy totally naked, ever. Only some Internet porn Sarah and I devoured for a while. That's it. I've always been scared of seeing all, seeing *it*. The first time Sarah saw one hard, she said more animal names came flying out of her mouth in that one moment than all other moments in her life combined. Not animals you'd think either. No pythons and eels. According to her it was a full-on menagerie: hippos, elephants, orangutans, tapirs, gazelles, etc.

All of a sudden I'm walloped with missing her. How could I be in Joe Fontaine's freaking bedroom without her knowing? How could I have blown her off like this? I take out my phone, text: *Call back the search party. Please. Forgive.*

I look around again, curbing all impulses to go through drawers, peek under the bed, read the notebook lying open at my feet. Okay, I curb two out of three of those impulses. It's been a bad day for morality. And it's not really reading someone's journal if it's open and you can glance down and make out your name, well, your name to him, in a sentence that says…

I bend my knees, and without touching the notebook in any way, read just the bit around the initials JL. *I've never met anyone as heartbroken as JL, I want to make her feel better, want to be around her all the time, it's crazy, it's like she's on full blast, and everyone else is just on mute, and she's honest, so honest, nothing like Genevieve, nothing at all like Genevieve...* I hear his steps in the hall, stand up. The phone is ringing yet again.

He comes back with two clarinets, a B flat and a bass, holds them up. I go for the soprano like I'm used to.

"What's the deal with the phone?" I say, instead of saying *Who's Genevieve?* Instead of falling to my knees and confessing that I'm anything but honest, that I'm probably just exactly like Genevieve, whoever she is, but without the exotic French part.

He shrugs. "We get a lot of calls," he says, then begins his tuning ritual that makes everything in the world but him and a handful of chords disappear.

The untapped duet of guitar and clarinet is awkward at first. We stumble around in sound, fall over each other, look up embarrassed, try again. But after a while, we begin to click and when we don't know where the other is going, we lock eyes and listen so intently that for fleeting moments it's like our souls are talking. One time after I improvise alone for a while, he exclaims, "Your tone is awesome, so, so lonely, like, I don't know, a day without birds or something," but I don't feel lonely at all. I feel like Bailey is listening.

"Well, you're no different late at night, exactly the same John Lennon." We're sitting on the grass, drinking some wine Joe swiped from his father. The front door is open and a French chanteuse is blasting out of it into the warm night. We're swigging out of the bottle and eating cheese and a baguette. I'm finally in France with Joe, I think, and it makes me smile.

"What?" he asks.

"I don't know. This is nice. I've never drunk wine before."

"I have my whole life. My dad mixed it with water for us when we were little."

"Really? Drunken little Fontaine boys running into walls?"

He laughs. "Yup, exactly. That's my theory of why French children are so well behaved. They're drunk off their *petits mignons* asses most of the time." He tips the bottle and takes a sip, passes it to me.

"Are both your parents French?"

"Dad is, born and raised in Paris. My mom's from around here originally. But Dad makes up for it, he's Central Casting French." There's a bitterness in his voice, but I don't pursue it. I've only just recovered from the consequences of my snooping, have almost forgotten about Genevieve and the importance of honesty to Joe, when he says, "Ever been in love?" He's lying on his back, looking up at a sky reeling with stars.

I don't holler, *Yes, right now, with you, stupid*, like I suddenly want to, but say, "No. I've never been anything."

He gets up on one elbow, looks over at me. "What do you mean?"

I sit, hugging my knees, looking out at the spattering of lights down in the valley.

"It's like I was sleeping or something, happy, but sleeping, for seventeen years, and then Bailey died..." The wine has made it easier to talk but I don't know if I'm making any sense. I look over at Joe. He's listening to me so carefully, like he wants to catch my words in his hands as they fall from my lips.

"And now?"

"Well, now I don't know. I feel so different." I pick up a pebble and toss it into the darkness. I think how things used to be: predictable, sensible. How I used to be the same. I think how there is no inevitability, how there never was, I just didn't know it then. "I'm awake, I guess, and maybe that's good, but it's more complicated than that because now I'm someone who knows the worst thing can happen at any time."

Joe's nodding like I'm making sense, which is good, because I have no idea what I just said. I know what I meant though. I meant that I know now how close death is. How it lurks. And who wants to know that? Who wants to know we are just one carefree breath away from the end? Who wants to know that the person you love and need the most can just vanish forever?

He says, "But if you're someone who knows the worst thing can happen at any time, aren't you also someone who knows the best thing can happen at any time too?"

I think about this and instantly feel elated. "Yeah, that's right," I say. "Like right now with you, actually..." It's out of my mouth before I can stop it, and I see the delight wash across his face.

"Are we drunk?" I ask.

He takes another swig. "Quite possibly."

"Anyway, have you ever..."

"I've never experienced anything like what you're going through."

"No, I mean, have you ever been in love?" My stomach clenches. I want him to say no so badly, but I know he won't, and he doesn't.

"Yeah, I was. I guess." He shakes his head. "I think so anyway."

"What happened?"

A siren sounds in the distance. Joe sits up. "During the summers, I boarded at school. I walked in on her and my roommate, killed me. I mean really killed me. I never talked to her again, or him, threw myself into music in kind of an insane way, swore off girls, well, until now, I guess..." He smiles, but not like usual. There's a vulnerability in it, a hesitancy; it's all over his face, swimming around in his beautiful green eyes too. I shut my eyes to not have to see it, because all I can think about is how he almost walked in on Toby and me today.

Joe grabs the bottle of wine and drinks. "Moral of the story: violinists are insane. I think it's that crazy-ass bow." Genevieve, the gorgeous French violinist. Ugh.

"Yeah? What about clarinettists?"

He smiles. "The most soulful." He trails his finger across my face, forehead to cheek to chin, then down my neck. "And so beautiful." Oh my, I totally get why King Edward VIII abdicated his throne for love. If I had a throne, I'd abdicate it just to relive the last three seconds.

"And horn players?" I ask, intertwining my fingers with his.

He shakes his head. "Crazy hellions, steer clear. All-or-nothing types, no middle ground for the blowhards." Uh-oh. "Never want to cross a horn player," he adds flippantly, but I don't hear it flippantly. I can't believe I lied to him today. I have to stay away from Toby. Far away.

A pair of coyotes howl in the distance, sending a shiver up my spine. Nice timing, dogs.

"Didn't know you horn guys were so scary," I say, letting go of his hand and taking a swig off the bottle. "And guitarists?"

"You tell me."

"Hmm, let me think..." I trail my finger over his face this time. "Homely and boring, and of course, talentless—" He cracks up. "I'm not done. But they make up for all that because they are so, so passionate—"

"Oh, God," he whispers, reaching his hand behind my neck and bringing my lips to his. "Let's let the whole fucking world explode this time."

And we do.

19

I'm lying in bed, hearing voices.

"What do you think is wrong with her?"

"Not sure. Could be the orange walls getting to her." A pause, then I hear: "Let's think about it logically. Symptoms: still in bed at noon on a sunny Saturday, goofy grin on her face, stains on her lips likely from red wine, a beverage she's not allowed to drink, which we will address later, and the giveaway, still in her clothes, a dress I might add, with flowers on it."

"Well, my expert opinion, which I draw from vast experience and five glorious, albeit flawed marriages, is that Lennie Walker aka John Lennon is out of her mind in love."

Big and Gram are smiling down at me. I feel like Dorothy waking in her bed, surrounded by her Kansans after having been over the rainbow.

"Do you think you're ever going to get up again?" Gram is sitting on the bed now, patting my hand, which is in hers.

"I don't know." I roll over to face her. "I just want to lie here forever and think about him." I haven't decided which is better: experiencing last night, or the blissed-out replay in my mind where I can hit pause and turn ecstatic seconds into whole hours, where I can loop certain moments until the sweet grassy taste of Joe is again in my mouth, the clove scent of his skin is in the air, until I can feel his hands running through my hair, all over my dress, just one thin, thin layer between us, until the moment when he slipped his hands under the fabric and I felt his fingers on my skin like music – all of it sending me again and again right off the cliff that is my heart.

This morning, for the first time, Bailey wasn't my first thought on waking and it had made me feel guilty. But the guilt didn't have much of a chance against the dawning realization that I was falling in love. I had stared out the window at the early-morning fog, wondering for a moment if she had sent Joe to me so I would know that in the same world where she could die, this could happen.

Big says, "Would you look at her. We've got to cut down those damn rosebushes." His hair is particularly coiled and springy today, and his mustache is unwaxed, so it looks like a squirrel is running across his face. In any fairy tale, Big plays the king.

Gram chides him, "Hush now, you don't even believe in that." She doesn't like anyone to perpetuate the rumor about the aphrodisiacal nature of her roses, because there was a time when desperate lovers would come and steal them to try to change the hearts of their beloveds. It made her crazy. There is not much Gram takes more seriously than proper pruning.

Big won't let it go though. "I follow the proof-is-in-the-pudding scientific method: Please examine the empirical evidence in this bed. She's worse than me."

"No one is worse than you, you're the town swain." Gram rolls her eyes.

"You say swain, but imply swine," Big retorts, twisting his squirrel for effect.

I sit up in bed, lean my back against the sill to better enjoy their verbal tennis match. I can feel the summery day through the window, deliciously warming my back. But when I look over at Bailey's bed, I'm leveled. How can something this momentous be happening to me without her? And what about all the momentous things to come? How will I go through each and every one of them without her? I don't care that she was keeping things from me – I want to tell her absolutely everything about last night, about everything that will ever happen to me! I'm crying before I even realize it, but I don't want us all to tailspin, so I swallow and swallow it all down, and try to focus on last night, on falling in love. I spot my clarinet across the room, half covered with the paisley scarf of Bailey's I recently started wearing.

"Joe didn't come by this morning?" I ask, wanting to play again, wanting to blow all this everything I'm feeling out my clarinet.

Big replies, "No, bet a million dollars he's exactly where you are, though he probably has his guitar with him. Have you asked him if he sleeps with it yet?"

"He's a musical genius," I say, feeling my earlier giddiness returning. Without a doubt, I've gone bipolar.

"Oh, jeez. C'mon Gram, she's a lost cause." Big winks at me, then heads for the door.

Gram stays seated next to me, ruffling my hair like I'm a little kid. She's looking at me closely and a little too long. Oh no. I've been in such a trance, I forget that I haven't really been talking to Gram lately, that we've hardly been alone like this in weeks.

"Len." This is definitely her Gramouncement tone, but I don't think it's going to be about Bailey. About expressing my feelings. About packing up Bailey's things. About going to the city for lunch. About resuming my lessons. About all the things I haven't wanted to do.

"Yeah?"

"We talked about birth control, diseases and all that..." Phew. This one's harmless.

"Yeah, like a million times."

"Okay, just as long as you haven't suddenly forgotten it all."

"Nope."

"Good." She's patting my hand again.

"Gram, there's no need yet, okay?" I feel the requisite blush from revealing this, but better to not have her freaking out about it and constantly questioning me.

"Even better, even better," she says, the relief evident in her voice, and it makes me think. Things with Joe last night were intense, but they were paced to savor. Not so with Toby. I worry what might've happened if we weren't interrupted. Would I have had the sense to stop us? Would he have? All I know is that everything was happening really quickly, I was totally out of control, and condoms were the furthest thing from my mind. God. How did that happen? How did Toby Shaw's hands ever end up on my breasts? Toby's! And only hours before Joe's. I want to dive under the bed, make it my permanent residence. How did I go from bookworm and band geek to two-guys-in-the-same-day hussy?

Gram smiles, oblivious of the sudden bile rising in my throat, the twisting in my guts. She ruffles my hair again. "In the middle of all this tragedy, you're growing up, sweet pea, and that is such a wonderful thing."

Groan.

20

Lennie! Lennie! Lennnnnnnnnnie! God, I've missed you!" I pull the cell phone away from my ear. Sarah hadn't texted me back, so I assumed she was really pissed. I cut in to say so, and she responds, "I *am* furious! And I'm *not* speaking to you!" then she launches into all the summer gossip I've missed. I soak it up but can tell there was some true vitriol in her words. I'm lying on my bed, wiped after practicing Cavallini's Adagio and Tarantella for two straight hours – it was incredible, like turning the air into colors. It made me think of the Charlie Parker quote Mr James liked to repeat: *If you don't live it, it can't come out of your horn*. It also made me think I might go to summer band practice after all.

Sarah and I make a plan to meet at Flying Man's. I'm dying to tell her about Joe. Not about Toby. I'm thinking if I don't talk about it, I can just pretend it didn't happen.

She's lying on a rock in the sun reading Simone de Beauvoir's *The Second Sex* – in preparation, I'm sure, for her very promising guy-poaching expedition to State's Women's Studies Department feminism symposium. She springs to her feet when she sees me, and hugs me like crazy despite the fact that she's completely naked. We have our own secret pool and mini-falls behind Flying Man's that we've been coming to for years. We've declared it clothing optional and we opt not. "God, it's been forever," she says.

"I'm so sorry, Sarah," I say, hugging her back.

"It's okay, really," she says. "I know I need to give you a free pass right now. So that's…" She pulls away for a second, studies my face. "Wait a minute? What's wrong with you? You look weird. I mean *really* weird."

I can't stop smiling. I must look like a Fontaine.

"What, Lennie? What happened?"

"I think I'm falling in love." The moment the words are out of my mouth, I feel my face go hot with shame. I'm supposed to be grieving, not falling in love. Not to mention everything else I've been doing.

"Whaaaaaaaaaaaaaaaaaaaaaat! That is so unfreakingfreakingfreakingfreakingbelieveable! Cows on the moon, Len! Cows. On. The. Moon!" Well, so much for my shame. Sarah is in full on cheerleader mode, arms flailing, hopping up and down. Then she stops abruptly. "Wait, with whom? NOT Toby, I hope."

"No, no, of course not," I say as a speeding eighteen-wheeler of guilt flattens me.

"Whew," Sarah, says, sweeping her hand off her brow dramatically. "Who then? Who could you be in love with? You haven't gone anywhere, at least that I know of, and this town is beyond Loserville, so where'd you find him?"

"Sarah, it's Joe."

"It's not."

"Yeah, it is."

"No!"

"Yup."

"Not true."

"Is true."

"Nah-uh, nah-uh, nah-uh."

"Uh-huh, uh-huh, uh-huh."

Etc.

Her previous display of enthusiasm was nothing compared to the one that is going on now. She's doing circles around me, saying, "Oh my God. I am soooooooooooooo jealous. Every girl in Clover is after one Fontaine or another. No wonder you've been a shut-in. I would be too, if I could shut in with one of them. God, let me live vicariously through you. Tell me every freaking detail. That beautiful, beautiful boy, those eyes, those *eyelashes*, that unfreakingbelievable smile, that trumpet playing, wow, Lennnnnnnnnie." She's pacing now, has lit another cigarette, is chain smoking in glee – a naked smokestack maniac. I'm so happy to be hanging out with the marvel that is my best friend Sarah. And I'm so happy to be happy about it.

I tell her every detail. How he came over every morning with croissants, how we played music together, how he made Gram and Big so happy just by being in the house, how we drank wine last night and kissed until I was sure I had walked right into the sky. I told her how I think I can hear his heart beating even when he's not there, how I feel like flowers – Gramgantuan ones – are blooming in my chest, how I'm sure I feel just the way Heathcliff did for Cathy before—

"Okay, stop for a second." She's still smiling but she looks a bit worried and surprised too. "Lennie, you're not in love, you're demented. I've never heard anyone talk about a guy like this."

I shrug. "Then I'm demented."

"Wow, I want to be demented too." She sits down next to me on the rock. "It's like you've hardly kissed three guys in your whole life and now this. Guess you were saving it up or something..."

I tell her my Rip Van Lennie theory of having slept my whole life until recently.

"I don't know, Len. You always seemed awake to me."

"Yeah, I don't know either. It was a wine-induced theory." Sarah picks up a stone, tosses it into the water with a little too much force. "What?" I ask.

She doesn't answer right away, picks up another stone and hurls it too. "I am mad at you, but I'm not allowed to be, you know?"

It's exactly how I feel toward Bailey sometimes lately.

"You've just been keeping so much from me, Lennie. I thought ... I don't know."

It's as if she were speaking my lines in a play.

"I'm sorry," I say again feebly. I want to say more, give her an explanation, but the truth is I don't know why I've felt so closed off to her since Bailey died.

"It's okay," she says again quietly.

"It'll be different now," I say, hoping it's true. "Promise."

I look out at the sun courting the river's surface, the green leaves, the wet rocks behind the falls. "Want to go swimming?"

"Not yet," she says. "I have news too. Not breaking news,

but still." It's a clear dig and I deserve it. I didn't even ask how she was.

She's smirking at me, quite dementedly, actually. "I hooked up with Luke Jacobus last night."

"Luke?" I'm surprised. Besides for his recent lapse in judgment, which resulted in his band-kill status, he's been devotedly, unrequitedly in love with Sarah since second grade. King of the Nerdiverse, she used to call him. "Didn't you make out with him in seventh grade and then drop him when that idiot surfer glistened at you?"

"Yeah, it's probably dumb," she says. "I agreed to do lyrics for this incredible music he wrote, and we were hanging out, and it just happened."

"What about the Jean-Paul Sartre rule?"

"Sense of humor trumps literacy, I've decided – and jumping giraffes, Len – growth geyser! The guy's like the Hulk these days."

"He is funny," I agree. "And green."

She laughs, just as my phone signals a text. I rifle through my bag and take it out hoping for a message from Joe.

Sarah's singing, "Lennie got a love note from a Fontaine," as she tries to read over my shoulder. "C'mon let me see it." She grabs the phone from me. I pull it out of her hands, but it's too late. It says: *I need to talk to you. T.*

"As in Toby?" she asks. "But I thought … I mean, you just said … Lennie, what're you doing?"

"Nothing," I tell her, shoving the phone back in my bag,

already breaking my promise. "Really. Nothing."

"Why don't I believe you?" she says, shaking her head. "I have a bad feeling about this."

"Don't," I say, swallowing my own atrocious feeling.

"Really. I'm demented, remember?" I touch her arm. "Let's go swimming."

We float on our backs in the pool for over an hour. I make her tell me everything about her night with Luke so I don't have to think about Toby's text, what might be so urgent. Then we climb up to the falls and get under them, screaming over and over into the roar like we've done since we were little.

I scream bloody murder.

21

There were once two sisters
who were not afraid of the dark
because the dark was full of the other's voice
across the room,
because even when the night was thick
and starless
they walked home together from the river
seeing who could last the longest
without turning on her flashlight,
not afraid
because sometimes in the pitch of night
~~[illegible] they'd lie on their backs~~
~~in the middle~~
they'd lie on their backs
in the middle of the path
~~and look up until the stars [illegible] back~~
and look up until the stars came back
and when they did,
they'd reach their arms up to touch them
and did.

(Found on an envelope stuck under the tire of a car on Main Street)

By the time I walk home from the river through the woods, I've decided Toby, like me, feels terrible about what happened, hence the urgency of the text. He probably just wants to make sure it will never happen again. Well, agreed. No argument from demented ol' *moi*.

Clouds have gathered and the air feels thick with the possibility of a rare summer rain. I see a takeaway cup on the ground, so I sit down, write a few lines on it, and then bury it under a mound of pine needles. Then I lie down on my back on the spongy forest floor. I love doing this – giving it all up to the enormity of the sky, or to the ceiling if the need arises while I'm indoors. As I reach my hands out and press my fingers into the loamy soil, I start wondering what I'd be doing right now, what I'd be feeling right this minute if Bailey were still alive. I realize something that scares me: I'd be happy, but in a mild kind of way, nothing demented about it. I'd be turtling along, like I always turtled, huddled in my shell, safe and sound.

But what if I'm a shell-less turtle now, demented and devastated in equal measure, an unfreakingbelievable mess of a girl, who wants to turn the air into colors with her clarinet, and what if somewhere inside I prefer this? What if as much as I fear having death as a shadow, I'm beginning to like how it quickens the pulse, not only mine, but the pulse of the whole world. I doubt Joe would even have noticed me if I'd still been in that hard shell of mild happiness. He wrote in his journal that he thinks I'm on full blast, me, and maybe I am now, but I never was before. How can the cost of this change in me be so great? It doesn't seem right that anything good should come out of Bailey's death. It doesn't seem right to even have these thoughts.

But then I think about my sister and what a shell-less turtle she was and how she wanted me to be one too. *C'mon, Lennie*, she used to say to me at least ten times a day. *C'mon, Len*. And that makes me feel better, like it's her life rather than her death that is now teaching me how to be, who to be.

I know Toby's there even before I go inside, because Lucy and Ethel are camped out on the porch. When I walk into the kitchen, I see him and Gram sitting at the table talking in hushed voices.

"Hi," I say, dumbfounded. Doesn't he realize he can't be here?

"Lucky me," Gram says. "I was walking home with armfuls of groceries and Toby came whizzing by on his skateboard." Gram hasn't driven since the 1900s. She walks everywhere in Clover, which is how she became Garden Guru. She couldn't help herself, started carrying her shears on her trips to town and people would come home and find her pruning their bushes to perfection: ironic yes, because of her hands-off policy with her own garden.

"Lucky," I say to Gram as I take in Toby. Fresh scrapes cover his arms, probably from wiping out on his board. He looks wild-eyed and disheveled, totally unmoored. I know two things in this moment: I was wrong about the text and I don't want to be unmoored with him anymore.

What I really want is to go up to The Sanctum and play my clarinet.

Gram looks at me, smiles. "You swam. Your hair looks like a cyclone. I'd like to paint it." She reaches her hand up and touches my cyclone. "Toby's going to have dinner with us."

I can't believe this. "I'm not hungry," I say. "I'm going upstairs."

Gram gasps at my rudeness, but I don't care. Under no circumstances am I sitting through dinner with Toby, *who touched my breasts*, and Gram and Big. What is he thinking?

I go up to The Sanctum, unpack and assemble my clarinet, then take out the Edith Piaf sheet music that I borrowed from a certain garçon, turn to "La Vie en Rose," and start playing. It's the song we listened to last night while the world exploded. I'm hoping I can just stay lost in a state of Joeliriousness, and I won't hear a knock at my door after they eat, but of course, I do.

Toby, *who touched my breasts and, let's not forget, put his hand down my jeans too*, opens the door, walks tentatively across the room, and sits on Bailey's bed. I stop playing, rest my clarinet on my stand. Go away, I think heartlessly, just go away. Let's pretend it didn't happen, none of it.

Neither of us says a word. He's rubbing his thighs so intently, I bet the friction is generating heat. His gaze is drifting all around the room. It finally locks on a photograph of Bailey and him on her dresser. He takes a breath, looks over at me.

His gaze lingers.

"Her shirt..."

I look down. I forgot I had it on. "Yeah." I've been wearing Bailey's clothes more and more outside The Sanctum as well as in it. I find myself going through my own drawers and thinking, Who was the girl who wore these things? I'm sure a shrink would love this, all of it, I think, looking over at Toby. She'd probably tell me I was trying to take Bailey's place. Or worse, competing with her in a way I never could when she was alive.

But is that it? It doesn't feel like it. When I wear her clothes, I just feel safer, like she's whispering in my ear.

I'm lost in thought, so it startles me when Toby says in an uncharacteristic shaky voice, "Len, I'm sorry. About everything." I glance at him. He looks so vulnerable, frightened. "I got way out of control, feel so bad." Is this what he needed to tell me? Relief tumbles out of my chest.

"Me too," I say, thawing immediately. We're in this together.

"Me more, trust me," he says, rubbing his thighs again. He's so distraught. Does he think it's all his fault or something?

"We both did it, Toby," I say. "Each time. We're both horrible."

He looks at me, his dark eyes warm. "You're not horrible, Lennie." His voice is gentle, intimate. I can tell he wants to reach out to me. I'm glad he's across the room. I wish he were across the equator. Do our bodies now think whenever they're together they get to touch? I tell mine that is most definitely not the case, no matter that I feel it again. No matter.

And then a renegade asteroid breaks through the earth's atmosphere and hurtles into The Sanctum: "It's just that I can't stop thinking about you," he says. "I can't. I just..." He's balling up Bailey's bedspread in his fists. "I want—"

"Please don't say more." I cross the room to my dresser, open the middle drawer, reach in and pull out a shirt, my shirt. I have to take Bailey's off. Because I'm suddenly thinking that imaginary shrink is spot on.

"It's not me," I say quietly as I open the closet door and slip inside. "I'm not her."

I stay in the dark quiet getting my breathing under control, my life under control, getting my own shirt on my own body. It's like there's a river under my feet tumbling me toward him, still, even with everything that's happened with Joe, a roaring, passionate, despairing river, but I don't want to go this time. I want to stay on the shore. We can't keep wrapping our arms around a ghost.

When I come out of the closet, he's gone.

"I'm so sorry," I say aloud to the empty orange room.

As if in response, thousands of hands begin tapping on the roof. I walk over to my bed, climb up to the window ledge and stick my hands out. Because we only get one or two storms a summer, rain is an event. I lean far over the ledge, palms to the sky, letting it all slip through my fingers, remembering what Big told Toby and me that afternoon. *No way out of this but through*. Who knew what through would be?

I see someone rushing down the road in the downpour. When the figure gets near the lit-up garden I realize it's Joe and am instantly uplifted. My life raft.

"Hey," I yell out and wave like a maniac.

He looks up at the window, smiles, and I can't get down the stairs, out the front door, into the rain and by his side fast enough.

"I missed you," I say, reaching up and touching his cheek with my fingers. Raindrops drip from his eyelashes, stream in rivulets all down his face.

"God, me too." Then his hands are on my cheeks and we are kissing and the rain is pouring all over our crazy heads and once again my whole being is aflame with joy.

I didn't know love felt like this, like turning into brightness.

"What are you doing?" I say, when I can finally bring myself to pull away for a moment.

"I saw it was raining – I snuck out, wanted to see you, just like this."

"Why'd you have to sneak out?" The rain's drenching us, my shirt clings to me, and Joe's hands to it, rubbing up and down my sides.

"I'm in prison," he says. "Got busted big-time, that wine we drank was like a four-hundred-dollar bottle. I had no idea. I wanted to impress you so took it from downstairs. My dad went ape-shit when he saw the empty bottle – he's making me sort wood all day and night in the workshop while he talks to his girlfriend on the phone the whole time. I think he forgets I speak French."

I'm not sure whether to address the four-hundred-dollar bottle of wine we drank or the girlfriend, decide on the latter. "His girlfriend?"

"Never mind. I had to see you, but now I have to go back, and I wanted to give you this." He pulls a piece of paper out of his pocket, stuffs it quickly into mine before it can get soaked.

He kisses me again. "Okay, I'm leaving." He doesn't move.

"I don't want to leave you."

"I don't want you to," I say. His hair's black and snaky all around his glistening face. It's like being in the shower with him. Wow – to be in the shower with him.

He turns to go for real then and I notice his eyes narrow as he peers over my shoulder. "Why's he always here?"

I turn around. Toby's in the doorframe, *watching us* – he looks like he's been hit by a wrecking ball. God. He must not have left, must have been in the art room with Gram or something. He pushes open the door, grabs his skateboard, and rushes past without a word, huddled against the downpour.

"What's going on?" Joe asks, X-raying me with his stare. His whole body has stiffened.

"Nothing. Really," I answer, just as I did with Sarah. "He's upset about Bailey." What else can I tell him? If I tell him what's going on, what went on even after he kissed me, I'll lose him.

So when he says, "I'm being stupid and paranoid?" I just say, "Yeah." And hear in my head: *Never cross a horn player.*

He smiles wide and open as a meadow. "Okay." Then he kisses me hard one last time and we are again drinking the rain off each other's lips. "Bye, John Lennon."

And he's off.

I hurry inside, worrying about what Toby said to me and what I didn't say to Joe, as the rain washes all those beautiful kisses off of me.

22

I'm lying down on my bed, holding in my hands the antidote to worrying about anything. It's a sheet of music, still damp from the rain. At the top, it says in Joe's box-like weirdo boy handwriting: *For a soulful, beautiful clarinettist, from a homely, boring, talentless though passionate guitarist. Part 1, Part 2 to come.*

I try to hear it in my head, but my facility to hear without playing is terrible. I get up, find my clarinet, and moments later the melody spills into the room. I remember as I play what he said about my tone being so lonely, like a day without birds, but it's as if the melody he wrote is nothing but birds and they are flying out of the end of my clarinet and filling the air of a still summer day, filling the trees and sky – it's exquisite. I play it over and over again, until I know it by heart.

It's 2 a.m. and if I play the song one more time, my fingers will fall off, but I'm too Joelirious to sleep. I go downstairs to get something to eat, and when I come back into The Sanctum, I'm blindsided by a want so urgent I have to cover my mouth to stifle a shriek. I want Bails to be sprawled out on her bed reading. I want to talk to her about Joe, want to play her this song.

I want my sister.

I want to hurl a building at God.

I take a breath and exhale with enough force to blow the orange paint right off the walls.

It's no longer raining – the scrubbed newness of the night rolls in through the open window. I don't know what to do, so

I walk over to Bailey's desk and sit down like usual. I look at the detective's business card again. I thought about calling him but haven't yet, haven't packed up a thing either. I pull over a carton, decide to do one or two drawers. I hate looking at the empty boxes almost more than I hate the idea of packing up her things.

The bottom drawer's full of school notebooks, years of work, now useless. I take one out, glide my fingers over the cover, hold it to my chest, and then put it in the carton. All her knowledge is gone now. Everything she ever learned, or heard, or saw. Her particular way of looking at *Hamlet* or daisies or thinking about love, all her private intricate thoughts, her inconsequential secret musings – they're gone too. I heard this expression once: Each time someone dies, a library burns. I'm watching it burn right to the ground.

I stack the rest of the notebooks on top of the first, close the drawer, and do the same with the one above it. I close the carton and start a new one. There are more school notebooks in this drawer, some journals, which I will not read. I flip through the stack, putting them, one by one, into the box. At the very bottom of the drawer, there is an open one. It has Bailey's chicken scrawl handwriting all over it; columns of words cover the whole page, with lines crossing out most of them. I take it out, feel a pang of guilt, but then my guilt turns to surprise, then fear, when I see what the words are.

They're all combinations of our mother's name combined with other names and things. There is a whole section of the name Paige combined with people and things related to John Lennon, my namesake, and we assume her favorite musician because of it. We know practically nothing about Mom. It's like when she left, she took all traces of her life with her, leaving only a story behind. Gram rarely talks about anything but her amazing wanderlust, and Big isn't much better.

"At five years old," Gram would tell us over and over again, holding up her fingers for emphasis, "your mother snuck out of her bed one night and I found her halfway to town, with her little blue backpack and a walking stick. She said she was on an adventure – at five years old, girls!"

So that was all we had, except for a box of belongings we kept in The Sanctum. It's full of books we foraged over the years from the shelves downstairs, ones that had her name in them: *Oliver Twist, On the Road, Siddhartha, The Collected Poems of William Blake*, and some Harlequins, which threw us for a loop, book snobs that we are. None of them are dog-eared or annotated. We have some yearbooks, but there are no scribbles from friends in them. There's a copy of *The Joy of Cooking* with food spattered all over it. (Gram did once tell us that Mom was magical in the kitchen and that she suspects she makes her living on the road by cooking.)

But mostly, what we have are maps, lots and lots of them: road maps, topographic maps, maps of Clover, of California, of the forty-nine other states, of country after country, continent after continent. There are also several atlases, each of which look as read and reread as my copy of *Wuthering Heights*. The maps and atlases reveal the most about her: a girl for whom the world beckoned. When we were younger, Bailey and I would spend countless hours poring over the atlases imagining routes and adventures for her.

I start leafing through the notebook. There are pages and pages of these combinations: Paige/Lennon/Walker, Paige/Lennon/Yoko, Paige/Lennon/Imagine, Paige/Dakota/Ono, and on and on. Sometimes there are notes under a name combination. For instance, scribbled under the words Paige/Dakota is an address in North Hampton, Massachusetts. But then that's crossed out and the words *too young* are scrawled in.

I'm shocked. We'd both put our mother's name into search engines many times to no avail, and we would sometimes try to think of pseudonyms she might have chosen and search them to no avail as well, but never like this, never methodically, never with this kind of thoroughness and persistence. The notebook is practically full. Bailey must have been doing this in every free moment, every moment I wasn't around, because I so rarely saw her at the computer. But now that I'm thinking about it, I did see her in front of The Half Mom an awful lot before she died, studying it, intently, almost like she was waiting for it to speak to her.

I turn to the first page of the notebook. It's dated February 27, less than two months before she died. How could she have done all this in that amount of time? No wonder she needed St Anthony's help. I wish she'd asked for mine.

I put the notebook back in the drawer, walk back over to

my bed, take my clarinet out of the case again, and play Joe's song. I want to be in that summer day again, I want to be there with my sister.

At night,
when we were little,
we tented Bailey's covers,
crawled underneath with our flashlights
and played cards: Hearts,
Whist, Crazy Eights,
and our favorite: Bloody Knuckles.
The competition was vicious.
All day, every day,
we were the Walker Girls—
two peas in a pod
thick as thieves—
but when Gram closed the door
for the night,
we bared our teeth.
We played for chores,
for slave duty,
for truths and ~~[illegible]~~ dares and money.
~~We played for~~
We played to be better, brighter,
to be more beautiful,
more,
just more.
But it was all a ruse—
we played
so we could fall asleep ~~in the same bed~~
in the same bed
without having to ask,
so we could wrap together
like a braid,
so while we slept
our dreams could switch bodies.

(Found written on the inside cover of Wuthering Heights*,*
Lennie's room)

23

I used to talk to The Half Mom a lot,
but I'd wait until no one else was home
and then I'd say:

I imagine you
up there
not like a cloud or a bird or a star
not like a mother;
but like a mother;
except one who lives in the sky
who doesn't make a fuss
about gravity
who just goes about her business
drifting around with the wind.

(Found on a piece of newspaper under the Walkers' porch)

When I come down to the kitchen the next morning, Gram is at the stove cooking sausages, her shoulders hunched into a broad frown. Big slouches over his coffee at the table. Behind them the morning fog shrouds the window, like the house is hovering inside a cloud. Standing in the doorway I'm filled with the same scared, hollow feeling I get when I see abandoned houses, ones with weeds growing through the front steps, paint cracked and dirty, windows broken and boarded up.

"Where's Joe?" Big asks. I realize then why the despair is so naked this morning: Joe's not here.

"In prison," I say.

Big looks up, smirks. "What'd he do?" Instantly, the mood is lifted. Wow. I guess he's not only my life raft.

"Took a four-hundred-dollar bottle of wine from his father and drank it one night with a girl named John Lennon."

At the same time, Gram and Big gasp, then exclaim, "Four hundred dollars?!"

"He had no idea."

"Lennie, I don't like you drinking." Gram waves her spatula at me. The sausages sizzle and sputter in the pan behind her.

"I don't drink, well hardly. Don't worry."

"Damn, Len. Was it good?" Big's face is a study of wonder.

"I don't know. I've never had red wine before, guess so." I'm pouring a cup of coffee that is thin as tea. I've gotten used to the mud Joe makes.

"Damn," Big repeats, taking a sip of his coffee and making

a disgusted face. I guess he now prefers Joe's sludge too. "Don't suppose you will drink it again either, with the bar set that high."

I'm wondering if Joe will be at the first band practice today – I've decided to go – when suddenly he walks through the door with croissants, dead bugs for Big, and a smile as big as God for me…

"Hey!" I say.

"They let you out," says Big. "That's terrific. Is it a conjugal visit or is your sentence over?"

"Big!" Gram chastises. "Please."

Joe laughs. "It's over. My father is a very romantic man, it's his best and worst trait, when I explained to him how I was feeling—" Joe looks at me, proceeds to turn red, which of course makes me go full-on tomato. It surely must be against the rules to feel like this when your sister is dead!

Gram shakes her head. "Who would have thought Lennie such a romantic?"

"Are you kidding?" Joe exclaims. "Her reading *Wuthering Heights* twenty-three times didn't give it away?" I look down. I'm embarrassed at how moved I am by this. *He knows me.* Somehow better than they do.

"Touché, Mr Fontaine," Gram says, hiding her grin as she goes back to the stove. Joe comes up behind me, wraps his arms around my waist. I close my eyes, think about his body, naked under his clothes, pressing into me, naked under mine. I turn my head to look up at him. "The melody you wrote is so beautiful. I want to play it for you." Before the last word is out of my mouth, he kisses me. I twist around in his arms so that we are facing each other, then throw my arms around his neck while his find the small of my back, and sweep me into him. Oh God, I don't care if this is wrong of me, if I'm breaking every rule in the Western World, I don't care about freaking anything, because our mouths, which momentarily separated, have met again and anything but that ecstatic fact ceases to matter.

How do people function when they're feeling like this?

How do they tie their shoes?

Or drive cars?

Or operate heavy machinery?

How does civilization continue when this is going on?

A voice, ten decibels quieter than its normal register, stutters out of Uncle Big. "Uh, kids. Might want to, I don't know, mmmm..." Everything screeches to a halt in my mind. Is Big stammering? Uh, Lennie? Probably not cool to make out like this in the middle of the kitchen in front of your grandmother and uncle. I pull away from Joe; it's like breaking suction. I look at Gram and Big, who are standing there fiddly and sheepish while the sausages burn. Is it possible that we've succeeded in embarrassing the Emperor and Empress of Weird?

I glance back at Joe. He looks totally cartoon-dopey, like he's been bonked on the head with a club. The whole scene strikes me as hysterical, and I collapse into a chair laughing. Joe smiles an embarrassed half smile at Gram and Big, leans against the counter, his trumpet case now strategically held over his crotch. Thank God I don't have one of those. Who'd want a lust-o-meter sticking out the middle of their body?

"You're going to rehearsal, right?" he asks.

Bat. Bat. Bat.

Yes, if we make it.

We do make it, though in my case, in body only. I'm surprised my fingers can find the keys as I glide through the pieces Mr James has chosen for us to play at the upcoming River Festival. Even with Rachel sending me death-darts about Joe and repeatedly turning the stand so I can't see it, I'm lost in the music, feel like I'm playing with Joe alone, improvising, reveling in not knowing what is going to happen note to note … but mid-practice, mid-song, mid-note, a feeling of dread sweeps over me as I start thinking about Toby, how he looked when he left last night. What he said in The Sanctum. He has to know we need to stay away from each other now. He has to. I tuck the panic away but spend the rest of rehearsal painfully alert, following the arrangement without the slightest deviation.

After practice, Joe and I have the whole afternoon together because he's out of prison and I'm off work. We're walking back to my house, the wind whipping us around like leaves.

"I know what we should do," I say.

"Didn't you want to play me the song?"

"I do, but I want to play it for you somewhere else. Remember I dared you in the woods that night to brave the forest with me on a really windy day? Today is it."

We veer off the road and hike in, bushwhacking through thickets of brush until we find the trail I'm looking for. The sun filters sporadically through the trees, casting a dim and shadowy light over the forest floor. Because of the wind, the trees are creaking symphonically – it's a veritable philharmonic of squeaking doors. Perfect.

After a while, he says, "I think I'm holding up remarkably well, considering, don't you?"

"Considering what?"

"Considering we're hiking to the soundtrack of the creepiest horror movie ever made and all the world's tree trolls have gathered above us to open and close their front doors."

"It's broad daylight, you can't be scared."

"I can be, actually, but I'm trying not to be a wuss. I have a very low eerie threshold."

"You're going to love where I'm taking you, I promise."

"I'm going to love it if you take off all your clothes there, I promise, or at least some of them, maybe even just a sock." He comes over to me, drops his horn, and swings me around so we are facing each other.

I say, "You're very repressed, you know? It's maddening."

"Can't help it. I'm half French, *joie de vivre* and all. In all seriousness though, I haven't yet seen you in any state of undress, and it's been three whole days since our first kiss, *quelle catastrophe*, you know?" He tries to get my wind-blown hair out of my face, then kisses me until my heart busts out of my chest like a wild horse. "Though I do have a very good imagination…"

"*Quel dork*," I say, pulling him forward.

"You know, I only act like a dork so you'll say *quel dork*," he replies.

The trail climbs to where the old growth redwoods rocket into the sky and turn the forest into their private cathedral. The wind has died down and the woods have grown unearthly still and peaceful. Leaves flicker all around us like tiny pieces of light.

"So, what about your mom?" Joe asks all of a sudden.

"What?" My head couldn't have been further away from thoughts of my mother.

"The first day I came over, Gram said she'd finish the portrait when your mother comes back. Where is she?"

"I don't know." Usually I leave it at that and don't fill in the spare details, but he hasn't run away yet from all our other family oddities. "I've never met my mother," I say. "Well, I met her, but she left when I was one. She has a restless nature, guess it runs in the family."

He stops walking. "That's it? That's the explanation? For her leaving? And *never coming back*?"

Yes, it's nutso, but this Walker nutso has always made sense to me.

"Gram says she'll come back," I say, my stomach knotting up, thinking of her coming back right now. Thinking of Bailey trying so hard to find her. Thinking of slamming the door in her face if she did come back, of screaming, *You're too late*. Thinking of her never coming back. Thinking I'm not sure how to believe all this anymore without Bailey believing it with me.

"Gram's Aunt Sylvie had it too," I add, feeling imbecilic. "She came back after twenty years away."

"Wow," Joe says. I've never seen his brow so furrowed.

"Look, I don't know my mother, so I don't miss her or anything..." I say, but I feel like I'm trying to convince myself more than Joe. "She's this intrepid, free-spirited woman who took off to traipse all around the globe alone. She's mysterious. It's cool." *It's cool?* God, I'm a ninny. But when did everything change? Because it did used to be cool, super-cool, in fact – she was our Magellan, our Marco Polo, one of the wayward Walker women whose restless boundless spirit propels her from place to place, love to love, moment to unpredictable moment.

Joe smiles, looks at me so warmly, I forget everything else. "You're cool," he says. "Forgiving. Unlike dickhead me." Forgiving? I take his hand, wondering from his reaction, and my own, if I'm cool and forgiving or totally delusional. And what about this dickhead him? Who is it? Is it the Joe that never talked to that violinist again? If so, I don't want to meet that guy, ever. We continue in silence, both of us soaring around in the sky of our minds for another mile or so and then we are there, and all thoughts of dickhead him and my mysterious missing mother are gone.

"Okay, close your eyes," I say. "I'll lead you." I reach up from behind him and cover my hands over his eyes and steer him down the path. "Okay, open them."

There is a bedroom. A whole bedroom in the middle of the forest.

"Wow, where's Sleeping Beauty?" Joe asks.

"That would be me," I say, and take a running leap onto the fluffy bed. It's like jumping into a cloud. He follows me. "You're too awake to be her, we've already covered this." He stands at the edge of the bed, looking around. "This is unbelievable, how is this here?"

"There's an inn about a mile away on the river. It was a commune in the sixties, and the owner Sam's an old hippie. He set up this forest bedroom for his guests to happen upon if they hike up here, for surprise romance, I guess, but I've never seen a soul pass through and I've been coming forever. Actually, I did see someone here once: Sam, changing the sheets. He throws this tarp over when it rains. I write at that desk, read in that rocker, lie here on this bed and daydream. I've never brought a guy here before though."

He smiles, sits on the bed next to where I'm lying on my back and starts trailing his fingers over my belly.

"What do you daydream about?" he asks.

"This," I say as his hand spreads across my midriff under my shirt. My breathing's getting faster – I want his hands everywhere.

"John Lennon, can I ask you something?"

"Uh-oh, whenever people say that, something scary comes next."

"Are you a virgin?"

"You see – scary question came next," I mumble, mortified – what a mood-killer. I squirm out from under his hand. "Is it that obvious?"

"Sort of." Ugh. I want to crawl under the covers. He tries to backtrack. "No, I mean, I think it's cool that you are."

"It's decidedly uncool."

"For you maybe, but not for me, if…"

"If what?" My stomach is suddenly churning. Roiling.

Now he looks embarrassed – good. "Well, if sometime, not now, but sometime, you might not want to be one anymore, and I could be your first, that's where the cool part comes in, you know, for me." His expression is shy and sweet, but what he's saying makes me feel scared and excited and overwhelmed and like I'm going to burst into tears, which I do, and for once, I don't even know why.

"Oh, Lennie, I'm sorry, was that bad to say? Don't cry, there's no pressure at all, kissing you, being with you in any way is amazing—"

"No," I say, now laughing and crying at the same time. "I'm crying because … well, I don't know why I'm crying, but I'm happy, not sad…" I reach for his arm, and he lies down on his side next to me, his elbow resting by my head, our bodies touching length to length. He's peering into my eyes in a way that's making me tremble.

"Just looking into your eyes…" he whispers. "I've never felt anything like this."

I think about Genevieve. He'd said he was in love with her, does that mean…

"Me neither," I say, not able to stop the tears from spilling over again.

"Don't cry." His voice is weightless, mist. He kisses my eyes, gently grazes my lips.

He looks at me then so nakedly, it makes me lightheaded, like I need to lie down even though I'm lying down. "I know it hasn't been that long, Len, but I think … I don't know … I might be…"

He doesn't have to say it, I feel it too; it's not subtle – like every bell for miles and miles is ringing at once, loud, clanging, hungry ones, and tiny, happy, chiming ones, all of them sounding off in this moment. I put my hands around his neck, pull him to me, and then he's kissing me hard and so deep, and I am flying, sailing, soaring…

He murmurs into my hair, "Forget what I said earlier, let's stick with this, I might not survive anything more." I laugh. Then he jumps up, finds my wrists, and pins them over my head. "Yeah, right. Totally joking, I want to do *everything* with you, whenever you're ready, I'm the one, promise?" He's above me, batting and grinning like a total hooplehead.

"I promise," I say.

"Good. Glad that's decided." He raises an eyebrow. "I'm going to deflower you, John Lennon."

"Oh my God, so, so embarrassing, *quel, quel major dork*." I try to cover my face with my hands, but he won't let me. And then we are wrestling and laughing and it's many, many minutes before I remember that my sister has died.

24

THE. WORLD. IS. NOT. A. SAFE. PLACE.

(Found on a candy wrapper half-buried by the roses, Gram's Garden)

I see Toby's truck out front and a bolt of anger shoots through me. Why can't he just stay away from me for one freaking day even? I just want to hang on to this happiness. *Please*.

I find Gram in the art room, cleaning her brushes. Toby is nowhere in sight.

"Why is he always here?" I hiss at Gram.

She looks at me, surprised. "What's wrong with you, Lennie? I called him to help me fix the trellising around my garden and he said he would stop by after he was done at the ranch."

"Can't you call someone else?" My voice is seething with anger and exasperation, and I'm sure I sound completely bonkers to Gram. I am bonkers – I just want to be in love. I want to feel this joy. I don't want to deal with Toby, with sorrow and grief and guilt and DEATH. I'm so sick of DEATH.

Gram does not look pleased. "God, Len, have a heart, the guy's destroyed. It makes him feel better to be around us. We're the only ones who understand. He said as much last night." She is drying her brushes over the sink, snapping her wrist dramatically with each shake. "I asked you once if everything was all right between you two and you said yes. I believed you."

I take a deep breath and let it out slowly, trying to coerce Mr Hyde back into my body. "It's okay, it's fine, I'm sorry. I don't know what's wrong with me." Then I pull a Gram and walk right out of the room.

I go up to The Sanctum and put on the most obnoxious head-banging punk music I have, a San Francisco band called

Filth. I know Toby hates any kind of punk because it was always a point of contention with Bailey, who loved it. He finally won her over to the alt-country he likes, and to Willie Nelson, Hank Williams and Johnny Cash, his holy trinity, but he never came around to punk.

The music is not helping. I'm jumping up and down on the blue dance rug, banging around to the incessant beat, but I'm too angry to even bang around BECAUSE I DON'T WANT TO DANCE IN THE INNER PUMPKIN SANCTUM ALONE. In one instant, all the rage that I felt moments before for Toby has transferred to Bailey. I don't understand how she could have done this to me, left me here all alone. Especially because she promised me her whole life that she would never EVER disappear like Mom did, that we would always have each other, always, ALWAYS, ALWAYS. "It's the only pact that mattered, Bailey!" I cry out, taking the pillow and pounding it again and again into the bed, until finally, many songs later, I feel a little bit calmer.

I drop on my back on the bed, panting and sweating. How will I survive this missing? How do others do it? People die all the time. Every day. Every hour. There are families all over the world staring at beds that are no longer slept in, shoes that are no longer worn. Families that no longer have to buy a particular cereal, a kind of shampoo. There are people everywhere standing in line at the movies, buying curtains, walking dogs, while inside, their hearts are ripping to shreds. For years. For their whole lives. I don't believe time heals. I don't want it to. If I heal, doesn't that mean I've accepted the world without her?

I remember the notebook then. I get up, turn off Filth, put on a Chopin Nocturne to see if that'll settle me down, and go over to the desk. I take out the notebook, turn to the last page, where there are a few combinations that haven't yet been crossed out. The whole page is combinations of Mom's name with Dickens characters. Paige/Twist, Paige/Fagan, Walker/Havisham, Walker/Oliver/Paige, Pip/Paige.

I turn on the computer, plug in *Paige Twist* and then search through pages of docs, finding nothing that could relate to our mom, then I put in *Paige Dickens* and find some possibilities, but the documents are mostly from high school athletic teams and college alumni magazines, none that could have anything to do with her. I go through more Dickens combinations but don't find even the remotest possibility.

An hour's passed and I've just done a handful of searches. I look back over the pages and pages that Bailey did, and wonder again when she did it all and where she did it, maybe at the computer lab at the State, because how could I not have noticed her bleary-eyed at this computer for hours on end? It strikes me again how badly she wanted to find Mom, because why else would she have devoted all this time to it? What could have happened in February to take her down this road? I wonder if that was when Toby asked her to marry him. Maybe she wanted Mom to come to the wedding. But Toby said he had asked her right before she died. I need to talk to him.

I go downstairs, apologize to Gram, tell her I've been

emotional all day, which is true every freaking day lately. She looks at me, strokes my hair, says, "It's okay, sweet pea, maybe we could go on a walk together tomorrow, talk some—" When will she *get* it? I don't want to talk to her about Bailey, about anything.

When I come out of the house, Toby's standing on a ladder, working on the trellis in the front of the garden. Streamers of gold and pink peel across the sky. The whole yard is glowing with the setting sun, the roses look lit from within, like lanterns. He looks over at me, exhales dramatically, then climbs slowly down the ladder, leaning against it with arms crossed in front of his chest. "Wanted to say sorry … again." He sighs.

"I'm half out of my mind lately." His eyes search mine. "You okay?"

"Yeah, except for the half out of my mind part," I say.

He smiles at that, his whole face alighting with kindness and understanding. I relax a little, feel bad for wanting to behead him an hour before.

"I found this notebook in Bailey's desk," I tell him, eager to find out if he knows anything and very eager not to talk or think about yesterday. "It's like she was looking for Mom, but feverishly, Toby, page after page of possible pseudonyms that she must have been putting in search engines. She'd tried everything, must have done it around the clock. I don't know where she did it, don't know why she did it…"

"Don't know either," he says, his voice trembling slightly. He looks down. Is he hiding something from me?

"The notebook is dated. She started doing this at the end of February – did anything happen then that you know of?"

Toby's bones unhinge and he slides down the trellis, and drops his head into his hands and starts to cry.

What's going on?

I lower to him, kneel in front of him, put my hands on his arms. "Toby," I say gently. "It's okay." I'm stroking his hair with my hand. Fear prickles my neck and arms.

He shakes his head. "It's not okay." He can barely get the words out. "I wasn't ever going to tell you."

"What? What weren't you going to tell me?" My voice comes out shrill, crazy.

"It makes it worse, Len, and I didn't want it to be any harder for you."

"What?" Every hair on my body is on end. I'm really frightened now. What could possibly make Bailey's death any worse?

He reaches for my hand, holds it tight in his. "We were going to have a baby." I hear myself gasp. "She was pregnant when she died." No, I think, this can't be. "Maybe she was looking for your mom because of that. The end of February would have been around the time when we found out."

The idea begins to avalanche inside me, gaining speed and mass. My other hand has landed on his shoulder and although I'm looking at his face, I'm watching my sister hold their baby up in the air, making ferret faces at it, watching as she and Toby each take a hand of their child and walk him to the river. Or her. God. I can see in Toby's eyes all that he has been carrying alone, and for the first time since Bailey's death I feel more sorry for someone else than I do for myself. I close my arms around him and rock him. And then, when our eyes meet and we are again there in that helpless house of grief, a place where Bailey can never be and Joe Fontaine does not exist, a place where it's only Toby and me left behind, I kiss him. I kiss him to comfort him, to tell him how sorry I am, to show him I'm here and that I'm alive and so is he. I kiss him because I'm in way over my head and have been for months. I kiss him and keep kissing and holding and caressing him, because for whatever screwed-up reason, that is what I do.

The moment Toby's body stiffens in my arms, I know.

I know, but I don't know who it is.

At first, I think it's Gram, it must be. But it's not.

It's not Big either.

I turn around and there he is, a few yards away, motionless, a statue.

Our eyes hold, and then, he stumbles backward. I jump out of Toby's grasp, find my legs, and rush toward Joe, but he turns away, starts to run.

"Wait, please," I yell out. "Please."

He freezes, his back to me – a silhouette against a sky now burning up, a wildfire racing out of control toward the horizon. I feel like I'm falling down stairs, hurtling and tumbling with no ability to stop. Still, I force myself forward and go to him. I take his hand to try to turn him around, but he rips it away as if my touch disgusts him. Then he's turning, slowly, like he's moving underwater. I wait, scared out of my mind to look at him, to see what I've done. When he finally faces me, his eyes are lifeless, his face like stone. It's as if his marvelous spirit has evacuated his flesh.

Words fly out of my mouth. "It's not like us, I don't feel – it's something else, my sister…" *My sister was pregnant*, I'm about to say in explanation, but how would that explain anything? I'm desperate for him to get it, but I don't get it.

"It's not what you think," I say predictably, pathetically. I watch the rage and hurt erupt simultaneously in his face.

"Yes, it *is*. It's *exactly* what I think, it's exactly what I *thought*." He spits his words at me. "How could you… I thought you—"

"I do, I do." I'm crying hard now, tears streaming down my face. "You don't understand."

His face is a riot of disappointment. "You're right, I *don't*. Here."

He pulls a piece of paper out of his pocket. "This is what I came to give you." He crumples it up and throws it at me, then turns around and runs as fast as he can away into the falling night.

I bend over and grab the crumpled piece of paper, smooth it out. At the top it says *Part 2: Duet for aforementioned clarinettist and guitarist*. I fold it carefully, put it in my pocket, then sit down on the grass, a heap of bones. I realize I'm in the same exact spot Joe and I kissed last night in the rain. The sky's lost its fury, just some straggling gold wisps steadily being consumed by darkness. I try to hear the melody he wrote for me in my head, but can't. All I hear is him saying: *How could you?*

How could I?

Someone might as well roll up the whole sky, pack it away for good.

Soon, there's a hand on my shoulder. Toby. I reach up and rest my hand on his. He squats down on one knee next to me. "I'm sorry," he says quietly, and a moment later, "I'm going to go, Len." Then just the coldness on my shoulder where his hand had been. I hear his truck start and listen to the engine hum as it follows Joe down the road.

Just me. Or so I think until I look up at the house to see Gram silhouetted in the doorway like Toby was last night. I don't know how long she's been there, don't know what she's seen and what she hasn't. She swings open the door, walks to the end of the porch, leans on the railing with both hands.

"Come in, sweet pea."

I don't tell her what happened with Joe, just as I never told her what has been going on with Toby. Yet I can see in her mournful eyes as she looks into mine that she most likely already knows it all.

"One day, you'll talk to me again." She takes my hands. "I miss you, you know. So does Big."

"She was pregnant," I whisper.

Gram nods.

"She told you?"

“The autopsy.”

“They were engaged,” I say. This, I can tell from her face, she didn’t know.

She encloses me in her arms and I stay in her safe and sound embrace and let the tears rise and rise and fall and fall until her dress is soaked with them and night has filled the house.

25

I do not go to the altar of the desk to talk to Bailey on the mountaintop. I do not even turn on the light. I go straight into bed with all my clothes on and pray for sleep. It doesn't come.

What comes is shame, weeks of it, waves of it, rushing through me in quick hot flashes like nausea, making me groan into my pillow. The lies and half-truths and abbreviations I told and didn't tell Joe tackle and hold me down until I can hardly breathe. How could I have hurt him like this, done to him just what Genevieve did? All the love I have for him clobbers around in my body. My chest aches. All of me aches. He looked like a completely different person. He is a different person. Not the one who loved me.

I see Joe's face, then Bailey's, the two of them looming above me with only three words on their lips: *How could you?*

I have no answer.

I'm sorry, I write with my finger on the sheets over and over until I can't stand it anymore and flip on the light.

But the light brings actual nausea and with it all the moments with my sister that will now remain unlived: holding her baby in my arms. Teaching her child to play the clarinet. Just getting older together day by day. All the future we will not have rips and retches out of me into the trash bin I am crouched over until there's nothing left inside, nothing but me in this ghastly orange room.

And that's when it hits.

Without the harbor and mayhem of Toby's arms, the

sublime distraction of Joe's, there's only me.

Me, like a small seashell with the loneliness of the whole ocean roaring invisibly within.

Me.

Without.

Bailey.

Always.

I throw my head into my pillow and scream into it as if my soul itself is being ripped in half, because it is.

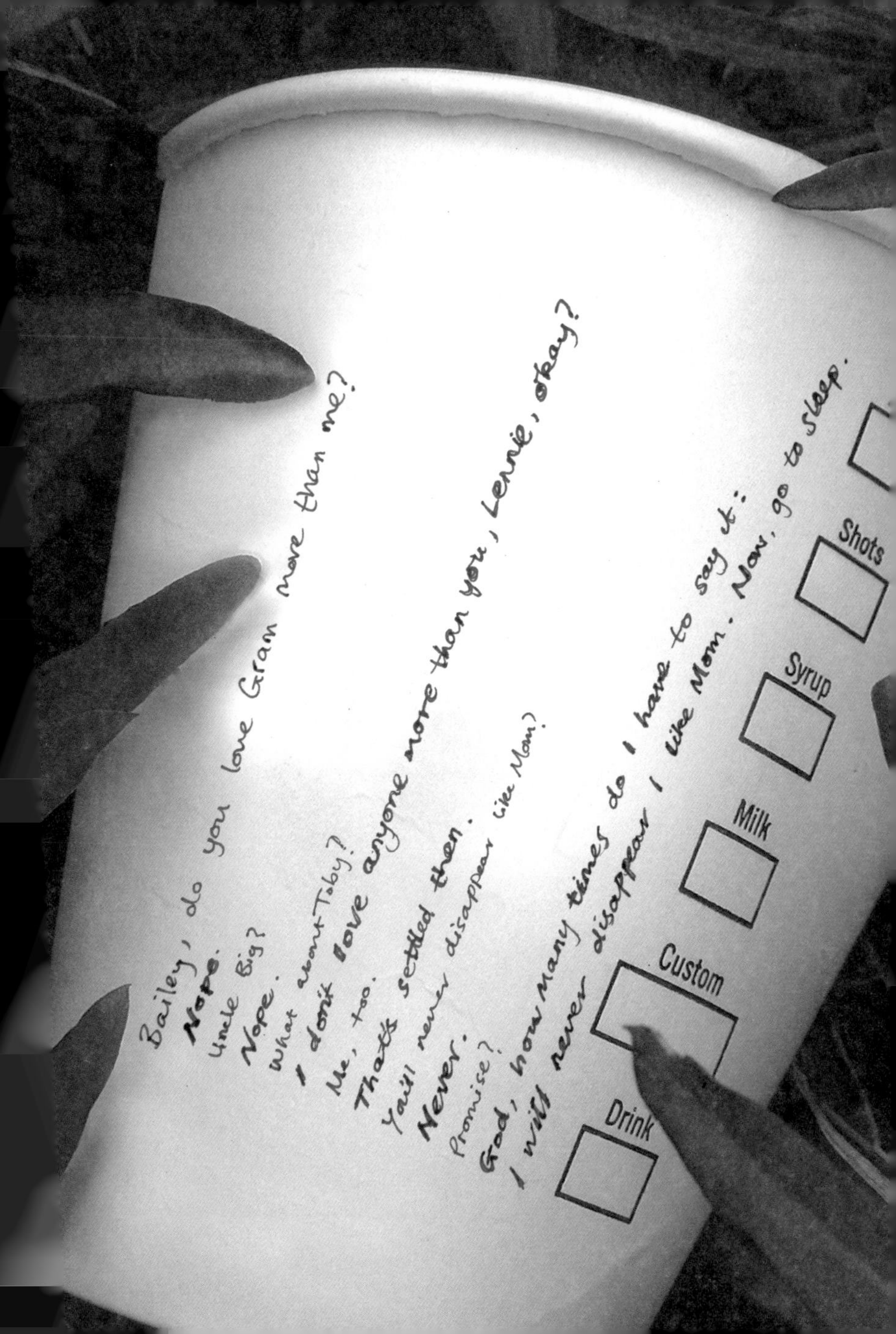
Bailey, do you love Gram more than me?
Nope.
Uncle Big?
Nope.
What about Toby?
I don't love anyone more than you, Lennie, okay?
Me, too.
That's settled then.
You'll never disappear like Mom?
Never.
Promise?
God, how many times do I have to say it:
I will never disappear like Mom. Now, go to sleep.
Drink
Custom
Milk
Syrup
Shots

(Found on a takeaway cup, Rain River)

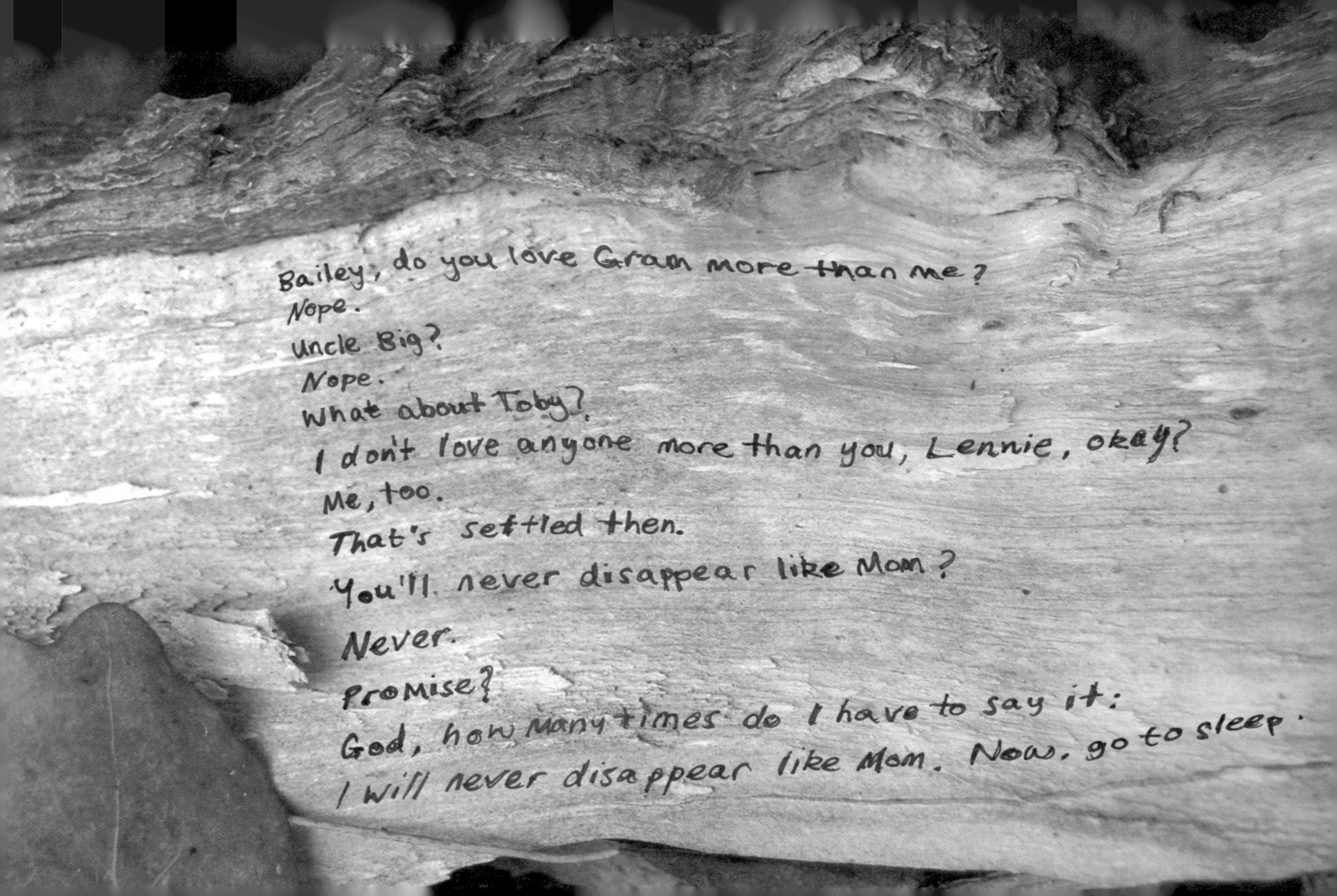
Bailey, do you love Gram more than me?
Nope.
Uncle Big?
Nope.
What about Toby?
I don't love anyone more than you, Lennie, okay?
Me, too.
That's settled then.
You'll never disappear like Mom?
Never.
Promise?
God, how many times do I have to say it:
I will never disappear like Mom. Now, go to sleep.

(Found scrawled on the branch of a tree outside Clover High)

Bailey, do you love Gram more than me?

Nope.

Uncle Big?

Nope.

What about Toby?

I don't love anyone more than you, Lennie, Okay?

Me, too.

That's settled ~~[illegible]~~ then.

You'll never disappear like Mom?

Never.

Promise?

God, how many times do I have to say it:

I will never disappear like Mom. Now, go to sleep.

(Found written on a desk, Clover Public Library)

Part 2

26

(Found on a piece of paper stuck between two rocks at Flying Man's)

I wake up later with my face mashed into the pillow. I lean up on my elbows and look out the window. The stars have bewitched the sky of darkness. It's a shimmery night. I open the window, and the sound of the river rides the rose-scented breeze right into our room. I'm shocked to realize that I feel a little better, like I've slept my way to a place with a little more air. I push away thoughts of Joe and Toby, take one more deep breath of the flowers, the river, the world, then I get up, take the trash bin into the bathroom, clean it and myself, and when I return head straight over to Bailey's desk.

I turn on the computer, pull out the notebook from the top desk drawer where I keep it now, and decide to continue from where I left off the other day. I need to do something for my sister and all I can think to do is to find our mother for her.

I start plugging in the remaining combinations in Bailey's notebook. I can understand why becoming a mother herself would have compelled Bailey to search for Mom like this. It makes sense to me somehow. But there is something else I suspect. In a far cramped corner of my mind, there is a dresser, and in that dresser there is a thought crammed into the back of the bottom-most drawer. I know it's there because I put it there where I wouldn't have to look at it. But tonight I open that creaky drawer and face what I've always believed and that is this: Bailey had it too. Restlessness stampeded through my sister her whole life, informing everything she did from running cross country to changing personas on stage. I've always thought that was the reason behind why she wanted to find our mother. And I know it was the reason I never wanted her to. I bet this is why she didn't tell me she was looking for Mom like this. She knew I'd try to stop her. I didn't want our mother to reveal to Bailey a way out of our lives.

One explorer is enough for any family.

But I can make up for that now by finding Mom. I put combination after combination into a mix of search engines. After an hour, however, I'm ready to toss the computer out the window. It's futile. I've gotten all the way to the end of Bailey's notebook and have started one of my own using words and symbols from Blake poems. I can see in the notebook that Bailey was working her way through Mom's box for clues to the pseudonym. She'd used references from *Oliver Twist*, *Siddhartha*, *On the Road*, but hadn't gotten to William Blake yet. I have his book of poems open and I'm combining words like *Tiger* or *Poison Tree* or *Devil* with *Paige* or *Walker* and the words chef, cook, restaurant, thinking as Gram did that that's how she might make money while traveling, but it's useless. After yet another hour of no possible matches, I tell the mountaintop Bailey in the explorer picture, I'm not giving up, I just need a break, and head downstairs to see if anyone is still awake.

Big's on the porch, sitting in the middle of the love seat like it's a throne. I squeeze in beside him.

"Unbelievable," he murmurs, goosing my knee. "Can't remember the last time you joined me for a nighttime chat. I was just thinking that I might play hooky tomorrow, see if a new lady-friend of mine wants to have lunch with me in a restaurant. I'm sick of dining in trees." He twirls his mustache a little too dreamily.

Uh-oh.

"Remember," I warn. "You're not allowed to ask anyone to marry you until you've been with her a whole year. Those were your rules after your last divorce." I reach over and tug on his mustache, add for effect, "Your fifth divorce."

"I know, I know," he says. "But boy do I miss proposing, nothing so romantic. Make sure you try it, at least once, Len – it's skydiving with your feet on the ground." He laughs in a tinkly way that might be called a giggle if he weren't thirty feet tall. He's told Bailey and me this our whole lives. In fact, until Sarah went into a diatribe about the inequities of marriage in sixth grade, I had no idea proposing wasn't always considered an equal-opportunity endeavor.

I look out over the small yard where hours before Joe left me, probably forever. I think for a minute about telling Big that Joe probably won't be around anymore, but I can't face breaking it to him. He's almost as attached to him as I am. And anyway, I want to talk to him about something else.

"Big?"

"Hmmm?"

"Do you really believe in this restless gene stuff?"

He looks at me, surprised, then says, "Sounds like a fine load of crap, doesn't it?"

I think about Joe's incredulous response today in the woods, about my own doubts, about everybody's, always. Even in this town where free-spiritedness is a fundamental family value, the few times I've ever told anyone my mother took off when I was one year old to live a life of freedom and itinerancy, they looked like they wanted to commit me to a nice rubber room somewhere. Even so, to me, this Walker family gospel never seemed all that unlikely. Anyone who's read a novel or walked down the street or stepped through the front door of my house knows that people are all kinds of weird, especially my people, I think, glancing at Big, who does God knows what in trees, marries perennially, tries to resurrect dead bugs, smokes more pot than the whole eleventh grade, and looks like he should reign over some fairy tale kingdom. So why wouldn't his sister be an adventurer, a blithe spirit? Why shouldn't my mother be like the hero in so many stories, the brave one who left? Like Luke Skywalker, Gulliver, Captain Kirk, Don Quixote, Odysseus. Not quite real to me, okay, but mythical and magical, not unlike my favorite saints or the characters in novels I hang on to perhaps a little too tightly.

"I don't know," I answer honestly. "Is it all crap?"

Big doesn't say anything for a long time, just twirls away at his mustache, thinking. "Nah, it's all about classification, know what I mean?" I don't, but won't interrupt. "Lots of things run through families, right? And this tendency, whatever it is, for whatever reason, runs through ours. Could be worse, we could have depression or alcoholism or bitterness. Our afflicted kin just hit the road—"

"I think Bailey had it, Big," I say, the words tumbling out of me before I can catch them, revealing just how much I might actually believe in it after all. "I've always thought so."

"Bailey?" His brow creases. "Nah, don't see it. In fact, I've never seen a girl so relieved as when she got rejected from that school in New York City."

"Relieved?" Now *this* is a fine load of crap! "Are you kidding? She *always* wanted to go to Juilliard. She worked sooooooooo hard. It was her dream!"

Big studies my burning face, then says gently. "Whose dream, Len?" He positions his hands like he's playing an invisible clarinet. "Because the only one I used to see working sooooooooo hard around here was you."

God.

Marguerite's trilling voice fills my head: *Your playing is ravishing. You work on the nerves, Lennie, you go to Juilliard.*

Instead, I quit.

Instead, I shoved and crammed myself into a jack-in-the box of my own making.

"C'mere." Big opens his arm like a giant wing and – closes it over me as I snuggle in beside him and try not to think about how terrified I'd felt each time Marguerite mentioned Juilliard, each time I'd imagine myself—

"Dreams change," Big says. "I think hers did."

Dreams change, yes, that makes sense, but I didn't know dreams could hide inside a person.

He wraps his other arm around me too and I sink into the bear of him, breathing in the thick scent of pot that infuses his clothes. He squeezes me tight, strokes my hair with his enormous hand. I'd forgotten how comforting Big is, a human furnace. I peek up at his face. A tear runs down his cheek.

After a few minutes, he says, "Bails might have had some ants in the pants, like most people do, but I think she was more like me, and you lately, for that matter – *a slave to love.*" He smiles at me like he's inducting me into a secret society. "Maybe it's those damn roses, and for the record, those I believe in: hook, line and sinker. They're deadly on the heart – I swear, we're like lab rats breathing in that aroma all season long…" He twirls his mustache, seems to have forgotten what he was saying. I wait, remembering that he's stoned. The rose scent ribbons through the air between us. I breathe it in, thinking of Joe, knowing full well that it's not the roses that have spurred this love in my heart, but the boy, such an amazing boy. *How could I?*

Far away, an owl calls – a hollow, lonesome sound that makes me feel the same.

Big continues talking as if no time has passed. "Nah, it wasn't Bails who had it—"

"What do you mean?" I ask, straightening up.

He stops twirling. His face has grown serious. "Gram was different when we were growing up," he says. "If anyone else had it, she did."

"Gram hardly leaves the neighborhood," I say, not following.

He chuckles. "I know. Guess that's how much I don't believe in the gene though. I always thought my mother had it. I thought she just bottled it up somehow, trapped herself in that art room for weeks on end, and threw it onto those canvases."

"Well, if that's the case, why didn't *my mother* just bottle it up, then?" I try to keep my voice down but I feel suddenly infuriated. "Why'd she have to leave if Gram just had to make some paintings?"

"I don't know, honey, maybe Paige had it worse."

"Had *what* worse?"

"I don't know!" And I can tell he doesn't know, that he's as frustrated and bewildered as I am. "Whatever makes a woman leave two little kids, her brother, and her mother, and not come back for sixteen years. That's what! I mean, we call it wanderlust, other families might not be so kind."

"What would other families call it?" I ask. He's never intimated anything like this before about Mom. Is it all a cover story for crazy? Was she really and truly out of her tree?

"Doesn't matter what anyone else would call it, Len," he says. "This is our story to tell."

This is our story to tell. He says it in his Ten Commandments way and it hits me that way: profoundly. You'd think for all the reading I do, I would have thought about this before, but I haven't. I've never once thought about the interpretative, the storytelling aspect of life, of my life. I always felt like I was in a story, yes, but not like I was the author of it, or like I had any say in its telling whatsoever.

You can tell your story any way you damn well please.

It's your solo.

27

This is the secret I kept from you, Bails,
from myself, too:
I think I liked that Mom was gone,
that she could be anybody,
anywhere,
doing anything.
I liked that she was our invention,
a woman living
on the last page of the story
with only what we imagined
spread out before her.
I liked that she was ours, alone.

(Found on a page ripped out of Wuthering Heights, *spiked on a branch, in the woods)*

Joelessness settles over the morning like a pall. Gram and I are slumped spineless over the kitchen table, staring off in opposite directions.

When I got back to The Sanctum last night, I put Bailey's notebook into the carton with the others and closed up the box. Then I returned St Anthony to the mantel in front of The Half Mom. I'm not sure how I'm going to find our mother, but I know it isn't going to be on the Internet. All night, I thought about what Big said. It's possible no one in this family is quite who I believed, especially me. I'm pretty sure he hit the jackpot with me.

And maybe with Bailey too. Maybe he's right and she didn't have it – whatever *it* is. Maybe what my sister wanted was to stay here and get married and have a family.

Maybe that was her color of extraordinary.

"Bailey had all these secrets," I say to Gram.

"Seems to run in the family," she replies with a tired sigh.

I want to ask her what she means, remembering what Big said about her too last night, but can't because he's just stomped in, dressed for work after all, a dead ringer for Paul Bunyan. He takes one look at us and says, "Who died?" Then stops midstep, shakes his head. "I *cannot* believe I just said that." He knocks on his head nobody-home-style. Then he looks around. "Hey, where's Joe this morning?"

Gram and I both look down.

"What?" he asks.

"I don't think he'll be around anymore," I say.

"Really?" Big shrinks from Gulliver to Lilliputian before my eyes. "Why, honey?"

I feel tears brimming. "I don't know."

Thankfully, he lets it drop and leaves the kitchen to check on the bugs.

The whole way to the deli I think of the crazy French violinist Genevieve with whom Joe was in love and how he never spoke to her again. I think of his assessment of horn players as all-or-nothing types. I think how I had all of him and now I'm going to have none of him unless I can somehow make him understand what happened last night and all the other nights with Toby. But how? I already left two messages on his cell this morning and even called the Fontaine house once. It went like this:

Lennie (shaking in her flip-flops): Is Joe home?

Marcus: Wow, Lennie, shocker … brave girl.

Lennie (looks down to see scarlet letter emblazoned on her T-shirt): Is he around?

Marcus: Nope, left early.

Marcus and Lennie: Awkward Silence

Marcus: He's taking it pretty hard. I've never seen him so upset about a girl before, about anything, actually…

Lennie (close to tears): Will you tell him I called?

Marcus: Will do.

Marcus and Lennie: Awkward Silence

Marcus (tentative): Lennie, if you like him, well, don't give up.

Dial tone.

And that's the problem, I madly like him. I make an SOS call to Sarah to come down to the deli during my shift.

Normally, I am The Zen Lasagna Maker. After three and a half summers, four shifts a week, eight lasagnas a shift: 896 lasagnas to date – done the math – I have it down. It's my meditation.

I separate noodle after noodle from the glutinous lump that comes out of the refrigerator with the patience and precision of a surgeon. I plunge my hands into the ricotta and spices and fold the mixture until fluffy as a cloud. I slice the cheese into cuts as thin as paper. I spice the sauce until it sings. And then I layer it all together into a mountain of perfection. My lasagnas are sublime. Today, however, my lasagnas are not singing. After nearly chopping off a finger on the slicer, dropping the glutinous lump of noodles onto the floor, overcooking the new batch of pasta, dumping a truck-load of salt into the tomato sauce, Maria has me on moron-duty stuffing cannolis with a blunt object while she makes the lasagnas by my side. I'm cornered. It's too early for customers, so it's just us trapped inside the *National Enquirer* – Maria's the town crier, chatters nonstop about the lewd and lascivious goings-on in Clover, including, of course, the arboreal escapades of the town Romeo: my uncle Big.

"How's he doing?"

"You know."

"Everyone's been asking about him. He used to stop at The Saloon every night after he returned to earth from the treetops."

Maria's stirring a vat of sauce beside me, a witch at her cauldron, as I try to cover the fact that I've broken yet another pastry shell. I'm a lovesick mess with a dead sister. "The place isn't the same without him. He holding up?" Maria turns to me, brushes a dark curl of hair from her perspiring brow, notes with irritation the growing pile of broken cannoli shells.

"He's just okay, like the rest of us," I say. "He's been coming home after work." I don't add, *and smoking three bowls of weed to numb the pain.* I keep looking up at the door, imagining Joe sailing through it.

"I did hear he had a treetop visitor the other day," Maria singsongs, back to everyone else's business.

"No way," I say, knowing full well that this is most likely the case.

"Yup. Dorothy Rodriguez, you know her, right? She teaches second grade. Last night at the bar, I heard that she rode up with him in the barrel high into the canopy, and *you know*…"

She winks at me. "They picnicked."

I groan. "Maria, it's my uncle, please."

She laughs, then blathers on about a dozen more Clover trysts until at last Sarah floats in dressed like a fabric shop specializing in paisley. She stands in the doorway, puts her arms up, and makes peace signs with both hands.

"Sarah! If you don't look like the spitting image of me twenty years – sheesh, almost thirty years ago," Maria says, heading into the walk-in refridgerator. I hear the door thump behind her.

"Why the SOS?" Sarah says to me. The summer day has

followed her in. Her hair is still wet from swimming. When I called earlier she and Luke were at Flying Man's "working" on some song. I can smell the river on her as she hugs me over the counter.

"Are you wearing toe rings?" I ask to postpone my confession a little longer.

"Of course." She lifts her kaleidoscopic pantalooned leg into the air to show me.

"Impressive."

She hops on the stool across the counter from where I'm working, throws down her book. It's by a Hélène Cixous. "Lennie, these French feminists are so much cooler than those stupid existentialists. I'm so into this concept of *jouissance*, it means transcendent rapture, which I'm sure you and Joe know all about—" She plays the air with invisible sticks.

"Knew." I take a deep breath. Prepare for the *I told you so* of the century.

Her face is stuck somewhere between disbelief and shock. "What do you mean, *knew*?"

"I mean, *knew*."

"But yesterday…" She's shaking her head, trying to catch up to the news. "You guys frolicked off from practice making the rest of us sick on account of the indisputable, irrefutable, unmistakable true love that was seeping out of every pore of your attached-at-the-hip bodies. Rachel nearly exploded. It was so beautiful." And then it dawns on her. "You didn't."

"Please don't have a cow or a horse or an aardvark or any

other animal about it. No morality police, okay?"

"Okay, promise. Now tell me you didn't. I told you I had a bad feeling."

"I did." I cover my face with my hands. "Joe saw us kissing last night."

"You've got to be kidding?"

I shake my head.

As if on cue, a gang of miniature Toby skate rats whiz by on their boards, tearing apart the sidewalk, quiet as a 747.

"But why, Len? Why would you do that?" Her voice is surprisingly without judgment. She really wants to know. "You don't love Toby."

"No."

"And you're dementoid over Joe."

"Totally."

"Then why?" This is the million-dollar question.

I stuff two cannolis, deciding how to phrase it. "I think it has to do with how much we both love Bailey, as crazy as that sounds."

Sarah stares at me. "You're right, that does sound crazy. Bailey would kill you."

My heart races wild in my chest. "I know. But Bailey is dead, Sarah. And Toby and I don't know how to deal with it. And that's what happened. Okay?" I've never yelled at Sarah in my life and that was definitely approaching a yell. But I'm furious at her for saying what I know is true. Bailey would kill me, and it just makes me want to yell at Sarah more, which I do.

"What should I do? Penance? Should I mortify the flesh, soak my hands in lye, rub pepper into my face like St Rose? Wear a hair shirt?"

Her eyes bug out. "Yes, that's exactly what I think you should do!" she cries, but then her mouth twitches a little. "That's right, wear a hair shirt! A hair hat! A whole hair ensemble!" Her face is scrunching up. She bleats out, "St Lennie," and then folds in half in hysterics. Followed by me, all our anger morphing into uncontrollable spectacular laughter – we're both bent over trying to breathe and it feels so great even though I might die from lack of oxygen.

"I'm sorry," I say between gasps.

She manages, "No, me. I promised I wouldn't get like that. Felt good though to let you have it."

"Likewise," I squeal.

Maria sweeps back in, apron loaded with tomatoes, peppers, and onions, takes one look at us, and says, "You and your crazy cohort get out of here. Take a break."

Sarah and I drop onto our bench in front of the deli. The street's coming to life with sunburned couples from San Francisco stumbling out of B&Bs, swaddled in black, looking for pancakes or river rafts or weed.

Sarah shakes her head as she lights up. I've confounded her. A hard thing to do. I know she'd still like to holler: *What in flying foxes were you thinking, Lennie?* but she doesn't.

"Okay, the matter at hand is getting that Fontaine boy back," she says calmly.

"Exactly."

"Clearly making him jealous is out of the question."

"Clearly." I sink my chin into my palms, look up at the thousand-year-old redwood across the street – it's peering down at me in consternation. It wants to kick my sorry newbie-to-the-earth ass.

"I know!" Sarah exclaims. "You'll seduce him." She lowers her eyelids, puckers her lips into a pout around her cigarette, inhales deeply, and then exhales a perfect smoke blob. "Seduction always works. I can't even think of one movie where it doesn't work, can you?"

"You can't be serious. He's so hurt and pissed. He's not even speaking to me, I called three times today … and it's me, not you, remember? I don't know how to seduce anyone." I'm miserable – I keep seeing Joe's face, stony and lifeless, like it was last night. If ever there was a face impervious to seduction, it's that one.

Sarah twirls her scarf with one hand, smokes with the other. "You don't have to *do* anything, Len, just show up to band practice tomorrow looking F-I-N-E, looking *irresistible*." She says irresistible like it has ten syllables. "His raging hormones and wild passion for you will do the rest."

"Isn't that incredibly superficial, Ms French Feminist?"

"*Au contraire, ma petite*. These feminists are all about celebrating the body, its *langage*." She whips the scarf in the air. "Like I said, they're all after *jouissance*. As a means, of course, of subverting the dominant patriarchal paradigm and the white male literary canon, but we can get into that another time." She flicks her cigarette into the street. "Anyway, it can't hurt, Len. And it'll be fun. For me, that is..." A cloud of sadness crosses her face.

We exchange a glance that holds weeks of unsaid words.

"I just didn't think you could understand me anymore," I blurt out. I'd felt like a different person and Sarah had felt like the same old one, and I bet Bailey had felt similarly about me, and she was right to. Sometimes you just have to soldier through in your own private messy way.

"I couldn't understand," Sarah exclaims. "Not really. Felt—*feel* so useless, Lennie. And man, those grief books suck, so formulaic, total hundred percent garbage."

"Thanks," I say. "For reading them."

She looks down at her feet. "I miss her too." Until this moment, it hadn't occurred to me she might've read those books for herself also. But of course. She revered Bailey. I've left her to grieve all on her own. I don't know what to say, so I reach across the bench and hug her. Hard.

A car honks with a bunch of hooting doofuses from Clover High in it. Way to ruin the moment. We disengage, Sarah waving her feminist book at them like a religious zealot – it makes me laugh.

When they pass, she takes another cigarette out of her pack, then gently touches my knee with it. "This Toby thing, I just don't get it." She lights the smoke, keeps shaking the match after it's out, like a metronome. "Were you competitive with Bailey? You guys never seemed like those King Lear type of sisters. I never thought so anyway."

"No we weren't. No … but … I don't know, I ask myself the same thing—"

I've crashed head-on into that something Big said last night, that awfully huge something.

"Remember that time we watched the Kentucky Derby?" I ask Sarah, not sure if this will make sense to anyone but me.

She looks at me like I'm crazy. "Yeah, uh, why?"

"Did you notice the racehorses had these companion ponies that didn't leave their sides?"

"I guess."

"Well, I think that was us, me and Bails."

She pauses a minute, exhales a long plume of smoke, before she says, "You were both racehorses, Len." I can tell she doesn't believe it though, that she's just trying to be nice.

I shake my head. "C'mon, be real, I wasn't. God, no way. I'm not." And it's been no one's doing but my own. Bailey went as crazy as Gram when I quit my lessons.

"Do you want to be?" Sarah asks.

"Maybe," I say, unable to quite manage a yes.

She smiles, then in silence, we both watch car after car creep along, most of them filled with ridiculously bright rubber river gear: giraffe boats, elephant canoes and the like. Finally she says, "Being a companion pony must suck. Not metaphorically, I mean, you know, if you're a horse. Think about it. Self-sacrifice twenty-four/seven, no glory, no glamour … they should start a union, have their own Companion Pony Derby."

"A good new cause for you."

"No. My new cause is turning St Lennon into a femme fatale." She smirks. "C'mon, Len, say yes."

Her *C'mon, Len* reminds me of Bails, and the next thing I know, I hear myself saying, "Okay, fine."

"It'll be subtle, I promise."

"Your strong-suit."

She laughs. "Yeah, you're so screwed."

It's a hopeless idea, but I have no other. I have to do something, and Sarah's right, looking sexy, assuming I can look sexy, can't hurt, can it? I mean it is true that seduction hardly ever fails in movies, especially French ones. So I defer to Sarah's expertise, experience, to the concept of *jouissance*, and Operation Seduction is officially under way.

I have cleavage. Melons. Bazumbas. Bodacious tatas. Handfuls of bosom pouring out of a minuscule black dress that I'm going to wear in broad daylight to band practice. I can't stop looking down. I'm stacked, a buxom babe. My scrawny self is positively zaftig. How can a bra possibly do this? Note to the physicists: Matter can indeed be created. Not to mention that I'm in platforms, so I look nine feet tall, and my lips are red as pomegranates.

Sarah and I have ducked into a classroom next to the music room.

"Are you sure, Sarah?" I don't know how I got myself into this ridiculous *I Love Lucy* episode.

"Never been more sure of anything. No guy will be able to resist you. I'm a little worried Mr James won't survive it though."

"All right. Let's go," I say.

The way I get down the hallway is to pretend I'm someone else. Someone in a movie, a black-and-white French movie where everyone smokes and is mysterious and alluring. I'm a woman, not a girl, and I'm going to seduce a man. Who am I kidding? I freak out and run back to the classroom. Sarah follows, my bridesmaid.

"Lennie, c'mon." She's exasperated.

There it is again, *Lennie, c'mon*. I try again. This time I think of Bailey, the way she sashayed, making the ground work for her, and I glide effortlessly through the door of the music room.

I notice right away that Joe isn't there, but there's still time until rehearsal starts, like fifteen seconds, and he's always early, but maybe something held him up.

Fourteen seconds: Sarah was right, all the boys are staring at me like I've popped out of a centerfold. Rachel almost drops her clarinet.

Thirteen, Twelve, Eleven: Mr James throws his arms up in celebration. "Lennie, you look ravishing!" I make it to my seat.

Ten, Nine: I put my clarinet together but don't want to get lipstick all over my mouthpiece. I do anyway.

Eight, Seven: tuning.

Six, Five: tuning still.

Four, Three: I turn around. Sarah shakes her head, mouths *unfreakingbelievable*.

Two, One: the announcement I now am expecting. "Let's begin class. Sorry to say we've lost our only trumpet player for the festival. Joe's going to perform with his brothers instead. Take out your pencils, I have changes."

I drop my glamorous head into my hands, hear Rachel say, "I told you he was out of your league, Lennie."

28

There once was a girl who found herself dead.
She peered over the ledge of heaven
and saw that back on earth
her sister missed her too much,
was way too sad,
so she crossed some paths
that would not have crossed,
took some moments in her hand
shook them up
and spilled them like dice
over the living world.
It worked.
The boy with the guitar collided
with her sister.
"There you go, Len," she whispered.
"The rest is up to you."

(Found on a folded up flyer on the sidewalk, Main Street)

"May the force be with you," Sarah says, and sends me on my way, which is up the hill to the Fontaines' in aforementioned black cocktail dress, platforms and bodacious tatas. The whole way up I repeat a mantra: *I am the author of my story and I can tell it any way I want. I am a solo artist. I am a racehorse.* Yes, this puts me into the major freaker category of human, but it does the trick and gets me up the hill, because fifteen minutes later I am looking up at Maison Fontaine, the dry summer grass crackling all around me, humming with hidden insects, which reminds me: how in the world does Rachel know what happened with Joe?

When I get to the driveway, I see a man dressed all in black with a shuck of white hair, waving his arms around like a dervish, shouting in French at a stylish woman in a black dress (hers fits her), who looks equally peeved. She is hissing back at him in English. I definitely do not want to walk past those two panthers, so I sneak around the far side of the property and then duck under the enormous willow tree that reigns like a queen over the yard, the thick drapes of leaves falling like a shimmering green ball gown around the ancient trunk and branches, creating the perfect skulk den.

I need a moment to bolster my nerve, so I pace around in my new glimmery green apartment trying to figure out what I'm going to actually say to Joe, a point both Sarah and I forgot to consider.

That's when I hear it: clarinet music drifting out from the house, the melody Joe wrote for me. My heart does a hopeful flip. I walk over to the side of Maison Fontaine that abuts the tree and, still concealed by a drape of leaves, I stand up on tiptoe and see through the open window a sliver of Joe playing a bass clarinet in the living room.

And thus begins my life as a spy.

I tell myself, after this song, I will ring the doorbell and literally face the music. But then, he plays the melody again and again and the next thing I know I'm lying on my back listening to the amazing music, reaching into Sarah's purse for a pen, which I find as well as a scrap of paper. I jot down a poem, spike it with a stick into the ground. The music is making me rapturous; I slip back into that kiss, again drinking the sweet rain off his lips—

To be rudely interrupted by DougFred's exasperated voice. "Dude, you're driving me berserk – this same song over and over again, for two days now, I can't deal. We're all going to jump off the bridge right after you. Why don't you just talk to her?" I jump up and scurry over to the window: Harriet the Spy in drag. *Please say you'll talk to her*, I mind-beam to Joe.

"No way," he says.

"Joe, it's pathetic … c'mon."

Joe's voice is pinched, tight. "I *am so* pathetic. She was lying to me the whole time … just like Genevieve, just like Dad to Mom for that matter…"

Ugh. Ugh. Ugh. Boy, did I blow it.

"Whatever, already, with all of that – shit's complicated sometimes, man." *Hallelujah, DougFred*.

"Not for me."

"Just get your horn, we need to practice."

Still concealed under the tree, I listen to Joe, Marcus and DougFred practicing: it goes like this, three notes, then a cell phone rings: Marcus: *Hey Ami*, then five minutes later, another ring: Marcus: *Salut Sophie*, then DougFred: *Hey Chloe*, then fifteen minutes later: *Hi Nicole*. These guys are Clover catnip. I remember how the phone rang pretty much continually the evening I spent here. Finally, Joe says: *Turn off the cell phones or we won't even get through a song* – but just as he finishes the sentence, his own cell goes off and his brothers laugh. I hear him say, *Hey Rachel*. And that's the end of me. *Hey Rachel* in a voice that sounds happy to hear from her, like he was expecting the call, waiting for it even.

I think of St Wilgefortis, who went to sleep beautiful and woke up with a full beard and mustache, and wish that fate on Rachel. Tonight.

Then I hear: *You were totally right. The Throat Singers of Tuva are awesome.*

Call 911.

Okay, calm down, Lennie. Stop pacing. Don't think about him batting his eyelashes at Rachel Brazile! Grinning at her, kissing her, making her feel like she's part sky… *What have I done?* I lie down on my back in the grass under the umbrella of trembling sunlit leaves. I'm leveled by a phone call. How must it have been for him to actually see me kiss Toby?

I suck, there's no other way to put it.

There's also no other way to put this: I'm so freaking in love – it's just blaring every which way inside me, like some psycho opera.

But back to BITCHZILLA!?

Be rational, I tell myself, systematic, think of all the many innocuous unromantic reasons she could be calling him. I can't think of one, though I'm so consumed with trying I don't even hear the truck pull up, just a door slamming. I get up, peek out through the thick curtain of leaves, and almost pass out to see Toby walking toward the front door. WTF-asaurus? He hesitates before ringing the bell, takes a deep breath, then presses the button, waits, then presses it again. He steps back, looks toward the living room, where the music is now blasting, then knocks hard. The music stops and I hear the pounding of feet, then watch the door open and hear Toby say: "Is Joe here?"

Gulp.

Next, I hear Joe still in the living room: "What's his problem? I didn't want to talk to him yesterday and I don't want to talk to him today."

Marcus is back in the living room. "Just talk to the guy."

"No."

But Joe must have gone to the door, because I hear muffled words and see Toby's mouth moving, although he's quieted down too much for me to make out the words.

I don't plan what happens next. It just happens. I just happen to have that stupid it's-my-story-I'm-a-racehorse mantra back on repeat in my head and so I somehow decide that whatever is going to happen, good or bad, I don't want to be hiding in a tree when it does. I muster all my courage and part the curtain of leaves.

The first thing I notice is the sky, so full of blue and the kind of brilliant white clouds that make you ecstatic to have eyes. Nothing can go wrong under this sky, I think as I make my way across the lawn, trying not to wobble in my platforms. The Fontaine panther-parents are nowhere in sight; probably they took their hissing match into the barn. Toby must hear my footsteps; he turns around.

"Lennie?"

The door swings open and three Fontaines pile out like they've been stuffed in a car.

Marcus speaks first: "Va-va-voom."

Joe's mouth drops open.

Toby's too, for that matter.

"Holy shit" comes out of DougFred's perpetually deranged with-glee face. The four of them are like a row of dumbfounded ducks. I'm acutely aware of how short my dress is, how tight it is across my chest, how wild my hair is, how red my lips are. I might die. I want to wrap my arms around my body. For the rest of my life, I'm going to leave the femme fatale-ing to other femmes. All I want is to flee, but I don't want them to stare at my butt as I fly into the woods in this tiny piece of fabric masquerading as a dress. Wait a second here – one by one, I take in their idiotic faces. Was Sarah right? Might this work? Could guys be this simple-minded?

Marcus is ebullient. "One hot tamale, John Lennon."

Joe glares at him. "Shut the hell up, Marcus." He has regained his composure and rage. Nope, Joe is definitely not this simpleminded. I know immediately this was a bad, bad move.

"What's wrong with you two?" he says to Toby and me, throwing up his arms in a perfect mimicry of his father's dervishness.

He pushes past his brothers and Toby, jumps off the stoop, comes up to me, so close that I can smell his fury. "Don't you get it? What you did? It's done, Lennie, we're done." Joe's beautiful lips, the ones that kissed me and whispered in my hair, they are twisting and contorting around words I hate. The ground beneath me begins to tilt. People don't really faint, do they? "Get it, because I mean it. It's ruined. *Everything* is."

I'm mortified. I'm going to kill Sarah. And what a total companion-pony move on my part. I knew this wouldn't work. There was no way he was going to toss aside this behemoth betrayal because I squeezed myself into this ridiculously small dress. How could I be so stupid?

And it's just dawned on me that I might be the author of my own story, but so is everyone else the author of their own stories, and sometimes, like now, there's no overlap.

He's walking away from me. I don't care that there are six pairs of eyes and ears on us. He can't leave before I have a chance to say something, have a chance to make him understand what happened, how I feel about him. I grab the bottom of his T-shirt. He snaps around, flings my hand away, meets my eyes. I don't know what he sees in them, but he softens a little. I watch some of the rage slip off of him as he looks at me. Without it, he looks unnerved and vulnerable, like a small disheartened boy. It makes me ache with tenderness. I want to touch his beautiful face. I look at his hands; they are shaking.

As is all of me.

He's waiting for me to speak. But I realize the perfect thing to say must be in another girl's mind, because it's not in mine. Nothing is in mine.

"I'm sorry," I manage out.

"I don't care," he says, his voice cracking a little. He looks down at the ground. I follow his gaze, see his bare feet sticking out of jeans; they are long and thin and monkey-toed. I've never seen his feet out of shoes and socks before. They're perfectly simian – toes so long he could play the piano with them.

"Your feet," I say, before I realize it. "I've never seen them before."

My moronic words drum in the air between us, and for a split second, I know he wants to laugh, wants to reach out and pull me to him, wants to tease me about saying something so ridiculous when he's about to murder me. I can see this in his face as if his thoughts were scribbled across it. But then all that gets wiped away as quickly as it came, and what's left is the unwieldy hurt in his unbatting eyes, his grinless mouth. He will never forgive me.

I took the joy out of the most joyful person on planet Earth.

"I'm so sorry," I say. "I—"

"God, stop saying that." His hands swoop around me like lunatic bats. I've reignited his rage. "It doesn't matter to me that you're sorry. You just don't get it." He whips around and bolts into the house before I can say another word.

Marcus shakes his head and sighs, then follows his brother inside with DougFred in tow.

I stand there with Joe's words still scorching my skin, thinking what a terrible idea it was to come up here, in this tiny dress, these skyscraping heels. I wipe the siren song off my lips. I'm disgusted with myself. I didn't ask for his forgiveness, didn't explain a thing, didn't tell him that he is the most amazing thing that's ever happened to me, that I love him, that he's the only one for me. Instead, I talked about his feet. *His feet.*

Talk about choking under pressure. And then I remember *Hey Rachel*, which explodes a Molotov cocktail of jealousy into my misery, completing the dismal picture.

I want to kick the postcard-perfect sky.

I'm so absorbed in my self-flagellation, I forget Toby's there until he says, "Emotional guy."

I look up. He's sitting on the stoop now, leaning back on his arms, his legs kicked out. He must have come straight from work; he's out of his usual skate rat rags and has on mud-splattered jeans and boots and button-down shirt and is only missing the Stetson to complete the Marlboro Man picture. He looks like he did the day he whisked my sister's heart away: Bailey's Revolutionary.

"He almost attacked me with his guitar yesterday. I think we're making progress," he adds.

"Toby, what're you doing here?"

"What are you doing hiding in trees?" he asks back, nodding at the willow behind me.

"Trying to make amends," I say.

"Me, too," he says quickly, jumping to his feet. "But to you. Been trying to tell him what's what." His words surprise me.

"I'll take you home," he says.

We both get into his truck. I can't seem to curb the nausea overwhelming me as a result of the hands-down worst seduction in love's history. Ugh. And on top of it, I'm sure Joe is watching us from a window, all his suspicions seething in his hot head as I drive off with Toby.

"So, what'd you say to him?" I ask when we've cleared Fontaine territory.

"Well, the three words I got to say yesterday and the ten I got in today added up to pretty much telling him he should give you a second chance, that there's nothing going on with us, that we were just wrecked…"

"Wow, that was nice. Busybody as you like, but nice."

He looks over at me for a moment before returning his eyes to the road. "I watched you guys that night in the rain … I saw it, how you feel."

His voice is full of emotion that I can't decipher and probably don't want to. "Thanks," I say quietly, touched that he did this despite everything, because of everything.

He doesn't respond, just looks straight ahead into the sun, which is obliterating everything in our path with unruly splendor. The truck blasts through the trees and I stick my hand out the window, trying to catch the wind in my palm like Bails used to, missing her, missing the girl I used to be around her, missing who we all used to be. We will never be those people again. She took them all with her.

I notice Toby's tapping his fingers nervously on the wheel. He keeps doing it. Tap. Tap. Tap.

"What is it?" I ask.

He grips the wheel tight with both hands.

"I really love her," he says, his voice breaking. "More than anything."

"Oh, Toby, I know that." That's the only thing I do understand about this whole mess: that somehow what happened between us happened because there's too much love for Bailey between us, not too little.

"I know," I repeat.

He nods.

Something occurs to me then: Bailey loved both Toby and me so much – he and I almost make up her whole heart, and maybe that's it, what we were trying to do by being together, maybe we were trying to put her heart back together again.

He stops the truck in front of the house. The sun streams into the cab, bathing us in light. I look out my window, can see Bails rushing out of the house, flying off the porch, to jump into this very truck I am sitting in. It's so strange. I spent forever resenting Toby for taking my sister away from me, and now it seems like I count on him to bring her back.

I open the door, put one of my platforms onto the ground.

"Len?"

I turn around.

"You'll wear him down." His smile is warm and genuine. He rests the side of his head on the steering wheel. "I'm going to leave you alone for a bit, but if you need me … for anything, okay?"

"Same," I say, my throat knotting up.

Our conjoined love for Bailey trembles between us; it's like a living thing, as delicate as a small bird, and as breathtaking in its hunger for flight. My heart hurts for both of us.

"Don't do anything stupid on that board," I say.

"Nope."

"Okay." Then I slide out, close the door, and head into the house.

29

Sometimes I'd see Sarah and her mom
share a look across a room
and I'd want
to heave my life over like a table.
I'd tell myself not to feel that way
that I was lucky;
I had Bailey,
I had Gram and Big,
I had my clarinet, books, a river, the sky.
I'd tell myself that I had a mother too,
just not one anyone else could see
but Bailey and me.

(Found scribbled on the classified ads in The Clover Gazette *under the bench outside Maria's Deli)*

Sarah's at State, since the symposium is this afternoon, so I have no one on which to blame the *Hey Rachel* seduction fiasco but myself. I leave her a message telling her I've been totally mortified like a good saint because of her *jouissance* and am now seeking a last-resort miracle.

The house is quiet. Gram must have gone out, which is too bad because for the first time in ages, I'd like nothing more than to sit at the kitchen table with her and drink tea.

I go up to The Sanctum to brood about Joe, but once there, my eyes keep settling on the boxes I packed the other night. I can't stand looking at them, so after I change out of my ridiculous outfit, I take them up to the attic.

I haven't been up here in years. I don't like the tombishness, the burned smell of the trapped heat, the lack of air. It always seems so sad too, full of everything abandoned and forgotten. I look around at the lifeless clutter, feel deflated at the idea of bringing Bailey's things up here. This is what I've been avoiding for months now. I take a deep breath, look around. There's only one window, so I decide, despite the fact that the area around it is packed in with boxes and mountains of bric-à-brac, that Bailey's things should go where the sun will at least seep in each day.

I make my way over there through an obstacle course of broken furniture, boxes, and old canvases. I move a few cartons immediately so I can crack open the window and hear the river. Hints of rose and jasmine blow in on the afternoon breeze. I open it wider, climb up on an old desk so I can lean out. The sky is still spectacular and I hope Joe is gazing up at it. No matter where I look inside myself, I come across more love for him, for everything about him, his anger as much as his tenderness – he's so alive, he makes me feel like I could take a bite out of the whole earth. If only words hadn't eluded me today, if only I yelled back at him: *I do get it! I get that as long as you live no one will ever love you as much as I do – I have a heart so I can give it to you alone!* That's exactly the way I feel – but unfortunately, people don't talk like that outside of Victorian novels.

I take my head out of the sky and bring it back into the stuffy attic. I wait for my eyes to readjust, and when they do, I'm still convinced this is the only possible spot for Bailey's things. I start moving all the junk that's already there to the shelves on the back wall. After many trips back and forth, I finally reach down to pick up the last of it, which is a shoebox, and the top flips open. It's full of letters, all addressed to Big, probably love letters. I peek at one postcard from an Edie. I decide against snooping further; my karma is about as bad as it's ever been right now. I slip the lid back on, place it on one of the lower shelves where there's still some space. Just behind it, I notice an old letter box, its wood polished and shiny. I wonder what an antique like this is doing up here instead of downstairs with all Gram's other treasures. It looks like a showcase piece too. I slide it out; the wood is mahogany and there's a ring of galloping horses engraved into the top. Why isn't it covered in dust like everything else on these shelves? I lift the lid, see that it's full of folded notes on Gram's mint-green stationery, so many of them, and lots of letters as well. I'm about to put it back when I see written on the outside of an envelope in Gram's careful script the name *Paige*. I flip through the other envelopes. Each and every one says *Paige* with the year next to her name. Gram writes letters to Mom? Every year? All the envelopes are sealed. I know that I should put the box back, that this is private, but I can't. Karma be damned. I open one of the folded notes. It says:

> *Darling, The second the lilacs are in full bloom, I have to write you. I know I tell you this every year, but they haven't blossomed the same since you left. They're so stingy now. Maybe it's because no one comes close to loving them like you did – how could they? Each spring I wonder if I'm going to find the girls sleeping in the garden, like I'd find you, morning after morning. Did you know how I loved that, walking outside and seeing you asleep with my lilacs and roses all around you – I've never even tried to paint the image. I never will. I wouldn't want to ruin it for myself.*
>
> *Mom*

Wow – my mother loves lilacs, *really* loves them. Yes, yes, it's true, most people love lilacs, but my mother is so gaga about them that she used to sleep in Gram's garden, night after night, all spring long, so gaga she couldn't bear to be inside knowing all those flowers were raising hell outside her window. Did she bring her blankets out with her? A sleeping bag? Nothing? Did she sneak out when everyone else was asleep? Did she do this when she was my age? Did she like looking up at the sky as much as I do? I want to know more. I feel jittery and light-headed, like I'm meeting her for the first time. I sit down on a box, try to calm down. I can't. I pick up another note. It says:

Remember that pesto you made with walnuts instead
of pine nuts? Well, I tried pecans, and you know what?
Even better. The recipe:
2 cups packed fresh basil leaves
2/3 cup olive oil
1/2 cup pecans, toasted
1/3 cup freshly grated Parmesan
2 large garlic cloves, mashed
1/2 teaspoon salt

My mother makes pesto with walnuts! This is even better than sleeping with lilacs. So normal. *So I think I'll whip up some pasta with pesto for dinner.* My mother bangs around a kitchen. She puts walnuts and basil and olive oil in a food processor, and presses blend. She boils water for pasta! I have to tell Bails. I want to scream out the window at her: *Our mother boils water for pasta!* I'm going to. I'm going to tell Bailey. I make my way over to the window, climb back up on the desk, put my head out, holler up at the sky, and tell my sister everything I've just learned. I feel dizzy, and yes, a bit out of my tree, when I climb back into the attic, now hoping no one heard this girl screaming about pasta and lilacs at the top of her lungs. I take a deep breath. Open another one.

Paige,
I've been wearing the fragrance you wore for years.

The one you thought smelled like sunshine. I've just found out they've discontinued it. I feel as though I've lost you now completely. I can't bear it.

Mom

Oh.

But why didn't Gram tell us our mother wore a perfume that smelled like sunshine? That she slept in the garden in the springtime? That she made pesto with walnuts? Why did she keep this real-life mother from us? But as soon as I ask the question, I know the answer, because suddenly there is not blood pumping in my veins, coursing all throughout my body, but longing for a mother who loves lilacs. Longing like I've never had for the Paige Walker who wanders the world. That Paige Walker never made me feel like a daughter, but a mother who boils water for pasta does. Except don't you need to be claimed to be a daughter? Don't you need to be loved?

And now there's something worse than longing flooding me, because how could a mother who boils water for pasta leave two little girls behind?

How could she?

I close the lid, slide the box back on a shelf, quickly stack Bailey's boxes by the window, and go down the stairs into the empty house.

30

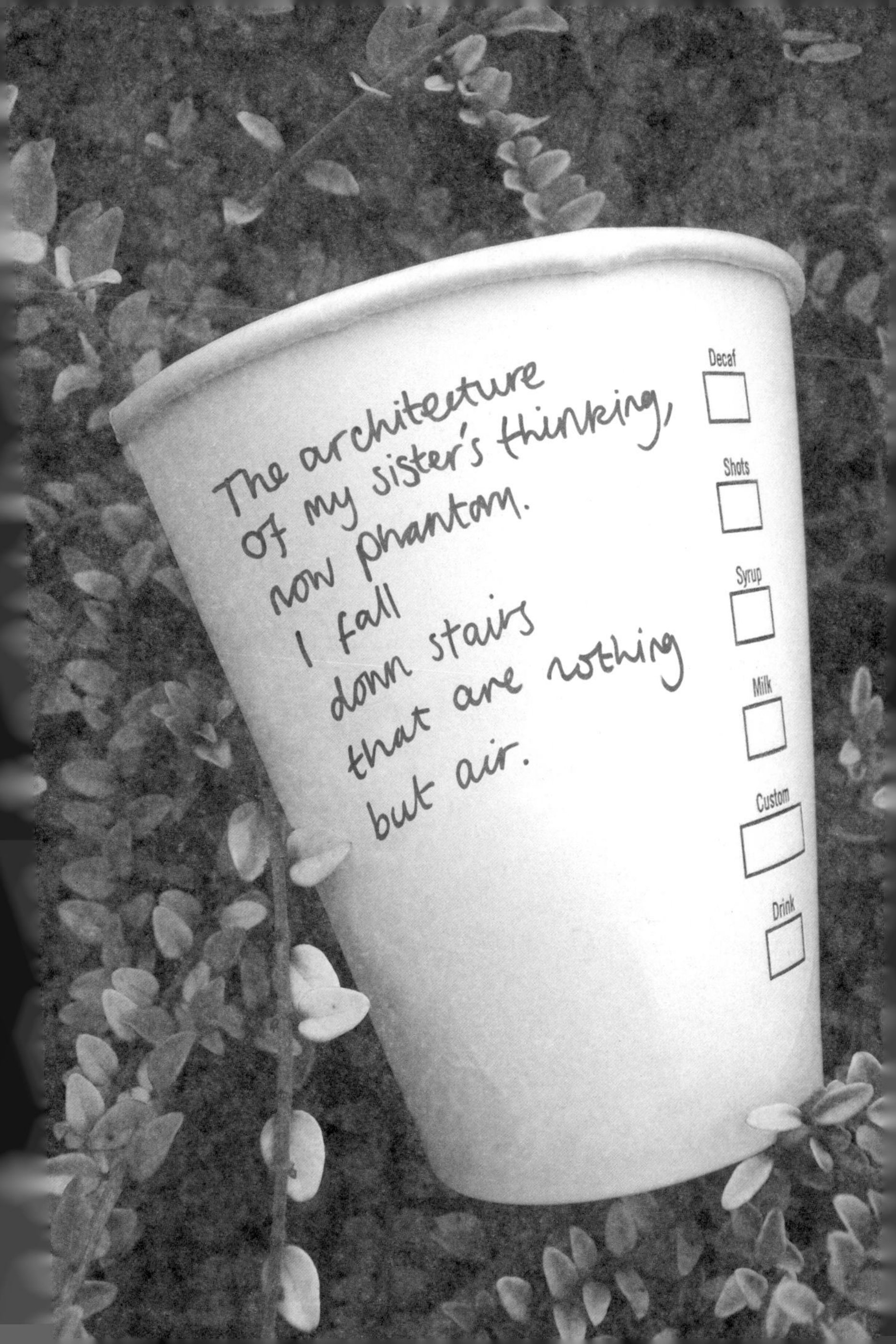
The architecture
of my sister's thinking,
now phantom.
I fall
down stairs
that are nothing
but air.
Decaf
Shots
Syrup
Milk
Custom
Drink

(Found on a takeaway cup by a grove of old growth redwoods)

The next few days inch by miserably. I skip band practice and confine myself to The Sanctum. Joe Fontaine does not stop by, or call, or text, or e-mail, or skywrite, or send Morse code, or telepathically communicate with me. Nothing. I'm quite certain he and *Hey Rachel* have moved to Paris, where they live on chocolate, music and red wine, while I sit at this window, peering down the road where no one comes bouncing along, guitar in hand, like they used to.

As the days pass, Paige Walker's love of lilacs and ability to boil water have the singular effect of washing sixteen years of myth right off of her. And without it, all that's left is this: our mother abandoned us. There's no way around it. And what kind of person does that? Rip Van Lennie is right. I've been living in a dream world, totally brainwashed by Gram. My mother's freaking nuts, and I am too, because what kind of ignoramus swallows such a cockamamie story? Those hypothetical families that Big spoke of the other night would've been right not to be kind. My mother is neglectful and irresponsible and probably mentally deficient too. She's not a heroine at all. She's just a selfish woman who couldn't hack it and left two toddlers on her mother's porch and *never came back*. That's who she is. And that's who we are too, two kids, discarded, just left there. I'm glad Bailey never had to see it this way.

I don't go back up to the attic.

It's all right. I'm used to a mother who rides around on a magic carpet. I can get used to this mother too, can't I? But what I can't get used to is that I no longer think Joe, despite my compounding love for him, is ever going to forgive me. How to get used to no one calling you John Lennon? Or making you believe the sky begins at your feet? Or acting like a dork so you'll say *quel dork*? How to get used to being without a boy who turns you into brightness?

I can't.

And what's worse is that with each day that passes, The Sanctum gets quieter, even when I'm blasting the stereo, even when I'm talking to Sarah, who's still apologizing for the seduction fiasco, even when I'm practicing Stravinsky, it just gets quieter and quieter, until it is so quiet that what I hear, again and again, is the cranking sound of the casket lowering into the ground.

With each day that passes, there are longer stretches when I don't think I hear Bailey's heels clunking down the hallway, or glimpse her lying on her bed reading, or catch her in my periphery reciting lines into the mirror. I'm becoming accustomed to The Sanctum without her, and I hate it. Hate that when I stand in her closet fumbling from piece to piece, my face pressed into the fabrics, that I can't find one shirt or dress that still has her scent, and it's my fault. They all smell like me now.

Hate that her cell phone finally has been shut down.

With each day that passes, more traces of my sister vanish, not only from the world, but from my very own mind, and there's nothing I can do about it, but sit in the soundless, scentless sanctum and cry.

On the sixth day of this, Sarah declares me a state of emergency and makes me promise to go to the movies with her that night.

She picks me up in Ennui, wearing a black miniskirt, black minier tank top that shows off a lot of tanned midriff, three-foot black heels, all topped off with a black ski hat, which I'm supposing is her attempt at practicality, because a chill blew in and it's arctic cold. I'm wearing a brown suede coat, turtleneck, and jeans. We look like we are spliced together from different weather systems.

"Hi!" she says, taking the cigarette out of her mouth to kiss me as I get in. "This movie really is supposed to be good. Not like that last one I made you go to where the woman sat in a chair with her cat for the first half. I admit that one was problematico." Sarah and I have opposite movie-going philosophies. All I want out of celluloid is to sit in the dark with a huge bucket of popcorn. Give me car chases, girl gets boy, underdogs triumphing; let me swoon and scream and weep. Sarah on the other hand can't tolerate such pedestrian fare and complains the whole time about how we're rotting our minds and soon won't be able to think our own thoughts because our brains will be lost to the dominant paradigm. Sarah's preference is The Guild, where they show bleak foreign films where nothing happens, no one talks, everyone loves the one who will never love them back, and then the movie ends. On the program tonight is some stultifyingly boring black-and-white film from Norway.

Her face drops as she studies mine. "You look miserable."

"Sucky week all around."

"It'll be fun tonight, promise." She takes one hand off the wheel and pulls a brown sack out of a backpack. "For the movie." She hands it to me. "Vodka."

"Hmm, then I'll for sure fall asleep in this action-packed, thrill-a-minute, black-and-white, silent movie from Norway."

She rolls her eyes. "It's not silent, Lennie."

While waiting in line, Sarah jumps around trying to keep warm. She's telling me how Luke held up remarkably well at the symposium despite being the only guy there, even made her ask a question about music, but then mid-sentence and mid-jump, her eyes bulge a little. I catch it, even though she's already resumed talking as if nothing has happened. I turn around and there's Joe across the street with Rachel.

They're so lost in conversation they don't even realize the light has changed.

Cross the street, I want to scream. *Cross the street before you fall in love*. Because that's what appears to be happening. I watch Joe lightly tug at her arm while he tells her something or other I'm sure about Paris. I can see the smile, all that radiance pouring over Rachel and I think I might fall like a tree.

"Let's go."

"Yup." Sarah's already walking toward the Jeep, fumbling in her bag for the keys. I follow her, but take one look back and meet Joe's eyes head on. Sarah disappears. Then Rachel. Then all the people waiting in line. Then the cars, the trees, the buildings, the ground, the sky until it is only Joe and me staring across empty space at each other. He does not smile. He antismiles. But I can't look away and he can't seem to either. Time has slowed so much that I wonder if when we stop staring at each other we will be old and our whole lives will be over with just a few measly kisses between us. I'm dizzy with missing him, dizzy with seeing him, dizzy with being just yards from him. I want to run across the street, I'm about to – I can feel my heart surge, pushing me toward him, but then he just shakes his head almost to himself and looks away from me and toward Rachel, who now comes back into focus. High-definition focus. Very deliberately, he puts his arm around her and together they cross the street and get in line for the movie. A searing pain claws through me. He doesn't look back, but Rachel does.

She salutes me, a triumphant smile on her face, then flips an insult of blond hair at me as she swings her arm around his waist and turns away.

My heart feels like it's been kicked into a dark corner of my body. *Okay I get it*, I want to holler at the sky. *This is how it feels*. Lesson learned. Come-uppance accepted. I watch them retreat into the theater arm in arm, wishing I had an eraser so I could wipe her out of this picture. Or a vacuum. A vacuum would be better, just suck her up, gone. Out of his arms. Out of my chair. For good.

"C'mon Len, let's get out of here," a familiar voice says. I guess Sarah still exists and she's talking to me, so I must still exist too. I look down, see my legs, realize I'm still standing. I put one foot in front of the other and make my way to Ennui.

There is no moon, no stars, just a brightless, lightless gray bowl over our heads as we drive home.

"I'm going to challenge her for first chair," I say.

"Finally."

"Not because of this—"

"I know. Because you're a racehorse, not some stupid pony." There's no irony in her voice.

I roll down the window and let the cold air slap me silly.

31

Remember
how it was
when
we
kissed?
Armfuls
and
armfuls
of
light
thrown
right
at
us.
A
rope
dropping
down
from
the
sky.
How
can
the
word
love
the
word
life
even
fit
in
the
mouth?

(Found on a piece of paper under the big willow)

Sarah and I are hanging half in, half out my bedroom window, passing the bottle of vodka back and forth.

"We could off her?" Sarah suggests, all her words slurring into one.

"How would we do it?" I ask, swigging a huge gulp of vodka.

"Poison. It's always the best choice, hard to trace."

"Let's poison him too, and all his stupid gorgeous brothers." I can feel the words sticking to the insides of my mouth. "He didn't even wait a week, Sarah."

"That doesn't mean anything. He's hurt."

"God, how can he like her?"

Sarah shakes her head. "I saw the way he looked at you in the street, like a crazy person, really out there, more demented than demented, holy Toledo tigers bonkers. You know what I think? I think he put his arm around her for your benefit."

"What if he has sex with her for my benefit?" Jealousy mad-dogs through me. Yet, that's not the worst part, neither is the remorse; the worst part is I keep thinking of the afternoon on the forest bed, how vulnerable I'd felt, how much I'd liked it, being that open, that *me*, with him. Had I ever felt so close to anyone?

"Can I have a cigarette?" I ask, taking one before she answers.

She cups a hand around the end of her smoke, lights it with the other, then hands it to me, takes mine, then lights it for herself. I drag on it, cough, don't care, take another and manage not to choke, blowing a gray trail of smoke into the night air.

"Bails would know what to do," I say.

"She would," Sarah agrees.

We smoke together quietly in the moonlight and I realize something I can never say to Sarah. There might've been another reason, a deeper one, why I didn't want to be around her. It's that she's not Bailey, and that's a bit unbearable for me – but I need to bear it. I concentrate on the music of the river, let myself drift along with it as it rushes steadily away.

After a few moments, I say, "You can revoke my free pass."

She tilts her head, smiles at me in a way that floods me with warmth. "Done deal."

She puts out her cigarette on the windowsill and slips back onto the bed. I put mine out too, but stay outside looking over Gram's lustrous garden, breathing it in and practically swooning from the bouquet that wafts up to me on the cool breeze.

And that's when I get the idea. The *brilliant* idea. I have to talk to Joe. I have to at least try to make him understand. But I could use a little help.

"Sarah," I say when I flop back onto the bed. "The roses, they're aphrodisiacal, remember?"

She gets it immediately. "Yes, Lennie! It's the last-resort miracle! Flying figs, yes!"

"Figs?"

"I couldn't think of an animal, I'm too wasted."

I'm on a mission. I've left Sarah sound asleep in Bailey's bed and I'm tiptoeing my thumping vodka head down the steps and out into the creeping morning light. The fog is thick and sad, the whole world an X-ray of itself. I have my weapon in hand and am about to begin my task. Gram is going to kill me, but this is the price I must pay.

I start at my favorite bush of all, the Magic Lanterns, roses with a symphony of color jammed into each petal. I snip the heads off the most extraordinary ones I can find. Then go to the Opening Nights and snip, snip, snip, merrily along to the Perfect Moments, the Sweet Surrenders, the Black Magics. My heart kicks around in my chest from both fear and excitement. I go from prize bush to bush, from the red velvet Lasting Loves to the pink Fragrant Clouds to the apricot Marilyn Monroes and end at the most beautiful orange-red rose on the planet, appropriately named: The Trumpeter. There I go for broke until I have at my feet a bundle of roses so ravishing that if God got married, there would be no other possible choice for the bouquet. I've cut so many I can't even fit the stems in one hand but have to carry them in both as I head down the road to find a place to stash them until later. I put them beside one of my favorite oaks, totally hidden from the house. Then I worry they'll wilt, so I run back to the house and prepare a basket with wet towels at the bottom and go back to the side of the road and wrap all the stems.

Later that morning, after Sarah leaves, Big goes off to the trees, and Gram retreats into the art room with her green women, I tiptoe out the door. I've convinced myself, despite all reason perhaps, that this is going to work. I keep thinking that Bails would be proud of this harebrained plan. *Extraordinary,* she'd say. In fact, maybe Bails would like that I fell in love with Joe so soon after she died. Maybe it's just the exact inappropriate way my sister would want to be mourned by me.

The flowers are still behind the oak where I left them. When I see them I am struck again by their extraordinary beauty. I've never seen a bouquet of them like this, never seen the explosive color of one bloom right beside another.

I walk up the hill to the Fontaines' in a cloud of exquisite fragrance. Who knows if it's the power of suggestion, or if the roses are truly charmed, but by the time I get to the house. I'm so in love with Joe, I can barely ring the bell. I have serious doubts if I'll be able to form a coherent sentence. If he answers I might just tackle him to the ground till he gives and be done with it.

But no such luck.

The same stylish woman who was in the yard squabbling the other day opens the door. "Don't tell me, you must be Lennie." It's immediately apparent that Fontaine spawn can't come close in the smile department to Mother Fontaine. I should tell Big – her smile has a better shot at reviving bugs than his pyramids.

"I am," I say. "Nice to meet you, Mrs Fontaine." She's being so friendly that I can't imagine she knows what's happened between her son and me. He probably talks to her about as much as I talk to Gram.

"And will you just look at those roses! I've never seen anything like them in my life. Where'd you pick them? The Garden of Eden?" Like mother, like son. I remember Joe said the same that first day.

"Something like that," I say. "My grandmother has a way with flowers. They're for Joe. Is he home?" All of a sudden, I'm nervous. Really nervous. My stomach seems to be hosting a symposium of bees.

"And the aroma! My God, what an aroma!" she cries. I think the flowers have hypnotized her. Wow. Maybe they do work. "Lucky Joe, what a gift, but I'm sorry dear, he's not home. He said he'd be back soon though. I can put them in water and leave them for him in his room if you like."

I'm too disappointed to answer. I just nod and hand them over to her. I bet he's at Rachel's feeding her family chocolate croissants. I have a dreadful thought – what if the roses actually are love-inducing and Joe comes back here with Rachel and both of them fall under their spell? This was another disastrous idea, but I can't take the roses back now. Actually, I think it would take an automatic weapon to get them back from Mrs Fontaine, who is leaning farther into the bouquet with each passing second.

"Thank you," I say. "For giving them to him." Will she be able to separate herself from these flowers?

"It was very nice to meet you, Lennie. I'd been looking forward to it. I'm sure Joe will *really* appreciate these."

"Lennie," an exasperated voice says from behind me. That symposium in my belly just opened its doors to wasps and hornets too. This is it. I turn around and see Joe making his way up the path. There is no bounce in his walk. It's as if gravity has a hand on his shoulder that it never did before.

"Oh, honey!" Mrs Fontaine exclaims. "Look what Lennie brought you. Have you ever seen such roses. I sure haven't. My word." Mrs Fontaine is speaking directly to the roses now, taking in deep aromatic breaths. "Well, I'll just bring these in, find a nice place for them. You kids have fun…"

I watch her head disappear completely in the bouquet as the door closes behind her. I want to lunge at her, grab the flowers, shriek, *I need those roses more than you do, lady*, but I have a more pressing concern: Joe's silent fuming beside me.

As soon as the door clicks closed, he says, "You still don't get it, do you?" His voice is full of menace, not quite if a shark could talk, but close. He points at the door behind which dozens of aphrodisiacal roses are filling the air with promise. "You've got to be kidding. You think it's that easy?" His face is getting flushed, his eyes bulgy and wild. "I don't want tiny dresses or stupid fucking magic flowers!" He flails in place like a marionette. "I'm *already* in love with you, Lennie, don't you get it? But I can't be with you. Every time I close my eyes I see you with *him*."

I stand there dumbstruck – sure, there were some discouraging things just said, but all of them seem to have fallen away. I'm left with six wonderful words: *I'm already in love with you*. Present tense, not past. Rachel Brazile be damned. A skyful of hope knocks into me.

"Let me explain," I say, intent on remembering my lines this time, intent on getting him to understand.

He makes a noise that's part groan, part roar, like *ahh-harrrrgh*, then says, "Nothing to explain. I saw you two. You lied to me over and over again."

"Toby and I were—"

He interrupts. "No way, I don't want to hear it. I told you what happened to me in France and you did this anyway. I can't forgive you. It's just the way I am. You have to leave me alone. I'm sorry."

My legs go weak as it sinks in that his hurt and anger, the sickness of having been deceived and betrayed, has already trumped his love.

He motions down the hill to where Toby and I were that night, and says, "What. Did. You. Expect?" What *did* I expect? One minute he's trying to tell me he loves me and the next he's watching me kiss another guy. Of course he feels this way.

I have to say something, so I say the only thing that makes sense in my mixed heart. "I'm so in love with you."

My words knock the wind out of him.

It's as if everything around us stops to see what's going to happen next – the trees lean in, birds hover, flowers hold their petals still. How could he not surrender to this crazy big love we both feel? He couldn't not, right?

I reach my hand out to touch him, but he moves his arm out of my reach.

He shakes his head, looks at the ground. "I can't be with

someone who could do that to me." Then he looks right in my eyes, and says, "I can't be with someone who could do that to *her sister.*"

The words have guillotine force. I stagger backward, splintering into pieces. His hand flies to his mouth. Maybe he's wishing his words back inside. Maybe he even thinks he went too far, but it doesn't matter. He wanted me to get it and I do.

I do the only thing I can. I turn around and run from him, hoping my trembling legs will keep me up until I can get away. Like Heathcliff and Cathy, I had the Big Bang, once-in-a-lifetime kind of love, and I destroyed it all.

All I want is to get up to The Sanctum so I can throw the covers over my head and disappear for several hundred years. Out of breath from racing down the hill, I push through the front door of the house. I blow past the kitchen, but backtrack when I glimpse Gram. She's sitting at the kitchen table, her arms folded in front of her chest, her face hard and stern. In front of her on the table are her garden shears and my copy of *Wuthering Heights*.

Uh-oh.

She jumps right in. "You have no idea how close I came to chopping your precious book to bits, but I have some self-control and respect for other people's things." She stands up. When Gram's mad, she practically doubles in size and all twelve feet of her is bulldozing across the kitchen right at me.

"What were you thinking, Lennie? You come like the Grim

Reaper and decimate my garden, my *roses*. How could you? You know how I feel about anyone but me touching my flowers. It's the one and only thing I ask. The one and only thing."

She's looming over me. "Well?"

"They'll grow back." I know this is the wrong thing to say, but holler-at-Lennie-day is taking its toll.

She throws her arms up, completely exasperated with me, and it strikes me how similar her expression and arm flailing resembles Joe's. "That is not the point and you know it." She points at me. "You've become very selfish, Lennie Walker."

This I was not expecting. No one's ever called me selfish in my life, least of all Gram – the never-ending fountain of praise and coddling. Are she and Joe testifying at the same trial?

Could this day get any worse?

Isn't the answer to that question always yes?

Gram's hands are on her hips now, face flushed, eyes blazing, double uh-oh – I lean back against the wall, brace myself for the impending assault. She leans in. "Yes, Lennie. You act like you're the only one in this house who has lost somebody. She was like my daughter, do you know what that's like? Do you? My *daughter*. No, you don't because you haven't once asked. Not once have you asked how I'm doing. Did it ever occur to you that I might need to talk?" She is yelling now. "I know you're devastated, but Lennie, you're not the only one."

All the air races out of the room, and I race out with it.

32

Bailey grabs my hand
and pulls me out of the window
into the sky,
pulls music out of my pockets.
"It's time you learned to fly,"
she says,
and vanishes.

(Found on a lollipop wrapper on the trail to the Rain River)

I bolt down the hallway and out the door and jump all four porch steps. I want to run into the woods, veer off the path, find a spot where no one can find me, sit down under an old craggy oak and cry. I want to cry and cry and cry and cry until all the dirt in the whole forest floor has turned to mud. And this is exactly what I'm about to do except that when I hit the path, I realize I can't. I can't run away from Gram, especially not after everything she just said. Because I know she's right. She and Big have been like background noise to me since Bailey died.

I've hardly given any thought to what they're going through. I made Toby my ally in grief, like he and I had an exclusionary right to it, an exclusionary right to Bailey herself. I think of all the times Gram hovered at the door to The Sanctum trying to get me to talk about Bailey, asking me to come down and have a cup of tea, and how I just assumed she wanted to comfort me. It never once occurred to me that she needed to talk herself, that she needed *me*.

How could I have been so careless with her feelings? With Joe's? With everyone's?

I take a deep breath, turn around, and make my way back to the kitchen. I can't make things right with Joe, but at least I can try to make them right with Gram. She's in the same chair at the table. I stand across from her, rest my fingers on the table, wait for her to look up at me. Not one window is open, and the hot stuffy kitchen smells almost rotten.

"I'm sorry," I say. "Really." She nods, looks down at her

hands. It occurs to me that I've disappointed or hurt or betrayed everyone I love in the last couple months: Gram, Bailey, Joe, Toby, Sarah, even Big. How did I manage that? Before Bailey died, I don't think I ever really disappointed anyone. Did Bailey just take care of everyone and everything for me? Or did no one expect anything of me before? Or did I just not do anything or want anything before, so I never had to deal with the consequences of my messed-up actions? Or have I become really selfish and self-absorbed? Or all of the above?

I look at the sickly Lennie houseplant on the counter and know that it's not me anymore. It's who I used to be, before, and that's why it's dying. That me is gone.

"I don't know who I am," I say, sitting down. "I can't be who I was, not without her, and who I'm becoming is a total screw-up."

Gram doesn't deny it. She's still mad, not twelve feet of mad, but plenty mad.

"We could go out to lunch in the city next week, spend the whole day together," I add, feeling puny, trying to make up for months of ignoring her with a lunch.

She nods, but that is not what's on her mind. "Just so you know, I don't know who I am without her either."

"Really?"

She shakes her head. "Nope. Every day, after you and Big leave, all I do is stand in front of a blank canvas thinking how much I despise the color green, how every single shade of it disgusts me or disappoints me or breaks my heart." Sadness fills me. I imagine all the green willowy women sliding out of their canvases and slinking their way out the front door.

"I get it," I say quietly.

Gram closes her eyes. Her hands are folded one on top of the other on the table. I reach out and put my hand over hers and she quickly sandwiches it.

"It's horrible," she whispers.

"It is," I say.

The early-afternoon light drains out the windows, zebra-ing the room with long dark shadows. Gram looks old and tired and it makes me feel desolate. Bailey, Uncle Big and I have been her whole life, except for a few generations of flowers and a lot of green paintings.

"You know what else I hate?" she says. "I hate that everyone keeps telling me that I carry Bailey in my heart. I want to holler at them: *I don't want her there*. I want her in the kitchen with Lennie and me. I want her at the river with Toby and their baby. I want her to be Juliet and Lady Macbeth, you stupid, stupid people. Bailey doesn't want to be trapped in my heart or anyone else's." Gram pounds her fist on the table. I squeeze it with my hands and nod *yes*, and feel *yes*, a giant, pulsing, angry yes that passes from her to me. I look down at our hands and catch sight of *Wuthering Heights* lying there silent and helpless and ornery as ever. I think about all the wasted lives, all the wasted love crammed inside it.

"Gram, do it."

"What? Do what?" she asks.

I pick up the book and the shears, hold them out to her. "Just do it, chop it to bits. Here." I slip my fingers and thumb into the handle of the garden shears just like I did this morning, but this time I feel no fear, just that wild, pulsing, pissed off *yes* coursing through me as I take a cut of a book that I've underlined and annotated, a book that is creased and soiled with years of me, years of river water, and summer sun, and sand from the beach, and sweat from my palms, a book bent to the curves of my waking and sleeping body. I take another cut, slicing through chunks of paper at a time, through all the tiny words, cutting the passionate, hopeless story to pieces, slashing their lives, their impossible love, the whole mess and tragedy of it. I'm attacking it now, enjoying the swish of the blades, the metal scrape after each delicious cut. I cut into Heathcliff, poor, heartsick, embittered Heathcliff and stupid Cathy for her bad choices and unforgivable compromises. And while I'm at it, I take a swipe at Joe's jealousy and anger and judgment, at his *dickhead-him* inability to forgive. I hack away at his ridiculous all-or-nothing-horn-player bullshit, and then I lay into my own duplicity and deceptiveness and confusion and hurt and bad judgment and overwhelming, never-ending grief. I cut and cut and cut at everything I can think of that is keeping Joe and me from having this great big beautiful love while we can.

Gram is wide-eyed, mouth agape. But then I see a faint smile find her lips. She says, "Here, let me have a go." She takes the shears and starts cutting, tentatively at first, but then she gets carried away just as I had, and starts hacking at handfuls and handfuls of pages until words fly all around us like confetti.

Gram's laughing. "Well, that was unexpected." We are both out of breath, spent, and smiling giddily.

"I am related to you, aren't I?" I say.

"Oh, Lennie, I have missed you." She pulls me into her lap like I'm five years old. I think I'm forgiven.

"Sorry I hollered, sweet pea," she says, hugging me into her warmth.

I squeeze her back. "Should I make us some tea?" I ask.

"You better, we have lots of catching up to do. But first things first, you destroyed my whole garden, I have to know if it worked."

I hear again: *I can't be with someone who could do that to her sister*, and my heart squeezes so tight in my chest, I can barely breathe. "Not a chance. It's over."

Gram says quietly, "I saw what happened that night." I tense up even more, slide out of her lap and go over to fill the tea kettle. I suspected Gram saw Toby and me kiss, but the reality of her witnessing it sends shame shifting around within me. I can't look at her. "Lennie?" Her voice isn't incriminating. I relax a little. "Listen to me."

I turn around slowly and face her.

She waves her hand around her head like she's shooing a fly. "I won't say it didn't render me speechless for a minute or two." She smiles. "But crazy things like that happen when people are this shocked and grief-stricken. I'm surprised we're all still standing."

I can't believe how readily Gram is pushing this aside, absolving me. I want to fall to her feet in gratitude. She definitely did not confer with Joe on the matter, but it makes his words sting less, and it gives me the courage to ask, "Do you think she'd ever forgive me?"

"Oh, sweet pea, trust me on this one, she already has." Gram wags her finger at me. "Now, Joe is another story. He'll need some time..."

"Like thirty years," I say.

"Woohoo – poor boy, that was an eyeful, Lennie Walker." Gram looks at me mischievously. She has snapped back into her sassy self. "Yes, Len, when you and Joe Fontaine are forty-seven—" She laughs. "We'll plan a beautiful, beautiful wedding—"

She stops mid-sentence because she must notice my face. I don't want to kill her cheer, so I'm using every muscle in it to hide my heartbreak, but I've lost the battle.

"Lennie." She comes over to me.

"He hates me," I tell her.

"No," she says warmly. "If ever there was a boy in love, sweet pea, it's Joe Fontaine."

33

Gram made me go to the doctor
to see if there was something wrong
with my heart.
After a bunch of tests, the doctor said:
Lennie, you lucked out.
I wanted to punch him in the face,
but instead I started to cry
in a drowning kind of way.
I couldn't believe
I had a lucky heart
when what I wanted
was the same kind of heart
as Bailey.
I didn't hear Gram come in,
or come up behind me,
just felt her arms slip around my shaking frame,
then the press of both her hands hard
against my chest, holding it all in,
holding me together.
Thank God, she whispered,
before the doctor or I could utter a word.
How could she have possibly known
that I'd gotten good news?

(Found on the back of an envelope on the trail to the forest bedroom)

When the tea is in the mugs, the window's opened, and Gram and I have relaxed into the waning light, I say quietly, "I want to talk to you about something."

"Anything, sweet pea."

"I want to talk about Mom."

She sighs, leans back in her chair. "I know." She crosses her arms, holding both elbows, cradling herself. "I was up in the attic. You put the box back on a different shelf—"

"I didn't read much … sorry."

"No, I'm the one who's sorry. I've wanted to talk to you about Paige these last few months, but…"

"I wouldn't let you talk to me about anything."

She nods slightly. Her face is about as serious as I've ever seen it. She says, "Bailey shouldn't have died knowing so little about her mother."

I drop my eyes. It's true – I was wrong to think Bailey wouldn't want to know everything that I do, whether it hurts or not. I rake my fingers around in the remains of *Wuthering Heights*, waiting for Gram to speak.

When she does, her voice is strained, tight. "I thought I was protecting you girls, but now I'm pretty sure I was just protecting myself." I lift my gaze to meet hers. "It's so hard for me to speak about her. I told myself the better you girls knew her, the more it would hurt." She sweeps some of the book to herself. "I focused on the restlessness, so you girls would wouldn't feel so abandoned, wouldn't blame her, or worse, blame yourselves.

I wanted you to admire her. That's it."

That's it? Heat rushes up my body. Gram reaches her hand to mine. I slip it away from her.

I say, "You just made up a story so we wouldn't feel abandoned…" I raise my eyes to hers, continue despite the pain in her face. "But we *were* abandoned, Gram, and we didn't know why, don't know anything about her except some crazy story." I feel like scooping up a fistful of *Wuthering Heights* and hurling it at her. "Why not just tell us she's crazy if she is? Why not tell the truth whatever it is? Wouldn't that have been better?"

She grabs my wrist, harder than I think she intended. "But there's not just one truth, Lennie, there never is. What I told you wasn't some story I made up." She's trying to be calm, but I can tell she's moments away from doubling in size. "Yes, it's true that Paige wasn't a stable girl. I mean, who in their proper tree leaves two little girls and doesn't come back?" She lets go of my wrist now that she has my full attention. She looks wildly around the room as if the words she needs might be on the walls. After a moment, she says, "Your mother was an irresponsible tornado of a girl and I'm sure she's an irresponsible tornado of a woman. But it's also true that she's not the first tornado to blast through this family, not the first one who's disappeared like this either. Sylvie swung back into town in that beat-up yellow Cadillac after twenty years drifting around. Twenty years!" She bangs her fist on the table, hard, the piles of *Wuthering Heights* jump with the impact. "Yes, maybe some doctor could give it a name, a diagnosis, but what difference does it make what we call it, it still is what it is, we call it the restless gene, so what? It's as true as anything else."

She takes a sip of her tea, burns her tongue. "Ow," she exclaims uncharacteristically, fanning her mouth.

"Big thinks you have it too," I say. "The restless gene." I'm rearranging words into new sentences on the table. I peek up at her, afraid by her silence that this admission might not have gone over very well.

Her brow's furrowed. "He said that?" Gram's joined me in mixing the words around on the table. I see she's put *under that benign sky* next to *so eternally secluded*.

"He thinks you just bottle it up," I say.

She's stopped shuffling words. There's something very un-Gram in her face, something darting and skittish. She won't meet my eyes, and then I recognize what it is because I've become quite familiar with it myself recently – it's shame.

"What, Gram?"

She's pressing her lips together so tightly, they've gone white; it's like she's trying to seal them, to make sure no words come out.

"What?"

She gets up, walks over to the counter, cradles up against it, looks out the window at a passing kingdom of clouds. I watch her back and wait. "I've been hiding inside that story, Lennie, and I made you girls, and Big, for that matter, hide in it with me."

"But you just said—"

"I know – it's not that it isn't true, but it's also true that blaming things on destiny and genes is a helluva lot easier than blaming them on myself."

"On yourself?"

She nods, doesn't say anything else, just continues to stare out the window.

I feel a chill creep up my spine. "Gram?"

She's turned away from me so I can't see the expression on her face. I don't know why, but I feel afraid of her, like she's slipped into the skin of someone else. Even the way she's holding her body is different, crumpled almost. When she finally speaks, her voice is too deep and calm. "I remember everything about that night..." she says, then pauses, and I think about running out of the room, away from this crumpled Gram who talks like she's in a trance. "I remember how cold it was, unseasonably so, how the kitchen was full of lilacs – I'd filled all the vases earlier in the day because she was coming." I can tell by Gram's voice she's smiling now and I relax a little. "She was wearing this long green dress, more like a giant scarf really, totally inappropriate, which was Paige – it's like she had her own weather around her always." I've never heard any of this about my mother, never heard about anything as real as a green dress, a kitchen full of flowers. But then Gram's tone changes again. "She was so upset that night, pacing around the kitchen, no not pacing, billowing back and forth in that scarf. I remember thinking she's like a trapped wind, a wild gale imprisoned in this kitchen with me, like if I opened a window she'd be gone."

Gram turns toward me as if finally remembering I'm in the room. "Your mother was at the end of her rope and she never was someone with a lot of rope on hand. She'd come for the weekend so I could see you girls. At least that's why I'd thought she'd come, until she began asking me what I'd do if she left. 'Left?' I said to her, 'Where? For how long?' which is when I found out she had a plane ticket to God knows where, she wouldn't say, and planned on using it – a one-way ticket. She told me she couldn't do it, that she didn't have it right inside to be a mother. I told her that her insides were right enough, that she couldn't leave, that you girls were her responsibility. I told her that she had to buck up like every other mother on this earth. I told her that you could all live here, that'd I'd help her, but she couldn't just up and go like those others in this crazy family, I wouldn't have it. 'But if I did leave,' she kept insisting, 'what would you do?' Over and over she asked it. I remember I kept trying to hold her by her arms, to get her to snap out of it, like I'd do when she was young and would get wound up, but she kept slipping out of my grasp like she was made of air." Gram takes a deep breath. "At this point, I was very upset myself, and you know how I get when I blow. I started shouting. I do have my share of the tornado inside, that's for sure, especially when I was younger, Big's right." She sighs. "I lost it, really lost it. 'What do you think I'd do if you left?' I hollered. 'They're my granddaughters, but Paige, if you leave you can never come back. Never. You'll be dead to them, dead in their hearts, and dead to me. Dead. To all of us.' My exact despicable words. Then I locked myself in my art room for the rest of the night. The next morning – she was gone."

I've fallen back into my chair, boneless. Gram stands across the room in a prison of shadows. "I told your mother to never come back."

She'll be back, girls.

A prayer, never a promise.

Her voice is barely above a whisper. "I'm sorry."

Her words have moved through me like fast-moving storm clouds, transforming the landscape. I look around at her framed green ladies, three of them in the kitchen alone, women caught somewhere between here and there – each one Paige, all of them Paige in a billowy green dress, I'm sure of it now. I think about the ways Gram made sure our mother never died in our hearts, made sure Paige Walker never bore any blame for leaving her children. I think about how, unbeknownst to us, Gram culled that blame for herself.

I remember the ugly thing I'd thought that night at the top of the stairs when I overheard her apologizing to The Half Mom. I'd blamed her too. For things even the almighty Gram can't control.

"It's not your fault," I say, with a certainty in my voice I've never heard before. "It never was, Gram. *She* left. *She* didn't come back – her choice, not yours, no matter what you said to her."

Gram exhales like she's been holding her breath for sixteen years.

"Oh Lennie," she cries. "I think you just opened the window" – she touches her chest – "and let her out."

I rise from my chair and walk over to her, realizing for the first time that she's lost two daughters – I don't know how she bears it. I realize something else too. I don't share this double grief. I have a mother and I'm standing so close to her, I can see the years weighing down her skin, can smell her tea-scented breath. I wonder if Bailey's search for Mom would have led her here too, right back to Gram. I hope so. I gently put my hand on her arm wondering how such a huge love for someone can fit in my tiny body. "Bailey and I are so lucky we got you," I say. "We scored."

She closes her eyes for a moment, and then the next thing I know I'm in her arms and she's squeezing me so as to crush every bone. "I'm the one who lucked out," she says into my hair. "And now I think we need to drink our tea. Enough of this."

As I make my way back to the table, something becomes clear: life's a freaking mess. In fact, I'm going to tell Sarah we need to start a new philosophical movement: messessentialism instead of existentialism: for those who revel in the essential mess that is life. Because Gram's right, there's not one truth ever, just a whole bunch of stories, all going on at once, in our heads, in our hearts, all getting in the way of each other. It's all a beautiful calamitous mess. It's like the day Mr James took us into the woods and cried triumphantly, "That's it! That's it!" to the dizzying cacophony of soloing instruments trying to make music together. That is it.

I look down at the piles of words that used to be my favorite book. I want to put the story back together again so Cathy and Heathcliff can make different choices, can stop getting in the way of themselves at every turn, can follow their raging, volcanic hearts right into each other's arms. But I can't. I go to the sink, pull out the trash can, and sweep Cathy and Heathcliff and the rest of their unhappy lot into it.

Later that evening, I'm playing Joe's melody over and over on the porch, trying to think of books where love actually triumphs in the end. There's Lizzie Bennet and Darcy, and Jane Eyre ends up with Mr Rochester, that's good, but he had that wife locked up for a while, which freaks me out. There's Florentino Aziza in *Love in the Time of Cholera*, but he had to wait over fifty years for Fermina, only for them to end up on a ship going nowhere. Ugh. I'd say there's slim literary pickings on this front, which depresses me; how could true love so infrequently prevail in the classics? And more importantly, how can I make it prevail for Joe and me? If only I could convert him to messessentialism … *If only I had wheels on my ass, I'd be a trolley cart.* After all that he said today, I think that about covers my chances.

I'm playing his song for probably the fiftieth time when I realize Gram's in the doorway listening to me. I thought she was locked away in the art room recovering from the emotional tumult of our afternoon. I stop mid-note, suddenly self-conscious. She opens the door, strides out with the mahogany box from the attic in her hands. "What a lovely melody. Bet I could play it myself at this point," she says, rolling her eyes as she puts the box on the table and drops into the love seat. "Though it's very nice to hear you playing again."

I decide to tell her. "I'm going to try for first chair again this fall."

"Oh, sweet pea," she sings. Literally. "Music to my tin ears."

I smile, but inside, my stomach is roiling. I'm planning on telling Rachel next practice. It'd be so much easier if I could just pour a bucket of water on her like the Wicked Witch of the West.

"Come sit down." Gram taps the cushion next to her. I join her, resting my clarinet across my knees. She puts her hand on the box. "Everything in here is yours to read. Open all the envelopes. Read my notes, the letters. Just be prepared, it's not all pretty, especially the earlier letters."

I nod. "Thank you."

"All right." She removes her hand from the box. "I'm going to take a walk to town, meet Big at The Saloon. I need a stiff drink." She ruffles my hair, then leaves the box and me to ourselves.

After putting my clarinet away, I sit with the box on my lap, trailing circles around the ring of galloping horses with my fingers. Around and around. I want to open it, and I also don't want to. It's probably the closest I'll ever get to knowing my mother, whoever she is – adventurer or wack job, heroine or villain, probably just a very troubled, complicated woman.

I look out at the gang of oaks across the road, at the Spanish moss hanging over their stooped shoulders like decrepit shawls, the gray, gnarled lot of them like a band of wise old men pondering a verdict—

The door squeaks. I turn to see that Gram has put on a bright pink floral no-clue-what – a coat? A cape? A shower curtain? – over an even brighter purple flowered frock. Her hair is down and wild; it looks like it conducts electricity. She has make-up on, an eggplant-color lipstick, cowboy boots to house her Big Foot feet. She looks beautiful and insane. It's the first time she's gone out at night since Bailey died. She waves at me, winks, then heads down the steps. I watch her stroll across the yard. Right as she hits the road, she turns back, holds her hair so the breeze doesn't blow it back into her eyes.

"Hey, I give Big one month, you?"

"Are you kidding? Two weeks, tops."

"It's your turn to be best man."

"That's fine," I say, smiling.

She smiles back at me, humor peeking out of her queenly face. Even though we pretend otherwise, nothing quite raises Walker spirits like the thought of another wedding for Uncle Big.

"Be okay, sweet pea," she says. "You know where we are..."

"I'll be fine," I say, feeling the weight of the box on my legs.

As soon as she's gone, I open the lid. I'm ready. All these

notes, all these letters, sixteen years' worth. I think about Gram jotting down a recipe, a thought, a silly or not-so-pretty something she wanted to share with her daughter, or just remember herself, maybe stuffing it in her pocket all day, and then sneaking up to the attic before bed, to put it in this box, this mailbox with no pickup, year after year, not knowing if her daughter would ever read them, not knowing if anyone would—

I gasp, because isn't that just exactly what I've been doing too: writing poems and scattering them to the winds with the same hope as Gram that someone, someday, somewhere might understand who I am, who my sister was, and what happened to us.

I take out the envelopes, count them – fifteen, all with the name *Paige* and the year. I find the first one, written sixteen years ago by Gram to her daughter. Slipping my finger under the seal, I imagine Bailey sitting beside me. *Okay*, I tell her, taking out the letter, *Let's meet our mother*.

Okay to everything. I'm a messessentialist – okay to it all.

34

The Shaw Ranch presides over Clover. Its acreage rolls in green and gold majesty from the ridge all the way down to town. I walk through the iron gate and make my way to the stables, where I find Toby inside talking to a beautiful black mare as he takes her saddle off.

"Don't mean to interrupt," I say, walking over to him.

He turns around. "Wow, Lennie."

We're smiling at each other like idiots. I thought it might be weird to see him, but we both seem to be acting pretty much thrilled. It embarrasses me, so I drop my gaze to the mare between us and stroke her warm moist coat. Heat radiates off her body.

Toby flicks the end of the reins lightly across my hand.

"I've missed you."

"Me too, you." But, I realize with some relief that my stomach isn't fluttering, even with our eyes locked as they now are. Not even a twitter. Is the spell broken? The horse snorts – perfect: thanks, Black Beauty.

"Want to go for a ride?" he asks. "We could go up on the ridge. I was just up there. There's a massive herd of elk roaming."

"Actually, Toby … I thought maybe we could visit Bailey."

"Okay," he says, without thinking, like I asked him to get an ice cream. Strange.

I told myself I would never go back to the cemetery. No one talks about decaying flesh and maggots and skeletons, but how can you not think of those things? I've done everything in my power to keep those thoughts out of my mind, and staying away from Bailey's grave has been crucial to that end. But last night, I was fingering all the things on her dresser like I always do before I go to sleep, and I realized that she wouldn't want me clinging to the black hair webbed in her hairbrush or the rank laundry I still refuse to wash. She'd think it was totally gross: Lady-Havisham-and-her-wedding-dress gross and dismal. I got an image of her then sitting on the hill at the Clover cemetery with its ancient oaks, firs and redwoods like a queen holding court, and I knew it was time.

Even though the cemetery is close enough to walk, when Toby's finished, we jump in his truck. He puts the key in the ignition, but doesn't turn it. He stares straight through the windshield at the golden meadows, tapping on the wheel with two fingers in a staccato rhythm. I can tell he's revving up to say something. I rest my head on the passenger window and look out at the fields, imagining his life here, how solitary it must be. A minute or two later, he starts talking in his low lulling bass. "I've always hated being an only child. Used to envy you guys. You were just so tight."

He grips his hands on the wheel, stares straight ahead. "I was so psyched to marry Bails, to have this baby … I was psyched to be part of your family. It's going to sound so lame now, but I thought I could help you through this. I wanted to. I know Bailey would've wanted me to." He shakes his head. "Sure screwed it all up. I just … I don't know. You understood… It's like you were the only one who did. I started to feel so close to you, too close. It got all mixed up in my head—"

"But you did help me," I interrupt. "You were the only one who could even find me. I felt that same closeness even if I didn't understand it. I don't know what I would have done without you."

He turns to me. "Yeah?"

"Yeah, Toby."

He smiles his squintiest, sweetest smile. "Well, I'm pretty sure I can keep my hands off you now. I don't know about your frisky self though…" He raises his eyebrows, gives me a look, then laughs an unburdened free laugh. I punch his arm. He goes on, "So, maybe we'll be able to hang out a little – I don't think I can keep saying no to Gram's dinner invitations without her sending out the National Guard."

"I can't believe you just made two jokes in one sentence. Amazing."

"I'm not a total doorknob, you know?"

"Guess not. There must have been some reason my sister wanted to spend the rest of her life with you!" And just like that, it feels right between us, finally.

"Well," he says, starting the truck. "Shall we cheer ourselves up with a trip to the cemetery?"

"Three jokes, unbelievable."

However, that was probably Toby's word allotment for the year, I'm thinking as we drive along now in silence. A silence that is full of jitters. Mine. I'm nervous. I'm not sure what I'm afraid of really. I keep telling myself, it's just a stone, it's just a pretty piece of land with gorgeous stately trees overlooking the falls. It's just a place where my beautiful sister's body is in a box decaying in a sexy black dress and sandals. Ugh. I can't help it. Everything I haven't allowed myself to imagine rushes me: I think about airless empty lungs. Lipstick on her unmoving mouth. The silver bracelet that Toby had given her on her pulseless wrist. Her belly ring. Hair and nails growing in the dark. Her body with no thoughts in it. No time in it. No love in it. Six feet of earth crushing down on her. I think about the phone ringing in the kitchen, the thump of Gram collapsing, then the inhuman sound sirening out of her, through the floorboards, up to our room.

I look over at Toby. He doesn't look nervous at all. Something occurs to me.

"Have you been?" I ask.

"Course," he answers. "Almost every day."

"Really?"

He looks over at me, the realization dawning on him. "You mean you haven't been since?"

"No." I look out the window. I'm a terrible sister. Good sisters visit graves despite gruesome thoughts.

"Gram goes," he says. "She planted a few rosebushes, a bunch of other flowers too. The grounds people told her she had to get rid of them, but every time they pulled out her plants, she just replanted more. They finally gave up."

I can't believe everyone's been going to Bailey's grave but me. I can't believe how left out it makes me feel.

"What about Big?" I ask.

"I find roaches from his joints a lot. We hung out there a couple times." He looks over at me, studies my face for what feels like forever. "It'll be okay, Len. Easier than you think. I was really scared the first time I went."

Something occurs to me then. "Toby," I say, tentatively, mustering my nerve. "You must be pretty used to being an only child..." My voice starts to shake. "But I'm really new at it." I look out the window. "Maybe we..." I feel too shy all of a sudden to finish my thought, but he knows what I'm getting at.

"I've always wanted a sister," he says as he swerves into a spot in the tiny parking lot.

"Good," I say, every inch of me relieved. I lean over and give him the world's most sexless peck on the cheek. "C'mon," I say. "Let's go tell her we're sorry."

35

There once was a girl who found herself dead.
She spent her days peering
over the ledge of heaven,
her chin in her palm.
She was bored as a brick,
hadn't adjusted yet
to the slower pace of ~~the~~ heavenly life.
Her sister would look up at her
and wave,
and the dead girl would wave back
but she was too far away
for her sister to see.
The dead girl thought her sister
might be writing her notes,
but it was too long a trip to make
for a few scattered notes here and there
so she let them be.
And then, one day, her earthbound sister finally realized
she could hear music up there in heaven,
so after that, everything her sister needed to tell her
she did through her clarinet
and each time she played, the dead girl
jumped up (no matter what else she was doing),
and danced.

(Found on a piece of paper in the stacks, B section, Clover Public Library)

I have a plan. I'm going to write Joe a poem, but first things first.

When I walk into the music room, I see that Rachel's already there unpacking her instrument. This is it. My hand is so clammy I'm afraid the handle on my case will slip out of it as I cross the room and stand in front of her.

"If it isn't John Lennon," she says without looking up. Could she be so awful as to rub Joe's nickname in my face? Obviously, yes. Well, good, because fury seems to calm my nerves. Race on.

"I'm challenging you for first chair," I say, and wild applause bursts from a spontaneous standing ovation in my brain. Never have words felt so good coming out of my mouth! Hmm. Even if Rachel doesn't appear to have heard them. She's still messing with her reed and ligature like the bell didn't go off, like the starting gate didn't just swing open.

I'm about to repeat myself, when she says, "There's nothing there, Lennie." She spits my name on the floor like it disgusts her. "He's so hung up on you. Who knows why?"

Could this moment get any better? No! I try to keep my cool. "This has nothing to do with him," I say, and nothing could be more true. It has nothing to do with her either, not really, though I don't say that. It's about me and my clarinet.

"Yeah, right," she says. "You're just doing this because you saw me with him."

"No." My voice surprises me again with its certainty. "I want the solos, Rachel." At that she stops fiddling with her clarinet, rests it on the stand, and looks up at me. "And I'm starting up again with Marguerite." This I decided on the way to rehearsal. I have her undivided totally freaked-out attention now. "I'm going to try for All-State too," I tell her. This, however, is news to me.

We stare at each other and for the first time I wonder if she's known all year that I threw the audition. I wonder if that's why she's been so horrible. Maybe she thought she could intimidate me into not challenging her. Maybe she thought that was the only way to keep her chair.

She bites her lip. "How about if I split the solos with you. And you can—"

I shake my head. I almost feel sorry for her. Almost.

"Come September," I say. "May the best clarinettist win."

Not just my ass, but every inch of me is in the wind as I fly out of the music room, away from school, and into the woods to go home and write the poem to Joe. Beside me, step for step, breath for breath, is the unbearable fact that I have a future and Bailey doesn't.

This is when I know it.

My sister will die over and over again for the rest of my life. Grief is forever. It doesn't go away; it becomes part of you, step for step, breath for breath. I will never stop grieving Bailey because I will never stop loving her. That's just how it is. Grief and love are conjoined, you don't get one without the other. All I can do is love her and love the world, emulate her by living with daring and spirit and joy.

Without thinking, I veer onto the trail to the forest bedroom. All around me, the woods are in an uproar of beauty. Sunlight cascades through the trees, making the fern-covered floor look jeweled and incandescent. Rhododendron bushes sweep past me right and left like women in fabulous dresses. I want to wrap my arms around all of it.

When I get to the forest bedroom, I hop onto the bed and make myself comfortable. I'm going to take my time with this poem, not like all the others I scribbled and scattered. I take the pen out of my pocket, a piece of blank sheet music out of my bag, and start writing.

I tell him everything – everything he means to me, everything I felt with him that I never felt before, everything I hear in his music. I want him to trust me so I bare all. I tell him I belong to him, that my heart is his, and even if he never forgives me it will still be the case.

It's my story, after all, and this is how I choose to tell it.

When I'm done, I scoot off the bed and as I do, I notice a blue guitar pick lying on the white comforter. I must have been sitting on it all afternoon. I lean over and pick it up, and recognize it right away as Joe's. He must've come here to play – a good sign. I decide to leave the poem here for him instead of sneaking it inside the Fontaine mailbox like I had planned. I fold it, write his name on it, and place it on the bed under a rock to secure it from the wind. I tuck his pick under the rock as well.

Walking home, I realize it's the first time since Bailey died that I've written words for someone to read.

36

I'm too mortified to sleep. What was I thinking? I keep imagining Joe reading my ridiculous poem to his brothers, and worse to Rachel, all of them laughing at poor lovelorn Lennie, who knows nothing about romance except what she learned from Emily Brontë. I told him: *I belong to him*. I told him: *My heart is his*. I told him: *I hear his soul in his music*. I'm going to jump off of a building. Who says things like this in the twenty-first century? No one! How is it possible that something can seem like such a brilliant idea one day and such a bonehead one the next?

As soon as there's enough light, I throw a sweatshirt over my pajamas, put on some sneakers, and run through the dawn to the forest bedroom to retrieve the note, but when I get there, it's gone. I tell myself that the wind blew it away like all the other poems. I mean, how likely is it that Joe showed up yesterday afternoon after I left? Not likely at all.

Sarah is keeping me company, providing humiliation support while I make lasagnas.

She can't stop squealing. "You're going to be first clarinet, Lennie. For sure."

"We'll see."

"It'll really help you get into a conservatory. Juilliard even."

I take a deep breath. How like an imposter I'd felt every time Marguerite mentioned it, how like a traitor, conspiring to steal my sister's dream, just as it got swiped from her. Why didn't it occur to me then I could dream alongside her? Why wasn't I brave enough to have a dream at all?

"I'd love to go to Juilliard," I tell Sarah. There. Finally. "But any good conservatory would be okay." I just want to study music: what life, what living itself sounds like.

"We could go together," Sarah's saying, while shoveling into her mouth each slice of mozzarella as I cut it. I slap her hand. She continues, "Get an apartment together in New York City." I think Sarah might rocket into outer space at the idea – me too, though, I, pathetically, keep thinking: What about Joe? "Or Berklee in Boston," she says, her big blue eyes boinging out of her head. "Don't forget Berklee. Either way, we could drive there in Ennui, zigzag our way across. Hang out at the Grand Canyon, go to New Orleans, maybe—"

"Ughhhhhhhhhhhhhhhh," I groan.

"Not the poem again. What could be a better distraction than the divine goddesses Juilliard and Berklee. Sheesh. Unfreakingbelievable..."

"You have no idea how dildonic it was."

"*Nice* word, Len." She's flipping through a magazine someone left on the counter.

"*Lame* isn't lame enough of a word for this poem," I mutter. "Sarah, I told a guy that *I belong to him*."

"That's what happens when you read *Wuthering Heights* eighteen times."

"Twenty-three."

I'm layering away: sauce, noodles, *I belong to you*, cheese, sauce, *my heart is yours*, noodles, cheese, *I hear your soul in your music*, cheese, cheese, CHEESE…

She's smiling at me. "You know, it might be okay, he seems kind of the same way."

"What way?"

"You know, like you."

37

⑤ Scales Practise thes

Bails?

Yeah.

Can you believe Cathy married Edgar Linton?

No.

I mean what she had with Heathcliff,

how could she have just thrown it away?

I don't know. What is it, Len?

What's what?

What's with you and that book already?

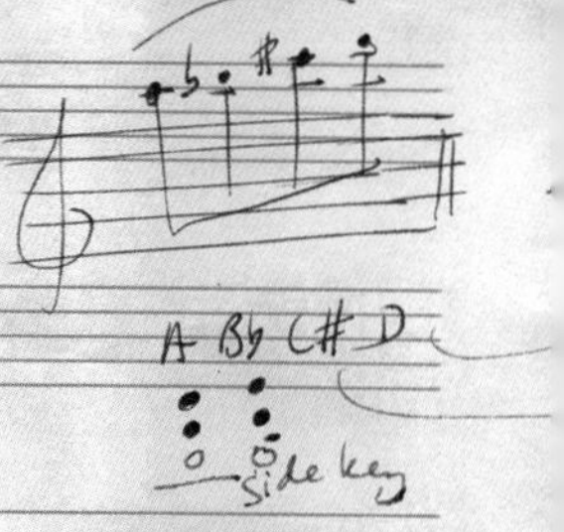

I don't know.

Yes you do. Tell me.

It's cornball.

C'mon, Len.

I guess I want it.

What?

① Gavotte Tongue quav

line 3

Put in the

To feel that kind of love.

You will.

How do you know?

Just do.

The toes knows?

The toes knows.

But if I find it, I don't want to screw it all up like they did.

You won't. The toes knows that, too.

Night, Bails.

Len, I was just thinking something...

What?

In, the end Cathy and Heathcliff are together,

Love is stronger than anything, even death.

Hmm...

Night, Len.

(Found on a folded up piece of music paper, in the parking lot, Clover High)

I tell myself it's ridiculous to go all the way back to the forest bedroom, that there's no way in the world he's going to be there, that no New Age meets Victorian Age poem is going to make him trust me, that I'm sure he still hates me, and now thinks I'm dildonic on top of it.

But here I am, and of course, here he's not. I flop onto my back on the bed. I look up at the patches of blue sky through the trees, and adhering to the regularly scheduled programming, I think some more about Joe. There's so much I don't know about him. I don't know if he believes in God, or likes macaroni and cheese, or what sign he is, or if he dreams in English or French, or what it would feel like – uh-oh. I'm headed from PG to XXX because, oh God, I really wish Joe didn't hate me so much, because I want to do *everything* with him. I'm so fed up with my virginity. It's like the whole world is in on this ecstatic secret but me—

I hear something then: a strange, mournful, decidedly unforest-like sound. I pick my head up and rest on my elbows so I can listen harder and try to isolate the sound from the rustling leaves and the distant river roar and the birds chattering all around me. The sound trickles through the trees, getting louder by the minute, closer. I keep listening, and then I recognize what it is, the notes, clear and perfect now, winding and wending their way to me – the melody from Joe's duet. I close my eyes and hope I'm really hearing a clarinet and it's not just some auditory hallucination inside my lovesick head. It's not, because now I hear steps shuffling through the brush and within a couple minutes the music stops and then the steps.

I'm afraid to open my eyes, but I do, and he's standing at the edge of the bed looking down at me – an army of ninja-cupids who must have all been hiding out in the canopy draw their bows and release – arrows fly at me from every which way.

"I thought you might be here." I can't read his expression. Nervous? Angry? His face seems restless like it doesn't know what to emote. "I got your poem..."

I can hear the blood rumbling through my body, drumming in my ears. What's he going to say? I got your poem and I'm sorry, I just can't ever forgive you. I got your poem and I feel the same way – *my heart is yours, John Lennon*. I got your poem and I've already called the psych ward – I have a straitjacket in this backpack. Strange. I've never seen Joe wear a backpack.

He's biting his lip, tapping his clarinet on his leg. Definitely nervous. This can't be good.

"Lennie, I got *all* your poems." What's he talking about? What does he mean *all* my poems? He slides the clarinet between his thighs to hold it and takes off his backpack, unzips it. Then he takes a deep breath, pulls out a box, hands it to me. "Well, probably not all of them, but these."

I open the lid. Inside are scraps of paper, napkins, takeaway cups, all with my words on them. The bits and pieces of Bailey and me that I scattered and buried and hid. This is not possible.

"How?" I ask, bewildered, and starting to get uneasy thinking about Joe reading everything in this box. All these private desperate moments. This is worse than having someone read your journal. This is like having someone read the journal that you thought you'd burned. And how did he get them all? Has he been following me around? That would be perfect. I finally fall in love with someone and he's a total freaking maniac.

I look at him. He's smirking a little and I see the faintest: bat. bat. bat. "I know what you're thinking," he says. "That I'm the creepy stalker dude."

Bingo.

He's amused. "I'm not, Len. It just kept happening. At first I kept finding them, and then, well, I started looking. I just couldn't help it. It became like this weird-ass treasure hunt. Remember that first day in the tree?"

I nod. But something even more amazing than Joe being a crazy stalker and finding my poems has just occurred to me – he's not angry anymore. Was it the dildonic poem? Whatever it was I'm caught in such a ferocious uprising of joy I'm not even listening to him as he tries to explain how in the world these poems ended up in this shoebox and not in some trash heap or blowing through Death Valley on a gust of wind.

I try to tune in to what he's saying. "Remember in the tree I told you that I'd seen you up at The Great Meadow? I told you that I'd watched you writing a note, watched you drop it as you walked away. But I didn't tell you that after you left, I went over and found the piece of paper caught in the fence. It was a poem about Bailey. I guess I shouldn't have kept it. I was going to give it back to you that day in the tree, I had it in my pocket, but then I thought you'd think it was strange that I took it in the first place, so I just kept it." He's biting his lip. I remember him telling me that day he saw me drop something I'd written, but it never occurred to me he would go *find* it and *read* it. He continues, "And then, while we were in the tree, I saw words scrawled on the branches, thought maybe you'd written something else, but I felt weird asking, so I went back another time and wrote it down in a notebook."

I can't believe this. I sit up, fish through the box, looking more closely this time. There are some scraps in his weirdo Unabomber handwriting – probably transcribed from walls or sides of barns or some of the other practical writing surfaces that I found. I'm not sure how to feel. He knows everything – I'm inside out.

His face is caught between worry and excitement, but excitement seems to be winning out. He's pretty much bursting to go on. "That first time I was at your house, I saw one sticking out from under a stone in Gram's garden, and then another one on the sole of your shoe, and then that day when we moved all the stuff, man … it's like your words were everywhere I looked. I went a little crazy, found myself looking for them all the time…" He shakes his head. "Even kept it up when I was so pissed at you. But the strangest part is that I'd found a couple before I'd even met you, the first was just a few words on the back of a candy wrapper, found it on the trail to the river, had no idea who wrote it, well, until later…"

He's staring at me, tapping the clarinet on his leg. He looks nervous again. "Okay, say something. Don't feel weird. They just made me fall more in love with you." And then he smiles, and in all the places around the globe where it's night, day breaks. "Aren't you at least going to say *quel dork*?"

I would say a lot of things right now if I could get any words past the smile that has taken over my face. There it is again his *I'm in love with you* obliterating all else that comes out of his mouth with it.

He points to the box. "They helped me. I'm kind of an unforgiving doltwad, if you haven't noticed. I'd read them – read them over and over after you came that day with the roses – trying to understand what happened, why you were with him, and I think maybe I do now. I don't know, reading all the poems together, I started to *really* imagine what you've been going through, how horrible it must be..." He swallows, looks down, shuffles his foot in the pine needles. "For him too. I guess I can see how it happened."

How can it be I was writing to Joe all these months without knowing it? When he looks up, he's smiling. "And then yesterday..." He tosses the clarinet onto the bed. "Found out you belong to me." He points at me. "I own your ass."

I smile. "Making fun of me?"

"Yeah, but it doesn't matter because you own my ass too." He shakes his head and his hair flops into his eyes so that I might die. "Totally."

A flock of hysterically happy birds busts out of my chest and into the world. I'm glad he read the poems. I want him to know all the inside things about me. I want him to know my sister, and now, in some way, he does. Now he knows before as well as after.

He sits down on the edge of the bed, picks up a stick and draws on the ground with it, then tosses it, looks off into the trees. "I'm sorry," he says.

"Don't be. I'm glad—"

He turns around to face me. "No, not about the poems. I'm sorry, what I said that day, about Bailey. From reading all these, I knew how much it would hurt you—"

I put my finger over his lips. "It's okay."

He takes my hand, holds it to his mouth, kisses it. I close my eyes, feel shivers run through me – it's been so long since we've touched. He rests my hand back down. I open my eyes. His are on me, questioning. He smiles, but the vulnerability and hurt still in his face tears into me. "You're not going to do it to me again, are you?" he asks.

"Never," I blurt out. "I want to be with you forever!" Okay, lesson learned twice in as many days: you can chop the Victorian novel to shreds with garden shears but you can't take it out of the girl.

He beams at me. "You're crazier than me."

We stare at each other for a long moment and inside that moment I feel like we are kissing more passionately than we ever have even though we aren't touching.

I reach out and brush my fingers across his arm. "Can't help it. I'm in love."

"First time," he says. "For me."

"I thought in France—"

He shakes his head. "No way, nothing like this." He touches my cheek in that tender way that he does that makes me believe in God and Buddha and Mohammed and Ganesh and Mary et al. "No one's like you, for me," he whispers.

"Same," I say, right as our lips meet. He lowers me back onto the bed, aligns himself on top of me so we are legs to legs, hips to hips, stomach to stomach. I can feel the weight of him pressing into every inch of me. I rake my fingers through his dark silky curls.

"I missed you," he murmurs into my ears, my neck and hair, and each time he does I say, "Me too," and then we are kissing again and I can't believe there is anything in this uncertain world that can feel this right and real and true.

Later, after we've come up for oxygen, I reach for the box, and start flipping through the scraps. There are a lot of them, but not near as many as I wrote. I'm glad there are some still out there, tucked away between rocks, in trash bins, on walls, in the margins of books, some washed away by rain, erased by the sun, transported by the wind, some never to be found, some to be found in years to come.

"Hey, where's the one from yesterday?" I ask, letting my residual embarrassment get the better of me, thinking I might still be able to accidentally rip it up, now that it's done its job.

"Not in there. That one's mine." Oh well. He's lazily brushing his hand across my neck and down my back. I feel like a tuning fork, my whole body humming.

"You're not going to believe this," he says. "But I think the roses worked. On my parents – I swear, they can't keep their hands off each other. It's disgusting. Marcus and Fred have been going down to your place at night and stealing roses to give to girls so they'll sleep with them." Gram is going to love this. It's a good thing she's so smitten with the Fontaine boys.

I put down the box, scoot around so I'm facing him. "I don't think *any* of you guys need Gram's roses for that."

"John Lennon?"

Bat. Bat. Bat.

I run my finger over his lips, say, "I want to do everything with you too."

"Oh man," he says, pulling me down to him, and then we are kissing so far into the sky I don't think we're ever coming back.

If anyone asks where we are, just tell them to look up.

38

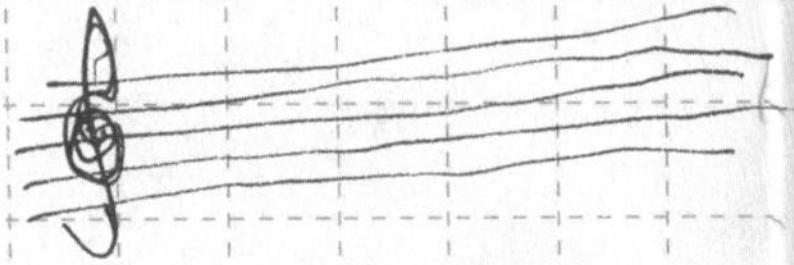

Bails?

Yeah?

Is it so dull being dead?

It was, not anymore.

What changed?

I stopped peering over the ledge...

What do you do now?

It's hard to explain – it's like swimming,

but not in water, in light.

Who do you swim with?

Mostly you and Toby, Gram, Big,

with Mom, too, sometimes.

How come I don't know it?

But you do, don't you?

I guess, like all those days we spent

at Flying Man's?

Exactly, only brighter.

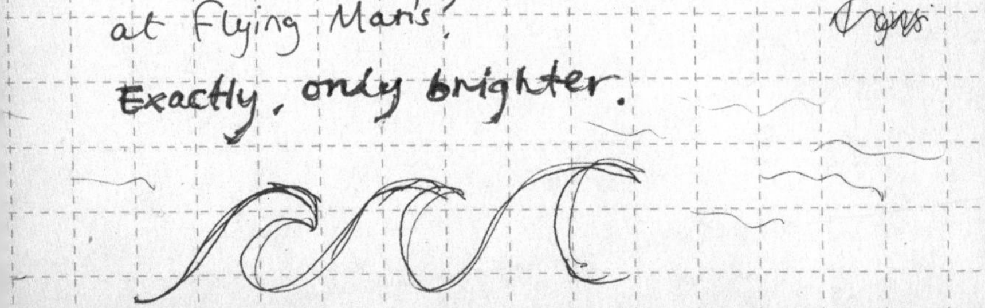

(Written in Lennie's journal)

Gram and I are baking the day away in preparation for Big's wedding. All the windows and doors are open and we can hear the river and smell the roses and feel the heat of the sun streaming in. We're chirping about the kitchen like sparrows.

We do this every wedding, only this is the first time we're doing it without Bailey. Yet, oddly, I feel her presence more today in the kitchen with Gram than I have since she died. When I roll the dough out, she comes up to me and sticks her hand in the flour and flicks it into my face. When Gram and I lean against the counter and sip our tea, she storms into the kitchen and pours herself a cup. She sits in every chair, blows in and out the doors, whisks in between Gram and me humming under her breath and dipping her finger into our batters. She's in every thought I think, every word I say, and I let her be. I let her enchant me as I roll the dough and think my thoughts and say my words, as we bake and bake – both of us having finally dissuaded Joe of the necessity of an exploding wedding cake – and talk about inanities like what Gram is going to wear for the big party. She is quite concerned with her outfit.

"Maybe I'll wear pants for a change." The earth has just slid off its axis. Gram has a floral frock for every occasion – I've never seen her out of one. "And I might straighten my hair." Okay, the earth has slid off its axis and is now hurtling toward a different galaxy. Imagine snake-haired Medusa with a blow-dryer. Straight hair is an impossibility for Gram or any Walker, even with thirty hours to go until party time.

"What gives?" I ask.

"I just want to look nice, no crime in that, is there? You know, sweet pea, it's not like I've lost my sex appeal." I can't believe Gram just said sex appeal. "Just a bit of a dry spell is all," she mutters under her breath. I turn to look at her. She's sugaring the raspberries and strawberries and flushing as crimson as they are.

"Oh my God, Gram! You have a crush."

"God no!"

"You're lying. I can see it."

Then she giggles in a wild cackley way. "I am lying! Well, what do you expect? With you so loopy all the time about Joe, and now Big and Dorothy … maybe I caught a little of it. Love is contagious, everyone knows that, Lennie."

She grins.

"So, who is it? Did you meet him at The Saloon that night?" That's the only time she's been out socializing in months. Gram is not the Internet dating type. At least I don't think she is.

I put my hands on my hips. "If you don't tell me, I'm just going to ask Maria tomorrow. There's nothing in Clover she doesn't know."

Gram squeals, "Mum's me, sweet pea."

No matter how I prod through hours more of pies, cakes and even a few batches of berry pudding, her smiling lips remain sealed.

After we're done, I get my backpack, which I loaded up earlier, and take off for the cemetery. When I hit the trailhead, I start running. The sun is breaking through the canopy in isolated blocks, so I fly through light and dark and dark and light, through the blazing unapologetic sunlight, into the ghostliest loneliest shade, and back again, back and forth, from one to the next, and through the places where it all blends together into a leafy-lit emerald dream. I run and run and as I do the fabric of death that has clung to me for months begins to loosen and slip away. I run fast and free, suspended in a moment of private raucous happiness, my feet barely touching the ground as I fly forward to the next second, minute, hour, day, week, year of my life.

I break out of the woods on the road to the cemetery. The hot afternoon sunlight is lazing over everything, meandering through the trees, casting long shadows. It's warm and the scent of eucalyptus and pine is thick, overpowering. I walk the footpath that winds through the graves listening to the rush of the falls, remembering how important it was for me, despite all reason, that Bailey's grave be where she could see and hear and even smell the river.

I'm the only person in the small hilltop cemetery and I'm glad. I drop my backpack and sit down beside the gravestone, rest my head against it, wrap my hands and arms around it like I'm playing a cello. The stone is so warm against my body. We chose this one because it had a little cabinet in it, a kind of reliquary, with a metal door that has an engraving of a bird on it. It sits under the chiseled words. I run my fingers across my sister's name, her nineteen years, then across the words I wrote on a piece of paper months ago and handed to Gram in the funeral parlor: *The Color of Extraordinary*.

I reach for my pack, pull a small notebook out of it. I transcribed all the letters Gram wrote to our mom over the last sixteen years. I want Bailey to have those words. I want her to know that there will never be a story that she won't be a part of, that she's everywhere like sky. I open the door and slide the book in the little cabinet, and as I do, I hear something scrape. I reach in and pull out a ring. My stomach drops. It's gorgeous, an orange topaz, big as an acorn. Perfect for Bailey. Toby must have had it made especially for her. I hold it in my palm and the certainty that she never got to see it pierces me. I bet the ring is what they were waiting for to finally tell us about their marriage, the baby. How Bails would've showed it off when they made the grand announcements. I rest it on the edge of the stone where it catches a glint of sun and throws amber prismatic light over all the engraved words.

I try to fend off the oceanic sadness, but I can't. It's such a colossal effort not to be haunted by what's lost, but to be enchanted by what was.

I miss you, I tell her, *I can't stand that you're going to miss so much.*

I don't know how the heart withstands it.

I kiss the ring, put it back into the cabinet next to the notebook, and close the door with the bird on it. Then I reach into my pack and take out the houseplant. It's so decrepit, just a few blackened leaves left. I walk over to the edge of the cliff, so I'm right over the falls. I take the plant out of its pot, shake the dirt off the roots, get a good grip, reach my arm back, take one deep breath before I pitch my arm forward, and let go.

Epilogue

[redacted]

I belong to you

[redacted]

My heart is yours

[redacted]

I hear your soul in your music

[redacted]

(Found on the bed, in the forest bedroom)

(Found again in the bombroom, in the trash can, ripped into pieces by Lennie)

(Found again on Joe's desk, taped together, with the word dildonic written over it)

(Found framed under glass in Joe's dresser drawer where it still is)

Acknowledgements

In loving memory of Barbie Stein, who is everywhere like sky

I'd like to thank:

First and foremost, my parents, all four of them, for their boundless love and support: my awesome father and Carol, my huge-hearted mother and Ken. My whole family for their rollicking humor and steadfastness: my brothers Bruce, Bobby, and Andy, my sisters-in-law Patricia and Monica, my niece and nephews Adam, Lena, and Jake, my grandparents, particularly the inimitable Cele.

Mark Routhier for so much joy, belief, love.

My amazing friends, my other family, for every day, in every way: Ami Hooker, Anne Rosenthal, Becky MacDonald, Emily Rubin, Jeremy Quittner, Larry Dwyer, Maggie Jones, Sarah Michelson, Julie Regan, Stacy Doris, Maritza Perez, David Booth, Alexander Stadler, Rick Heredia, Patricia Irvine, James Faerron, Lisa Steindler, and James Assatly, who is so missed, also my extended families: the Routhier, Green, and Block clans … and many others, too many to name.

Patricia Nelson for around the clock laughs and legal expertise, Paul Feuerwerker for glorious eccentricity, revelry, and invaluable insights into the band room, Mark H for sublime musicality, first love.

The faculty, staff and student body of Vermont College of Fine Arts, particularly my miracle-working mentors: Deborah Wiles, Brent Hartinger, Julie Larios, Tim Wynne-Jones, Margaret Bechard, and visiting faculty Jane Yolen. And my classmates: the Cliff-hangers, especially Jill Santopolo, Carol Lynch Williams, Erik Talkin, and Mari Jorgensen. Also, the San Francisco VCFA crew. And Marianna Baer – angel at the end of my keyboard.

My other incredible teachers and professors: Regina Wiegand, Bruce Boston, Will Erikson, Archie Ammons, Ken McClane, Phyllis Janowitz, C.D. Wright, among many others.

To those listed above who spirit in and out of this book – a special thank you.

Deepest appreciation and gratitude go to:

My clients at Manus & Associates Literary Agency, as well as my extraordinary colleagues: Stephanie Lee, Dena Fischer, Penny Nelson, Theresa van Eeghen, Janet and Justin Manus, and most especially, Jillian Manus, who doesn't walk, but dances on water.

Alisha Niehaus, my remarkable editor, for her ebullience, profundity, insight, kindness, sense of humor, and for making every part of the process a celebration. Everyone at Dial and Penguin Books for Young Readers for astounding me each jubilant step of the way.

Emily van Beek of Pippin Properties for being the best literary agent on earth! I am forever mesmerized by her joyfulness, brilliance, ferocity and grace. Holly McGhee for her enthusiasm, humor, savvy and soulfulness. Elena Mechlin for her behind-the-scenes magic and cheer. The Pippin Ladies are without peer. And Jason Dravis at Monteiro Rose Dravis Agency for his dazzling know-how.

In addition, I heartily thank:

At Walker UK, my wonderful editor, Helen Thomas, for her passion, astuteness, humor and all around delightfulness, who made 6,000 miles feel like none, and publisher Jane Winterbotham for her enthusiasm and vision. Jane and Helen took tremendously good care of this story and I am so grateful. Also, the incredible Katie Everson for her genius and creativity in making the book look more beautiful than in my wildest dreams. And of course, Vera the plant.

Much gratitude also goes to the amazing Alex Webb at Rights People.

And finally, an extra heartfelt double-whammy out-of-the-freaking-park thank you to my brother Bobby: True Believer.